Lion of God:

The Complete Trilogy

Stephen England

Episode I

Part One

"Whoever thinks of stopping the Intifada before it achieves its goals, I will give him ten bullets in the chest."—*Yasser Arafat*

6:30 A.M. Israel Standard Time, October 12ᵗʰ, 2000
An undisclosed location in the Negev
Israel

There. He saw a dim shape barely visible in the opening to the darkened corridor ahead—the outline of a Kalashnikov assault rifle carried at low ready.

Target identified. The suppressed Jericho 941 semiautomatic pistol came up in his hands, never breaking stride as he advanced—its nightsights centering on the man's head, the base of the skull where the spine connects to the brain stem.

The trigger broke under the pressure of his finger, the pistol recoiling into his palm as a single 9mm round spat from the barrel, the suppressor reducing the sound to the faintest of coughs.

Target down.

He reached the corner and paused, flat against the wall, feeling the breath of his teammate on the back of his neck—soft footsteps against the floor as the rest of the four-man Mossad kill team stacked up behind him.

Go right, he motioned silently, taking his right hand off the weapon—and gesturing with two fingers. He didn't need to look back to know that the rear

1

pair of officers were moving to take the opposite corner. They were every bit as well-trained as he was.

Another quick gesture. *Go, go, go.*

He sprung out from the wall, going wide—cutting the pie as he moved into the corridor, pistol at the ready. His partner following him out.

Clear.

There was the sound of another suppressed *cough* from behind him, along with the dull thud of a target hitting the floor. Clearly the rear pair of officers had encountered—and dealt with—opposition.

He didn't react, didn't look behind him. If their intel was accurate, they were well-nigh on top of the room where the hostage was secured. And their time was running out.

The outline of a door to the right appeared, maybe ten meters ahead. Just where it should have been, given the structural blueprints they had reviewed at the mission briefing. The layout of the building burned into his memory.

They stacked up once more at the door—two on either side—ready to go in hard. At his signal.

They could have mirrored the door, gotten a glimpse of what was on the other side, but that would have taken time. Time they didn't have.

Time to do this. He took a deep breath, calming himself as he nodded at the officer immediately opposite him, uttering the first words since they had entered the target structure four minutes earlier—his voice nothing more than a faint whisper. "Bang the room."

A nod of acknowledgement and the rear officer withdrew a long, cylindrical stun grenade from his vest as his partner took a step back from the door—preparing to kick it in.

Disorientation. *Chaos.* That's what this was all about—minimizing the time the assault team spent trapped in the fatal funnel. Getting to the hostage.

His fellow Mossad officer's combat-booted foot connected with the door, smashing it in on its hinges as the man behind him threw the grenade, the cylinder describing a slow arc in the darkness as it sailed into the room.

Look away. He tucked his chin to his chest, turning instinctively to the side to shield his eyes. And just in time.

The room exploded in a light bright as the sun, the noise of the detonation hammering his eardrums. *Flash-bang.*

He was back up before the last echoes had finished reverberating through the building, his gun up as he entered the room, going right. His partner, left. *Nothing.*

Feeling a cold fear grasp at his heart, he spun on heel—finding his partner just standing there, her weapon half-raised.

The room was empty.

6:36 A.M.
The United States Embassy
Tel Aviv

Patience, David Lay thought, glancing down the hallway. That was the single most important character trait for anyone with aspirations of working in the Middle East. Immeasurable, ineffable patience.

You couldn't work long in the region without coming to terms with precisely why the Torah contained so many references to the longsuffering of God. A lesson he'd had to learn time and again in his three years as the CIA's Chief of Station in Tel Aviv.

"We'll be out presently," he announced, speaking into the small two-way radio in his hand. "Pass it along to the Marines."

The acknowledgement came back along with a burst of static just as the door opened behind him to reveal the Director of Central Intelligence, George Tenet.

"You have everything ready?" Tenet asked, buttoning his suit jacket as he joined Lay in the hall. "Everything's in order?"

"It is," Lay responded quietly. He'd been in Tel Aviv for the entirety of Tenet's time as DCI, but this visit to Israel was the first time the two of them had even been in the same room, let alone met.

And so far. . .well, it was too early to say.

"I've arranged a police escort to the talks," he continued, leading the way down the hall toward the elevator. "They'll meet us at the Erez Crossing."

"Israeli police?"

Lay glanced back in surprise. "Of course. In light of the last few days, I thought it was wise to take additional security precautions."

That was, in his opinion, a massive understatement. The unrest that had been building ever since the summer had finally spilled over its brim two weeks earlier—with Palestinian rioters clashing with police in the wake of Israeli opposition leader Ariel Sharon's visit to the Temple Mount, or the *Haram al-Sharif* as it was known to members of the Muslim faith.

The visit of the former IDF paratrooper turned vocal critic of the peace process had not been. . .well-received, in spite of the care taken to coordinate the visit with the *Waqf*, the Islamic trust in charge of Jerusalem's holy sites. And things were getting more hostile by the day.

The DCI shook his head, stopping stock-still in the hallway behind him. "Look, David, perception is everything. I'm here to *chair* the talks, not take sides in them. We made progress at Camp David this past summer, and we continued that progress last week in Paris. I didn't come here just to piss that all away."

"Would you have preferred I ask Mohammed Dahlan to offer his protection?" Lay asked, turning calmly to face him.

Dahlan was the chief of the Palestinian Security Force in Gaza, responsible for keeping law and order—or at least the roughest Middle Eastern equivalent of it—in that sector of the Palestinian Authority.

"We've spent the last four years training Dahlan's people, so don't give me that." Tenet's eyes flashed. "They're solid. And a joint escort would have provided for the necessary security while providing an appropriate symbolism for the talks."

The politics of the intelligence business, Lay thought—meeting the director's eyes. It was enough to make him wish for the bad old days of the Cold War, when all such things had been way above his pay grade. "That's not an option. The Israeli police," he continued, measuring his words carefully, "have suspended all joint patrols with the NSF since the Qalqiliyah incident."

An Israeli Border Police superintendent, shot dead by one of his Palestinian counterparts. It seemed a reasonable justification for such measures.

The DCI started to reply, then seemed to think better of it—staring into Lay's eyes for the space of a full minute before his face relaxed into a smile. "All right, then. Let's go make peace."

6:37 A.M.
The Negev

The hostage wasn't here. It took a brief moment for that realization to filter through, his ears still ringing from the blast of the stun grenade. Their intel had been wrong, that all-too-frequent reality out in the field.

And then a siren began to wail. Now everyone knew they were there.

The man swore fiercely under his breath, motioning for the rest of the team to form up on him as he led the way back out into the corridor of the now seemingly-abandoned structure—the encrypted radio clipped to his tactical vest suddenly coming alive with static. A woman's voice.

"Ariel, Hachilah-1, requesting sitrep." *Ariel.* His Mossad codename. He had been born <u>David Shafron</u>, but it had been a long time since anyone had known him by that name. *Years.*

Another man, from a different time.

"The mission is blown, Hachilah-1," he responded angrily, more furious with himself than anyone else. He should have *known*. "I say again, the mission is blown. Moving to extract."

"Negative, Ariel. There's a truck near the rear entrance," came the woman's voice once more. "We're picking up a large number of hostiles in the vicinity—your hostage may be with them."

May. That was the operative word of that particular sentence. But they had come this far. Ariel grimaced, motioning with his hand to his team members to spread out as they advanced down the corridor—their eyes perfectly adjusted to the darkness.

Target. Target. A pair of silhouettes emerging from the darkness ahead, his pistol coming up to cover the threat in a motion born of years of practice, his finger closing around the trigger.

Target down. He couldn't hear the report of his partner's weapon over the cacophony of the sirens, but he saw the second silhouette fall. *Moving on.*

A corridor to the right led toward the back of the building, his steps hastening as they neared the exit. The sound of a truck's engine running faintly audible amidst the sirens.

"Ready?" he mouthed, exchanging a glance with the man opposite him.

A nod. *Ready.* He took a step back from the door, bouncing momentarily on the balls of his feet before lashing out with a booted foot—the blow splintering the wood of the doorframe as it slammed outward, his partner first through, her weapon already up.

He followed the third member of the stack into the fatal funnel and out into the open, careful not to allow the muzzle of his weapon to sweep any of his team members. *Instant disqualification.*

Target. Target. Target. Target.

He saw them fall one by one, cut down by the precision fire of his team members—his attention suddenly focusing itself toward the truck, taking in the sight of a middle-aged man in a suit forced to his knees at the rear of the vehicle. A terrorist, his face concealed by a black balaclava, standing over him. His weapon pointed at the man's head.

Ariel swung, the muzzle of his pistol coming to bear, the terrorist's head appearing, perfectly aligned in the twin rear posts of the nightsights. *There.*

The Jericho recoiled into his hand, the bullet smashing through paper and backing as the reactive target slammed into the ground.

He lowered his weapon and slipped the safety on, holstering it once more on his belt as the "hostage" rose to his feet, dusting himself off—his face now clearly visible. Ariel's breath catching in his throat as he recognized the general, or *aluf*, as they were known in the Israeli Defense Force.

"General Shoham," he began, unable to completely mask his own look of surprise, "They told me you were arriving today, but I was not informed you would be part of the live-fire exercise."

The expression on the older man's broad, stolid face might have been a smile, but it was impossible to judge.

And unsafe to guess. "Nor should you have been," he replied after a long, tense moment. "Have your team secure their weapons and regroup for the debrief."

9:35 A.M.
Ramallah, The West Bank

The human cost of war. That was what he had spent a career documenting, Simon Collins thought, the straps of the British man's backpack digging into his shoulders as he made his way down the dusty street, ahead of the crowds now leaving from the burial of a young man taken far too soon. The high-pitched, keening wail of the women piercing the air. An other-worldly sound.

Twenty-five years, across three continents, as a freelance journalist. Reporting on human sorrow. *Tragedy.* Africa, Eastern Europe—now the Middle East. Men with power and guns, leaving broken lives in their wake.

And this place was no different, for all its claim of being a "promised land." A claim rendered farcical by the history of the place, a history soaked in the blood of those viewed by one side or another as "God's enemies."

A pretext for the murder of the innocent—like the boy whose funeral procession he now found himself following. His notepad and pen in hand, trying to capture the enormity of it all. The loss.

Halil Zahran had been seventeen years old when he had been shot dead by Israeli soldiers two days earlier.

He hadn't been the first, and he wouldn't be the last—the anger palpable in the crowd of thousands who had attended his funeral, the angry chants against the Zionist state. The banners waving over their heads as they returned from his burial, the colors of Palestine—recalling to mind the words of the 13th-century Arab poet Safi a-Din al-Hili:

"White are our deeds, black are our battles, green are our fields. . .red are our swords."

Peace had seemed so bright only months before, with Ehud Barak and Yasser Arafat reaching out to shake each other's hand at Camp David.

His contacts in the Palestinian delegation had gotten him in, his piece on the summit making the front page of *The Guardian*.

Now it seemed farther away than ever.

Collins stopped short, his young Arab guide nearly tripping into him—his pulse quickening as he glanced down the street, taking in the sight of a red sedan parked in front of the local police station.

A red sedan. . .with yellow plates. *Israeli plates.*

Something was wrong.

9:47 A.M.
HaKirya
Tel Aviv

"Have you been able to confirm their identities?" Shaul Mofaz asked, not turning from the window, looking from the seventeen-story height of the Matkal Tower out over the military complex toward the Marganit Tower to the west and the glistening blue expanse of the Mediterranean beyond.

Born in Tehran, he had made his *aliyah*—his return to Zion—at the age of nine along with the rest of his family. Long before the darkness had descended over that country.

Since then, the majority of his fifty-one years had been spent in the service of the Jewish state, first as a young paratrooper—then as an infantry brigade commander as Israel pushed into Lebanon in the early '80s.

He had been the IDF's Chief of General Staff, the *Ramatkal,* for the last two years—as the "peace process" continued along at a snail's pace and the clouds of war gathered all around them.

Clouds he feared had just broken over the West Bank.

"No, we have not," his adjutant replied. "The word on the street is that they're Mossad."

Of course, Mofaz thought—the fluorescent light glistening off his balding head as he turned to face the young man. To the Palestinians, every Jew was Mossad. A "Zionist spy."

He'd heard it all a thousand times before. "And. . .are they?"

"We've reached out to the Mossad, but have heard nothing from Efraim yet."

And that wasn't likely to be forthcoming. At least not on the short-term. "So, barring that, what we have is a pair of IDF soldiers in Palestinian custody at the police station in Ramallah?"

"According to the best intelligence we have available at this time, yes."

Shaul Mofaz shook his head. "Get the Prime Minister on the phone. Whoever they work for, they're our people. We're going to need to go in and get them out."

9:59 A.M.
The police station
Ramallah, The West Bank

You didn't spend over a quarter-century in war zones around the world without being able to sense barely-repressed violence. To feel it in the air around you.

And that's what he was feeling, all around him—this was no longer a funeral procession. This was a mob. Chanting young men, their clenched fists raised to the sky. Full-throated shouts of anger. He didn't understand more than a few words of the Arabic, but the intent was coming through loud and clear.

"What are they saying?" Collins demanded, placing a rough hand on his guide's shoulder and pulling the young man around to face him. He'd never asked Nur his age, but he couldn't have been much older than a university student, if that.

The same age as most of the men in the crowd now surrounding them.

"They—they've captured a pair of Jewish assassins," the young man responded breathlessly, his face dark with anger. "Trying to sneak in past the checkpoint—to murder the old man."

The old man. Arafat. Collins nodded his understanding, glancing over his shoulder and back toward the Mukataa, just visible in the distance—it was a common Palestinian way of referring to their leader. But Nur wasn't done.

"They have to pay for their crimes—for all that they have done to us. They have to be made to *pay*."

10:03 A.M.
Erez Crossing
The Gaza Strip

"You understand, of course. . .I have to have something I can give to the Israelis if this is to work," Tenet said, glancing over at his counterpart as they walked between the concrete barriers and barbed wire. Soldiers in IDF uniforms standing watch only a few short meters away, loaded M-16s held at the ready. "Give and take—that's what we need. It's the whole reason I'm here."

"I grew up in the squalor of a refugee camp, Mr. Tenet, but this is something you would already know," Mohammed Dahlan began in thickly-accented English, seeming to measure his words carefully, "I have been deported by the Israelis. I have been jailed by the Israelis—five times. What we need from them—all we need—is peace. If this cannot be obtained. . .they lose, we lose, and my people," he said, waving his hand toward the Gaza Strip behind them, "will continue to suffer as they have for decades."

"And that's what we're hoping to avoid. I—" He stopped short as David Lay materialized at his side without warning.

"There's something that's come up, director." Tenet just stood there for a moment, waiting for him to go on, until the station chief glared pointedly at Dahlan.

"Mr. Dahlan," Tenet said, managing a tight smile, "would you give us a moment?"

The Palestinian security commander glanced searchingly from Tenet to Lay and back again before nodding wordlessly and moving away a few steps toward his bodyguards.

"Now what is this all about, David?" the CIA director demanded, his eyes flashing as he turned on his subordinate. "I was *getting* somewhere with him before you stepped in."

"I just received a call from Station Tel Aviv. . .one of our assets in the West Bank reached out—activating emergency protocols."

"And?"

"A pair of Israelis—we think they're IDF—were seized by Palestinian police entering Ramallah and taken to the police station."

Tenet murmured an obscenity beneath his breath, shaking his head. "What were they *doing* in Ramallah?"

"We don't know."

"So help me, if Prime Minister Barak decided to send one of Shin Bet's undercover squads into the PA while all *this* is going on—Albright is going to lose it." Tenet swore again, agitation distorting his face. "This could sabotage the entire peace process."

He paused. "This is an Israeli matter. . .why did our asset make contact?"

"Because there's a mob growing outside the police station," Lay replied, casting a careful glance in Dahlan's direction to ensure they were still speaking privately. "They're calling for blood."

10:08 A.M.
HaKirya
Tel Aviv

Vadim Novesche, Shaul Mofaz thought, staring down at the man's picture. Thirty-three years of age, only married for a week. *Yossi Avrahami*. Thirty-eight, father of three.

A toy salesman.

The general's body shuddered with emotion, his face hardening as he drew himself up, gaining the mastery of himself with an effort.

He had been committing men to battle for over twenty years, ever-armed with the knowledge that they weren't all going to be coming back. It came with the territory, the price of command.

But this was different, somehow. These men weren't Mossad, weren't Shin Bet. They weren't even battle-hardened veterans. They were reservists, family men.

And now they were in trouble, as the last field report from Ramallah made all too clear. Their time was running out. "The Prime Minister?" he asked, glancing up from the jacket photos into his adjutant's face. "Has he given his approval to the operation?"

The younger man shook his head, his eyes dark and empty. The eyes of someone old before his time. "He's still deliberating with his advisers. Sending a military force into the West Bank at this time is perceived as. . .problematic. The mob surrounding the police station is mostly young men, teenagers."

Kids. Nothing more than kids in the eyes of a naive Western media which had never grasped the reality of the Middle East.

A place that made old men of them all.

Mofaz placed both hands before him on his desk, swearing softly beneath his breath as he rose. "I'm going to go see the Prime Minister myself."

10:11 A.M.
An undisclosed location
The Negev

"Upon reaching the room where your intelligence indicated the hostage was being held, you elected to stage a direct assault—without first mirroring the door." The small man's voice was soft like a woman's—raised scarce above a whisper—but there was steel in his eyes as he lifted them to look over his glasses at Ariel. "Why did you make that decision?"

There was no accusation in his voice, and Ariel knew better than to take it as one. The debriefing after every mission, every training exercise like this one, was the place where every sin was laid bare, every decision analyzed and re-analyzed through the prism of not just whether it had but how it *could* have gone wrong.

In that respect, Mossad's *Kidon* units differed little from his time in *Sayeret Duvdevan*, conducting undercover operations into the West Bank.

He took a sip from the bottle of water at his side, considering his answer carefully.

"Speed, surprise, violence of action," he said, repeating the familiar litany of close-quarters battle. "Our briefing had indicated that the hostage could be executed at any moment. We needed to hit the room as quickly as possible. It was a calculated risk."

"A risk that could have gone very, very wrong indeed. The intel was *not* reliable. By choosing not to confirm its validity—"

The small man looked up as the door opened, another Mossad officer standing there in the entrance, dressed in black jeans and a khaki polo shirt. "Whatever you need," he began, clearing his throat, "it will have to wait. We're still in the middle of the debrief."

The new arrival shook his head. "It's not going to wait. Shoham's requested his presence. Immediately."

10:15 A.M.
The police station
Ramallah, The West Bank

"*Allahu akbar! Allahu akbar!*"

God is great. That much Arabic he knew *very* well. Collins felt a pair of young Palestinians push past him chanting the *takbir*, the mob growing ever more restless—crowding toward the door of the police station, their shouts drowning out the voices of the Palestinian policemen stationed there. Nur was long gone, joining the rest of his countrymen. There had to be at least a thousand of them now, maybe more, a sea of young men as far as he could see.

All hell was going to break loose any moment, and he was going to be in the middle of it. He knew that, but found himself unable to pull away.

This was a story. Feeling ever more exposed, he pushed his way through the crowd, catching sight of an older man standing near the edge, talking on a cellular phone as his eyes took in the scene. His bearing projecting the unmistakable air of command only solidified by his military uniform.

It was an impulse, nothing more, but the Leica came up in Collins' hand, snapping a couple of quick photos of the man, his face clearly framed in the lens. He wasn't your average Palestinian soldier, he was someone of authority.

Collins felt a hand on his shoulder and turned quickly, the camera dropping to hang from his neck as he raised his hands in a gesture of non-aggression. This mob was a powderkeg—all it would take is a single spark.

Instead, it was the face of ABC News producer Nasser Atta that greeted him.

"Simon—I thought I recognized you. It's been a long time. . .Sudan, was it?

Collins nodded, looking past Atta toward where he recognized the ABC News team setting up their cameras. "You're getting this?"

Atta nodded, his face grim. "You have to understand their anger—where they're coming from after all the death of the last few weeks, but—"

Whatever the ABC News producer might have said next, it was lost in that moment as a throaty roar came from the front of the mob, a surge of bodies toward the police station.

"My *God*," Collins breathed, his voice nearly lost amongst the cacophony of angry shouts. "They're in."

10:19 A.M.
An undisclosed location
The Negev

This had nothing to do with the exercise. As realistic as Mossad tried to make their training, you could always tell the difference given enough experience, Ariel thought—reading the tension in the older officer's body language as they moved down one of the long corridors of the facility.

Reaching a room off to the side of the corridor, the officer stepped to one side and motioned him on in.

Avi ben Shoham stood at the opposite end of the room looking at a gigantic map of Israel covering one wall—his back to Ariel as the Kidon officer entered, waiting for the older man to speak.

"Ariel," Shoham began, his voice seeming to fill the room with its resonance. "The Lion of God, eh?"

"The codename was chosen for me," he responded stiffly, his eyes meeting Shoham's as the *aluf* turned from the map.

The man was a legend, a hero of the Jewish state. He had been a young tank commander in 1973, one of the scant handful in the Golan when the Syrian Army came flooding into the heights.

Five full divisions against a pair of armored brigades—desperately grim odds.

But fight the Israeli tankers had, with Shoham personally destroying eighteen Syrian tanks until he was forced to bail out of his own burning Patton. His right forearm still bore the mark of the flames, a scar seared into his flesh as if with a brand.

"You're not a religious man?" Shoham asked, correctly judging the tone of his response.

Ariel shook his head, stone-faced. "Not anymore."

"I want you to assemble your team. Get them ready for immediate deployment," the older man said without further preamble. "The Prime Minister is monitoring a developing situation in the West Bank."

10:21 A.M.
The police station
Ramallah, The West Bank

He had seen a man's brains blown out right in front of him while reporting in the Zaire back in '96—a government loyalist executed at point-blank range by one of Laurent-Désiré Kabila's ADFL guerrillas.

A life extinguished in the space of a single, brutal instant—just like *that*—no build-up, no warning. A pistol to the head, blood and brains spattered in the dust of the street.

But even that. . .had been nothing like this, Collins thought as he pushed his way forward, moving through the crowd like a man caught in a dream.

A nightmare.

He could vaguely make out the forms of men in the open second-floor window of the police station, swinging viciously at something—or someone—beneath them. The sound drowned out by the jeering roar of the mob.

Suddenly something toppled from the window, Collins' breath catching in his throat as he saw the bloodied and mutilated body of a man in civilian clothes hit the shrubbery below, crushing branches and rolling into the street.

My God.

Even after all that he had seen, all the death and suffering he had born

15

witness to over the decades—he felt physically ill, unable to turn, to look away as the mob descended upon the man like animals, on him almost before his body had touched the ground. Fists, sticks—the glint of a knife in the morning sun.

A young Palestinian man standing in the open window above, blood covering his hands and forearms as he held them up for the crowd to see.

He saw one man, at the forefront of the mob, wielding the remnants of a ripped-out window frame, raising it high above his head with a bestial shout of praise to God as he brought it smashing down into the bloody pulp of the Israeli's face.

Again. And *again*. And again. And again. *"Allahu akbar!"*

Collins glanced back, his eyes searching as he tried to find Nasser Atta and his camera crew amidst the crush of rioters, but they were nowhere to be seen.

Someone had to record this, the British journalist thought, only too conscious of his own danger as he reached for the Leica around his neck and brought it up to his eye—snapping a quick photo of the brutality unfolding before him as protesters began tearing at the still-living man, dragging him across the street.

Another photo and another, the *click* of his shutter lost in the angry jubilation of the crowd. He felt rough hands grab at his shoulder, a man's voice in his ear—screaming in broken English. "No picture! No *pictures*!"

The impact of a blow in the ribs sent him reeling, another catching himself high on the cheek as he found himself turned about, face-to-face with a young Arab who couldn't have been much out of his teens. His face distorted with the same hatred that he was seeing aimed at the Israeli soldier on the ground barely twenty feet away.

His long, thin finger jabbing toward the camera in the journalist's hand, the meaning all too clear. *Hand it over.*

"All right, all right," Collins gasped, struggling to catch his breath—his heart beating rapidly against his chest—his hand out, gesturing for the young man to calm down as he removed the camera from its lanyard around his neck.

He made as if to extend the camera toward his attacker, then abruptly feinted, his free hand coming up—clenching into a fist just as it connected with the man's throat in a devastating blow, sending him stumbling back.

Run. And he ran—ran without looking back, without turning. Without even knowing where he was going. Or caring.

Just get away.

10:23 A.M.
The Negev

Ariel tore off a fresh strip of black electrical tape, winding it around the grip of the UZI submachine gun to fully depress the weapon's ever-finicky grip safety. No sense in taking a chance on a malfunction in the field.

He glanced up as Tzipporah entered the room, her IMI Galatz sniper rifle carried at the low ready, her long black hair tucked up under the American-style ball cap she wore. A more than competent assaulter, she came into her own on the long gun—a fact he knew so very well, from her past year as part of his team.

"Ready?" he asked, adjusting the three-point sling that secured the UZI to his tactical vest and checking his spare mags.

She merely nodded, her dark eyes betraying no emotion. They were flying blind here—it hadn't even been established who was to execute the operation, a decision that would ultimately rest in the hands of the IDF's General Staff.

If he knew the *alufim*, they would most likely favor his old comrades at *Duvdevan* over Mossad, but that wasn't going to stop Halevy from getting his people in place.

Pre-positioning.

He exchanged a last glance with the woman, pushing the door open and leading the way out into the courtyard of the training facility—toward the 125th Squadron *Saifaneet* light transport helicopter warming up on the helipad, its rotors whipping the dust and sand of the Negev into a blinding haze. Their roar making it almost impossible to hear without shouting.

Sand and grit biting into his face, Ariel pulled open the door and threw himself inside, landing in the seat next to his second-in-command, a grim-faced older man he knew only by his codename "Ze'ev." Himself a former member of *Shayetet-13*, the Israeli Navy's special operations unit.

He acknowledged Ariel with only a nod as the team's sniper levered herself up into the seat behind them alongside the fourth and final man, Nadir, reaching back to close the helo's door.

Finishing the final check of his personal equipment, Ariel leaned forward, placing his hand on the pilot's shoulder—his eyes conveying the unspoken message. *Let's get in the air.*

There was only one thing certain in all of this. The men in the West Bank were living on borrowed time.

He felt the helicopter lurch into the air, the sickening feeling of the ground dropping away from them as the *Saifaneet* tilted forward—racing over the desert flats toward the dried out wadi to the north.

They could be in the skies over Ramallah in just over thirty minutes.

Only a few moments had passed when the helicopter pulled up without warning, settling into a momentary hover before it banked left, describing an arc as it turned back toward the training facility.

Ariel reached forward and grabbed one of the comms headsets, slipping it over his ears just in time to hear the repeated order, ". . .say again, RTB immediately."

Return to base.

He exchanged a look with Ze'ev, the older man's face expressionless—only his eyes betraying the emotions roiling within. They both knew all too well what this could mean.

They came in hot, the *Saifaneet* flaring as it pulled into a hover above the courtyard.

And that's when Ariel saw him through the blinding whirlwind of sand— the figure of Avi ben Shoham standing there in front of the main building. Waiting for them.

And he knew—without even getting out of the helicopter, without a word being spoken. The reality hitting him like a blow across the face.

The soldiers they had been setting off to rescue. . .were dead.

10:51 A.M.
The highway
Gaza City, Gaza Strip

"I need to speak with Dahlan. *Now!*" Tenet's eyes were flashing fire, his face distorted with anger as he advanced toward the lead SUV.

"Easy there," David Lay murmured, his eyes locking with those of Dahlan's head of security, the man's stance by the open driver's side door betraying the tension in his body. *Don't do anything rash.*

It was a little late for that admonition, in reality. They shouldn't have stopped here—practically in the middle of the highway—the convoy exposed to possible attack from any direction. But after the call from Station Tel Aviv, Tenet hadn't been in a mood to listen.

"Please, Mr. Tenet—we need you to return to your vehicle immediately, sir," the young IDF *segen* serving as the officer in charge of their escort warned, advancing with his Galil assault rifle held at patrol ready, its buttstock tucked against his shoulder, his hand closed around the weapon's pistol grip.

Tenet shook his head, staring angrily at the Palestinian bodyguard in front of him. "Do I really have to repeat myself? I want to speak—"

"Do we have a problem here?" Mohammed Dahlan asked calmly, buttoning his suit jacket as he emerged from the interior of the Mercedes.

"We do," the CIA director retorted, mastering himself with an effort. He took a step forward as Dahlan motioned his bodyguards to stand down, lowering his voice. "You know how delicate the peace process has been these last few weeks—but you *know* how close we are. This will set us back *decades.*"

The Palestinian security chief shook his head. "I have no idea what you are talking about, Mr. Tenet. I—"

"I am talking," Tenet interrupted, jabbing a thick finger in Dahlan's direction, "about the bodies of murdered Israelis being paraded through the streets of Ramallah. As we speak."

11:16 A.M.
The training facility

"...the bodies to al-Manarah Square, where an impromptu victory celebration appears to be taking place. One of the bodies appears to have been dragged behind a car through the streets of Ramallah."

There was no way they could have gotten to them in time, Avi ben Shoham told himself, staring grimly at the TV screen as the news host continued, his voice trembling as he narrated the carnage. No way anyone could have gotten to them.

Staging a successful hostage rescue was something that took time, an abundance of it. And that was the one thing they hadn't had.

The one thing they never seemed to have. *And good men died.* As they ever had, a shadow passing across Shoham's face as he remembered his brothers in the Golan.

He'd managed to get clear of the tank before its fuel tanks cooked off. His loader hadn't been so lucky. The memory burned forever in his memory—realizing that the man was no longer with them—turning back toward the Patton just as it exploded, the fireball washing over him. *The screams.*

Weeks later, when they had pinned the Medal of Valor upon his chest. . .he had never felt less a hero in his life. It still sat in his desk drawer at his home in Galilee, its yellow ribbon a reminder of the Holocaust, the sword and olive branch forged into the plain metal Star of David, bearing stark witness. *Never again.*

"What are we hearing from Jerusalem, Ayelet?" He asked, turning to the uniformed woman standing a few feet away.

"Rumblings," she responded, "nothing more certain. But retaliation is going to be swift—Barak has no other choice. The talk is of a strike at selected security targets in Ramallah and Gaza."

A show of force. That's what this would be, he thought, glancing back toward the members of the Kidon team now filing into the communications center, their weapons stowed and tactical vests removed.

Retaliation. *Delivering a message.*

Finding the men actually responsible for the atrocity—that was going to take much longer.

And when they did. . .

Someone called out his name and Avi turned to see a young Mossad officer coming across the room toward him. "You have a call on the secure line," he announced, lowering his voice as he moved closer, his hand grasping Shoham's shoulder for a moment before he passed on. "It's Efraim."

11:41 A.M.
HaKirya
Tel Aviv

"Enough," Shaul Mofaz spat, throwing the folder back on the table, the images still visible. Images of a police station turned into a charnel house, members of Arafat's *Tanzim* militia posing for pictures, the fresh blood visible on the concrete walls. Smeared in bloody handprints. "Level the place."

"Shaul, I—" one of his fellow *alufim* began, but Mofaz cut him off angrily.

"As long as that building stands, pictures like this one are going to spread all over the Arab world—celebrating the murder of Jews. We level it, leave it in rubble, remove the monument to their 'victory.' And we launch a strike on the Mukataa."

"Arafat's headquarters?" The man shook his head. "If you attack him directly, this becomes war."

Mofaz reached forward, tapping one of the photos with a weathered forefinger. "This has *already* become war."

"The Prime Minister has already expressed his concern that warning be given to the Palestinian Authority in advance of the strikes—give them time to evacuate civilians from the area." The general exchanged an uncomfortable glance with one of his fellows. "I don't believe Barak will approve the kind of measures you're suggesting."

And that was the way it always was. Missiles into empty buildings. A token retaliation, theater for the benefit of onlookers.

Mofaz glared at both men for a long moment before turning away. "All right, then. But the police station stays on the strike list. Along with the marina in Gaza. And the broadcast center of the Voice of Palestine? Make sure they hear *us*."

12:35 P.M.
Gaza City

"The President will be furious," George Tenet mused aloud, staring out the tinted windows of the armored Agency Suburban as their convoy moved deeper into Gaza City, twisting through the narrow streets as they made their way toward the Mediterranean and Arafat's beachfront headquarters. "The political capital we've invested in bringing both sides to the table—in ensuring that the Palestinians had both the training and equipment for self-governance. And now *this* happens in the middle of an official visit. It's nothing less than a slap in the face."

And that was the Middle East, Lay thought, maintaining a studiously neutral expression. If he had learned one thing in his years in the region, it was that the Arab street was a force to itself, unpredictable and volatile as the desert. If you thought you could bend it to your will, you were wrong.

And likely to get kicked in the teeth as soon as you tried.

That was what was happening to the efforts of Tenet and the State Department now—months of planning and negotiations kicked into dust by the actions of a mob. Spontaneous and uncontrollable. But that was a problem for the higher-ups. So far above his paygrade that even offering advice would be ill-considered.

His only concern would be dealing with the chaos the peace-makers left in their wake when they returned stateside.

The cellular phone in the inside jacket pocket of his suit began to ring as they turned into the Arafat compound, the jangle drawing an annoyed look from Tenet. "Make sure you have that thing turned off."

"It's Langley," Lay announced, heedless of Tenet's words as he read the identifier code off the phone's tiny screen. This was. . .irregular, to say the least. "McLaughlin."

He punched the button to *Accept Call*, raising the phone to his ear as the Suburban rolled to a stop, armed guards in the green uniforms of the Palestinian Security Force moving forward to secure the convoy. *Dahlan's people.*

"Deputy Director," he began, "what can I do for you?"

He listened for what had to be only a few minutes before the call ended, but it seemed like an eternity—the color draining from his face the longer the acting deputy director spoke.

"What's going on, David?" he heard Tenet's voice ask as he returned the phone to his jacket, his hands moving sluggishly—as if in a dream.

"An hour ago," Lay said, a look of disbelief in his eyes as he glanced over at the DCI, "the USS *Cole* was bombed at harbor in Aden. More than twenty American sailors are believed dead."

1:17 P.M.
The training facility
The Negev

No one longs for peace more than the soldier. For no one knows the horrors of the alternative more keenly.

Ariel shook his head as the host on the television screen continued her newscast in Hebrew, her words playing over the looping images from Ramallah—each of them now as familiar as if he had been standing there.

His face twitching in uncontrollable anger as the video once more showed the broken body of the reservist being hurled from the second-floor window of the police station to land at the feet of the mob below.

The mutilated, barely recognizable bodies of Vadim Novesche and Yossi Avrahami had been returned to the custody of the IDF at the border of the West Bank an hour earlier. Once-bright hopes for peace shattered in the space of a morning.

For peace. . .was not to be the lot of the Jew.

He had been in the first year of his enlistment when a Palestinian traffic policeman from Khan Yunis named Ayman Radi had walked into a bus stop in Jerusalem, detonating his backpack full of explosives only meters from a bus filled with young Israeli soldiers returning to their bases from weekend leave.

Holy war is our path, a note left behind by Radi for his family had read. *My death will be martyrdom. I will knock on the gates of Paradise with the skulls of the sons of Zion.*

A harbinger of all that was to come.

He heard the door of the small meeting room open and close behind him, half-turned to see Tzipporah standing there, his own helplessness mirrored in her dark eyes. "Today they dragged the body of our brother through the streets," she began, looking past him to the television screen—her voice nearly choking with fury, "like that of a dog. How long until the Prime Minister *allows* us to respond?"

There was nothing within himself that he could offer in answer to her anger, no words of calm. He moved past on her on his way out the door, his voice trembling with barely suppressed rage. "Not soon enough."

2:39 P.M.
Arafat's Headquarters
Gaza City, Gaza Strip

". . .the casualty figures are still unclear, but the frigate HMS *Marlborough* has been diverted in answer to the *Cole's* distress call and is under full steam for Aden, with a full complement of medical and damage control personnel aboard."

Thank God for the Brits, David Lay thought, gazing out the window of the second-floor office toward the Mediterranean. "How long until we have US personnel on-scene?"

"Not long," Daniel Vukovic responded. Lay's second-in-command in Tel Aviv, he was now in charge of monitoring the situation. "There's a Marine FAST team in-bound from Qatar. They'll establish a secure perimeter as soon as they land."

"How bad are we talking?"

"It's bad, David—the photos look like someone placed a shaped charge against the hull and ripped it open, several hundred pounds of high explosive, minimum. The reports are all over the place—but near as we can assess at this time, a small boat was used as the delivery vehicle."

"Like the one back in January," Lay observed, taking a deep breath. There had been an attempt on the *Arleigh Burke*-class guided missile destroyer USS *The Sullivans* in port at Aden on the third day of the new year—part of the foiled Millenium attack plot—but the boat used by the terrorists had been overloaded with explosives and sank before it could even reach the ship.

"Right. This thing has al-Qaeda's fingerprints all over it."

You always knew you couldn't get lucky forever. And *they* only needed to get it right once.

Lay looked up to see the young IDF officer in charge of their escort standing in the doorway of the office and responded, "I have to go here, Dan. Keep me apprised."

"Mr. Lay," the officer began as he saw Lay return the phone to the pocket of his jacket, "my apologies, but I have to speak with your director."

Lay grimaced, gesturing back toward the closed door of the conference rooms behind him. "I'm afraid that's not going to be possible. He's meeting with President Arafat and they are not to be disturbed. Can I deliver a message to him?"

The young lieutenant shook his head. "Both of you need to come with my men and me. At once."

There was an urgency there in the soldier's words. Something he knew—wasn't willing to say. At least not to him.

"There's not—" Lay began, his words cut off as the door opened, Tenet emerging from the conference room behind him. An expression of weary anger written on the DCI's face.

It was the look of a man who was spending too much of his time beating his head against the wall. "Wrapping up?" Lay asked as his boss came up.

Tenet snorted. "We've barely even had time to begin—he's tied up on the phone—his third call from Mubarak. And Terje Larsen's due any minute."

The UN envoy. His head came up in that moment, noticing the Israeli officer. "What is he doing up here?"

"He asked to speak with you—said it was important that we leave. Right away."

Tenet's gaze shifted from Lay's face to that of the lieutenant. "Why? We're not done here."

"Sir," the young man began, his eyes meeting the CIA director's in an unflinching gaze. "I cannot order you to leave. But if you choose to stay, my men and I will no longer be able to protect you."

And there it was. "Are you saying—"

The door behind them opened once more and Lay turned to see the figure of Yasser Arafat standing there in the entry, the characteristic black-and-white checkered *keffiyeh* covering his head—his small, dark eyes flashing as they darted from one man to the next.

"Out," he ordered, gesturing peremptorily to Tenet with an angry wave of his hand. "Get out, all of you—leave my office at once. We are about to be bombed by the Israelis."

2:51 P.M.
A restaurant
Ramallah, The West Bank

Fear. Raw and visceral, eating away at him like a corrosive acid.

Simon Collins slammed the door of the restroom shut behind him, closing off the nearly deserted restaurant without. His fingers trembling uncontrollably as he moved to the sink, turning the faucet on full blast and thrusting both hands under its stream—rubbing them together as if he could cleanse himself of the memory.

The *horror* of what he had seen—of having come so close to death himself. The raw, barbaric hatred he had seen in the eyes of the young men in that crowd. In the words of a fifteen-year-old he had glimpsed later, bathing his hands in the blood of a slain soldier and chanting loudly, "This will teach the Jews to come to our land!" as the crowd cheered around him.

It hadn't ended when he had left the police station—making his way through the streets later, trying to sort out his next move, he had seen one of the bodies being dragged behind a car, the man's entrails spilling out into the dust.

Despite everything he had known—everything he had witnessed over the decades—he'd found himself nearly doubled over at the sight, convulsed in dry heaves.

He had worked in the territories for years, walked these streets many times. Ramallah wasn't a desolate backwater, but a bright, thriving city. A remarkably liberal place for the Middle East—a place where you could find Western restaurants like this one, clubs filled with young women in short cocktail dresses and high heels, rocking out to the latest Top 40 from the United States.

The last place on earth he would have expected to explode into such a display of medieval savagery, butchery more reminiscent of Rwanda, of the Zaire—than the city he had known and loved. But he had *seen* it with his own eyes. Captured it with his own lens.

He stood there for a long moment, his hands dripping with water as he gazed into the mirror above the sink—sunken, haunted eyes staring back at him.

There were some things a man's eyes were never meant to see. Some things which could never be unseen.

It was as Collins was drying his hands that he heard a low, throbbing sound—seeming to vibrate through the very walls, growing louder by the moment.

Building in intensity as he left the restroom, heading for the door leading out to the street. It was a sound he remembered well from Kosovo. A sound that had ever been accompanied by terror.

Helicopters.

2:55 P.M.
Gaza City, The Gaza Strip

You could feel the difference in the air as the three-vehicle convoy took a turn out the Arafat compound, the Agency Suburban in the middle as they headed back out toward Highway 4. A stillness, like the quiet before a summer thunderstorm.

Tension. About to be shattered.

"Is that—?" Lay's eyes followed the direction of Tenet's finger as he pointed through the tinted windows of the speeding SUV toward the Mediterranean, out past the marina where the small boats making up the Palestinian Security Force's "navy" rode at anchor.

And there it was, an Israeli warship outlined against the horizon, the afternoon sun reflected off the waves. "It is," Lay responded quietly, his eyes narrowing. "A *Sa'ar 5*-class corvette, from the looks of it."

The director shook his head, murmuring a curse as he glared out toward the vessel. "Everything we've done—everything we were *trying* to do to lay the groundwork for Sharm el-Sheikh next week. All of it gone. . .this is going to be war now, David. This—"

Whatever Tenet might have been about to say was lost as one of the NSF boats in the marina suddenly exploded, both men flinching at the noise—a gout of flame shooting toward the sky.

War. Lay glanced back in time to see a pair of AH-64 *"Peten"* gunships appear over the buildings behind them, pulling into a hover—weapons trained on the marina, smoke trails emerging in the sky as yet more rockets flashed from beneath the helicopters' stubby pylons.

He reached forward and gripped their driver firmly on the shoulder, squeezing hard as the man turned toward him. "Let's get out of here pronto, shall we?"

3:01 P.M.
Ramallah, The West Bank

Collins emerged from the entry of the restaurant into the streets of the city, hearing panicked shouts amidst the intensifying roar of helicopter rotors. A discarded bike lying by the side of the street. An abandoned bag of vegetables from a nearby market, strewn in the dust.

A young Palestinian nearly colliding with him as he ran for cover. *Chaos.*

Pandemonium everywhere.

A loud *boom* resounded over the city, a sound like that of a giant clapping his hands together, and Collins glanced up to see the front of the police station enveloped in smoke—a pair of American-manufactured Bell Cobra gunships coming into view over the rooftops of Ramallah, just hanging there for a moment.

A menacing presence.

He saw soldiers and police spilling out the front door of the police station in a panic—members of Arafat's *Tanzim* militia running for their lives.

Not fast enough. A scant moment later, another three rockets launched from beneath the Cobras' weapons pylons, screaming through the afternoon sky until they slammed into the police station—dust and debris billowing out into the streets as the building collapsed.

Rubble covering the spot where the Israeli soldier had been thrown from the window, the place where his blood had soaked the ground.

The gunships dipped forward, picking up airspeed as they emerged from the smoke, screaming past the rooftops over Collins' head like massive insects of prey.

Already stalking their next targets.

"Simon!" He looked up at the sound of his name called out in accented English—catching sight of Nasser Atta crouched on the other side of the street, beckoning to him as he took shelter behind the door of his sedan.

Collins sprinted across the street and dropped down on one knee beside the ABC News' producer, glancing back toward the police station to see the smoke and dust slowly clearing away from above the rubble—the Palestinian flag which had hung over its entry now shredded and lying in the dirt. The moans of the injured—a man lying on his back, his leg mangled below the knee. Trying painfully to lift himself, to reach the Kalashnikov assault rifle which lay only a few feet away.

"I knew there would be reprisals coming, I just didn't expect. . .this," Atta murmured, still seemingly shell-shocked as he stared toward the destruction, the throb of helicopter rotors still audible in the distance.

They weren't gone yet.

"You'll be safer with me," he added after a long moment, seeming to collect himself. "You need to stay with someone local, a face people know."

Fair enough. After the events of the morning, though, the offer of protection rang hollow on Collins' ears. Was anyone even *capable* of protecting any of them if something went wrong?

"Who's this?" The British journalist asked skeptically, watching a green Land Rover pull into the square before the rubble of the police station—a middle-aged man in military fatigues stepping out with a bullhorn in his hands, a maroon beret perched atop his head.

"That's Abu Awad," Atta breathed, taking a careful look over the hood of the car. Collins grimaced in recognition, keeping his own head down.

"Abu Awad", the *kunya* of Mahmoud Damra. The commander of Arafat's infamous Force 17 and one of the Palestinian president's closest associates, Damra had made a name for himself in the heavy fighting against the Israelis during the siege of Beirut back in the early '80s.

"Is this all the Jews can do?" Damra's thick, guttural voice boomed out through the bullhorn, resounding off the surrounding buildings. "This was nothing more than a firecracker. We do not fear them—we will turn Ramallah into a cemetery for the occupiers."

A distant explosion served as grim punctuation to his words, the helicopters hitting targets deeper in the city.

The sounds of war.

9:54 A.M. Eastern Time
The CNN Center
Atlanta, Georgia

"To the Middle East now," Bill Hemmer announced, adjusting his glasses as he stared directly into the red eye of the CNN cameras. "A lot of the information we're getting right now is still developing at this time—only about another hour of sunlight there in the Middle East. Again, the picture with the tank hunkered down is indeed in the West Bank, in the Palestinian town of Ramallah. Said to be just on the outskirts of that town. Daryn?"

"That's right, Bill," His co-anchor began, clearing her throat. "There right within Ramallah, we have one of our CNN producers, Sausan Ghosheh. We've been talking to her by phone."

A picture of Ghosheh came up on-screen as Daryn Kagan continued, "Sausan, what's the latest from where you are inside Ramallah?"

There was a moment's delay before the producer's voice came back over the line. "Daryn, I'm standing outside of this police station that was just bombed by Israeli helicopter gunships a few minutes ago. The top floor of that—it's a two-story building, and the top floor is completely destroyed. I am standing here with groups of people who walk by, hundreds of them, chanting—some of them carrying weapons—very angry, calling this a humiliation of Palestine."

Kagan nodded her understanding, momentarily consulting the notes before her on the desk. "So Sausan, the police station where you are standing—for our viewers who are just now joining our live coverage—please explain for us the significance of that particular building."

"Earlier today, according to the Palestinian officials, a Ford transit car carrying two Israeli undercover police agents came close to this police station. The police were suspicious of this car, and they tried to stop the car. The car wouldn't stop. So the police—" Ghosheh's voice broke off for a moment, faint shouts sounding in the distance, the connection filling with static. "As I am talking to you right now, people are running. People are running, because they're hearing helicopters, and, they're trying to find something to hide under, expecting the helicopters to attack."

"Sausan," Hemmer interjected, taking a sip from the silver container of ice water he always kept on his desk, "are you all right? Are you in a safe place?"

"All right," she responded, ignoring his question, "now they stopped, they're looking—and they're pointing up in the air. It was only a false alarm, but you can see how people are angry and very frightened here. They're terrified of another hit. They don't think this will be the end of it, and they are pointing toward the sky and calling for revenge against Israel."

The cycle of violence, the young CNN anchor mused, his brow furrowing. Never-ending in the Middle East.

"As to your previous question, Daryn," Ghosseh continued, sounding as though she was out of breath, "as I was saying, there was this Israeli transit car. They couldn't stop, they wouldn't stop—the people in the car. And the Palestinian youth, they surrounded the car. As I am talking now, there is a bomb. I heard the sound of a bomb, but I can't see where it is."

Kagan looked across at him, her eyes betraying her concern. "Sausan, most importantly—are you in a place that's safe for you to talk, or do we need to let you go so you can seek shelter?"

"I'm running as I'm talking to you," Ghosheh's voice came back after a moment, speaking in short gasps, "it's why I'm running out of breath."

"Okay, I think we're going to let you get to a safe place and we'll check back with you later on." She looked up into the cameras, her face grave. "That is Sausan Ghosheh, reporting live from Ramallah—obviously a place that is filled with tension today as the Israelis take action which they say is not retaliation; but which does follow the death of two Israeli soldiers earlier this morning. Bill?"

"And now, as we turn our attention to the Gulf of Aden, where fresh details are emerging regarding what the Pentagon is calling a terrorist attack on the USS *Cole*. . ."

6:18 P.M.
A residence
Tel Aviv, Israel

"I expect the civilized world to understand the difficult dilemma with which Israel is faced," Shlomo Ben-Ami stated, staring unflinchingly into the battery of news cameras facing him—the flashbulbs going off in the face of the acting Foreign Minister clearly visible on the television screen. "The desire for peace, and peace as a national interest, cannot co-exist with violence of the kind that Arafat has initiated in the recent weeks."

He paused, appearing to consult the written statement before him for a moment before looking up. "There is no self-respecting sovereign state that can conduct a peace process, when its supposed partner deliberately releases known terrorists and breaks all the rules of political behavior. Israel believes that the current deterioration of the situation can be stopped, but only if the world will say clearly and unequivocally to Arafat: 'Enough is enough.'"

And that would require a moral resolve that the world had never possessed, the old man thought—taking a sip of his whiskey as he stared at the television across the darkened room. They sat in their comfortable houses, paid token homage to the memory of the Holocaust and self-righteously assured themselves, *"Never again."*

But they did. . .nothing. That task had ever fallen to men like him, all the way back to the War of Independence—when the Jewish state had been born of fire and blood.

"The Palestinians are responsible for their fate," the Foreign Minister said, continuing to deliver his statement, "and they must therefore understand the full significance and implications—and especially the damage—which the continuation and escalation of the current situation will cause. Even at this difficult hour, we call upon the Palestinian people: Choose the course of peace, stop the firing and the riots, and return to the course of good neighborliness. Thank you."

The room exploded in a flurry of questions from the assembled members of the press, each of them drowning out the other until the old man saw Ben-Ami gesture to a *Haaretz* reporter near the front.

"Are we now, by your definition," the reporter asked, "in a state of war with the Palestinian Authority, and what will happen now? There were several waves of attacks in Ramallah and Gaza. Has the IDF now halted its fire and is waiting, or are we still in the midst of the attack?"

"We have defined this operation as a limited action, designed to respond to the situation created by the Palestinian Authority, and to convey a sharp message that Israel, as a sovereign state, cannot and will not react with self-restraint in the face of such a blatant and humiliating act against its citizens and soldiers. At the same time, this is a localized message. We will of course be the first to rejoice if this will mark the end of the wave of bloodshed. However, we are still at the beginning of this crisis. We do not seek confrontation. But if confrontation is forced upon us, we will be forced to respond similarly."

To respond similarly. The old man drained the last of his whiskey and returned the tumbler to the small endtable beside his chair, a small ring in the wood marking where it had rested for years.

Blood for blood, an eye for an eye. Ever the order of things in the Middle East, stretching back over the course of millennia.

Men were fools to think they could change it now. He heard footsteps behind him, and knew without turning who had entered. "It was good of you to come, Avi. Please, sit down."

"I came as soon as I was able, Efraim," Avi ben Shoham responded, moving across the room to take a seat opposite the Mossad director. "It's been. . .a dark day."

Efraim Halevy merely nodded by way of reply, his index finger rubbing gently across his clean-shaven lip as he stared at the now-muted television. "You know that his wife heard it happening, don't you?"

"What do you mean?"

Halevy let out a deep, heavy sigh. "Yossi Avrahami's wife Hani—she called his mobile phone to make sure he was safe. The voice that answered told her with a laugh, 'We are now slaughtering your husband.' And all she could hear was the screams."

Shoham flinched as if he had been slapped, his face tightening into a death mask, eyes burning with wrath. He opened his mouth to speak, but no words came out.

"You and I, Avi," the Mossad director began once more, "we are no longer young men. Our lives have been spent in defense of the Jewish state. And now, just as we might have thought ourselves on the very brink of securing peace for our children's children. . .all we have worked for is torn away. Our brothers butchered, and us helpless to save them. Paralyzed."

"We will have our vengeance."

"And it's not to be found by firing rockets into empty buildings," Halevy said, lifting his head to look Shoham in the face, his eyes glittering cold as death in the dim light. "As much as Barak would like to tell himself otherwise. But by finding and hunting down those responsible for their murders. Those *actually* responsible—the men behind this. . .what is the word? 'Lynching.'"

Shoham nodded his understanding. There was no word in Hebrew for the kind of evil that had taken place in Ramallah, so a horrible new loan word from the English had entered the lexicons of them all this day to fill the gap.

"We have known each other for decades, Avi," Halevy continued, "and you have ever proven to be someone upon whom I could rely. Which is why I am entrusting you with the responsibility of carrying this out. Find those responsible, track them down wherever they hide—and kill them. That the world may know. . .murder a Jew and you can expect to die the death of a dog, wallowing in your own blood in the street."

"It will be done."

"You will report directly to Eli Gerstman for this one—he's already been briefed and will be awaiting your contact. Anything you need will be provided."

"I will need a *Kidon* unit," Shoham replied, seeming to consider his words for a moment. "The field team, their support personnel—everything."

"Is there someone you had in mind?" Halevy asked, gazing at him keenly.

"There is, in fact. A young man who is known by the codename of 'Ariel.'"

"Ah, yes," Halevy nodded, rising to his feet and moving to the sideboard to refill his drink. "The Lion of God. . ."

Part Two

"There's no difference between one's killing and making decisions that will send others to kill. It's exactly the same thing, or even worse."—Golda Meir

8:09 A.M. December 9th, 2000 (Two months later)
Ben Gurion International Airport

"There'll be a car waiting for you at Dulles," Daniel Vukovic instructed, handing over the briefcase. "You're then to proceed straight to Langley for the debrief on RUMBLEWAY, where—"

"I have done this before," the dark-haired young man from the Operations Directorate smiled quietly, something of an edge glinting in his gunmetal-blue eyes. "A time or three."

Fair enough, Vukovic thought. The man couldn't have been much past his early twenties, but word in the community had it that he was one of Pavitt's rising stars in the DO's Special Operations Group—hard as that was to imagine.

Then again. . .it was the DO. Anything was possible over on that side of the house.

"All right then," he said finally, forcing a smile to his face as he turned to leave. "Enjoy the in-flight movie."

It would be about the only thing any of them enjoyed for some time to come, he thought, moving back through the terminal—in the wake of a field operation gone horribly wrong.

Which they tended to do, more often than not. It was why, as a careerist in the Intelligence Directorate, he viewed field ops at an absolute last resort—an option to be utilized only when all other options had been thoroughly exhausted.

Say what you would about photographic intelligence—and it *was* a means of intel-gathering not without its limitations—you'd never wake up one sunny morning to find that your spy satellite had been dropped off on your doorstep, genitals cut off and stuffed in its mouth.

Like they'd found the asset they had so carefully recruited from the West Bank, thrown out of a speeding car in the front of the Embassy only a week earlier.

His phone vibrated in the pocket of his light jacket as he left the concourse and he pulled it out, glancing momentarily at the screen before flipping it open. *The station chief.*

The outgoing station chief, he reminded himself, raising the phone to his ear. Cometh the New Year, cometh the new management. Still no word on whom the benevolent gods of the seventh floor had designated as Lay's replacement. If there was one good thing about a posting like Tel Aviv, it was that Langley generally gave it to an old hand.

It was no place for someone just learning to fly.

"Just saw Nichols off at the airport," he began, glancing about him as he made his way out toward his car, the morning rays of sun washing in over the city, through the palms off to the west. "On my way back. What do you need?"

"Avi ben Shoham has made contact, requested a meet. Hatraklin, at noon."

11:56 A.M.
Hatraklin

Always show up early. That was the maxim of any spy—it gave time to familiarize yourself with your surroundings. Prepare the battlespace.

It gave you an edge. Unless, of course, you were playing against another spy who was doing the same thing—on his home court.

"Have a seat, David," Avi ben Shoham advised in his thickly-accented English, the barest ghost of a smile playing around the Israeli's grave countenance. "This luncheon, it is. . .how do you say it? 'On me.'"

That was hardly a good sign, Lay thought, feeling himself tense at the words. Indigestion was likely going to keep him from abusing Shoham's. . .hospitality?

"Take it as a token of my friendship, a gesture in honor of your soon departure from our country," his counterpart continued as Lay pulled back the chair and sat down, glancing about the restaurant. "May your successor prove to be as reliable an ally."

"I'd drink to that," Lay assented, reaching for his menu. "I've recommended Vukovic for the post, but it's hard to say."

Shoham nodded. "Daniel is a good man—has excellent instincts for this work."

Vukovic was also a Jew—a Russian whose family had escaped to the States in the '50s—Lay thought, which was what made his appointment here in Tel Aviv unlikely. They couldn't risk the appearance of partiality.

A conflict of interest.

"I trust you have been well, David," the Israeli continued. "I heard about the. . .incident at your Embassy the other day."

"Indeed," Lay responded, grimacing as he glanced up from the menu. "That was a brutal piece of work."

It wasn't a sight he was likely to soon forget—the look of agonized horror frozen in the dead man's eyes, a face twisted in torment from the forcible castration.

And stuffed in his mouth. . .well, the less thought about that, the better.

"And that, David, is the reality of our business," Shoham returned soberly, reaching for the glass of ice water on the table before him. "Particularly here in the Middle East. We recruit assets like your man—and we know when we recruit them that it may well mean their death, sooner or later."

"I've lost assets before," Lay replied, remembering his early days with the Agency. Running agents first into Castro's Cuba, then Eastern Europe in the years before the Wall came down. He'd recruited more than one person only to have them disappear without a trace. As if they'd never even existed.

But never before this gruesomely, he didn't add, his eyes never leaving the Israeli's face.

The Soviet Union hadn't been given to the flashy displays of brutality favored by Middle Eastern thugs, preferring the silent terror that came from having neighbors vanish in the night.

"Your man, he was a homosexual, was he not?"

Lay nodded silently by way of response. That Shoham would know that shouldn't have surprised him, three years in to his tenure in Israel. The Mossad made it their business to *know*.

Who knows? Perhaps they had even considered recruiting the young man themselves. Perhaps they had. You never knew.

"Well then," the Israeli intelligence officer said, his voice as cold as the ice in his glass, "you can be certain that your involvement did not cause his death. It only hastened it."

"Like Abu Ammar?" Lay asked, using Yasser Arafat's old *kunya*.

A glint of humor entered Shoham's eyes, perhaps the closest Lay had seen him come to a laugh in three years. The Palestinian leader's proclivities were well-known to their community.

"For some men," he said finally, "no law applies." And that was true the world over.

Their waitress arrived a moment later to take their orders and refill Shoham's glass. Lay glanced after her retreating form, making sure she was out of earshot in the bustling restaurant before returning his attention to his counterpart. "But you and I both know, Avi—you didn't ask me here to discuss my departure, or the fate of my asset."

"No. . .I did not. During the summit at Sharm el-Sheikh," Shoham continued, "your government promised to aid us in bringing to justice those responsible for the murder of our soldiers in Ramallah, a promise reiterated by your Director to mine. Is that a promise the United States government intends to stand behind?"

"Of course," Lay responded, his eyes narrowing as he stared across the table—unable to escape the feeling that he was treading dangerously close to quicksand.

But that's how it always was when you found yourself tasked with keeping the promises of your betters.

"Tell me," the Israeli said after another long moment, sliding a photograph face-down across the tablecloth, "do you recognize this man?"

The image was that of an angry crowd of young Palestinians—the lens focused on the figure of a man in military uniform standing off to one side, a cellular phone held up to his ear.

"I do," Lay breathed, looking up into Shoham's eyes. "It's Mustafa al-Shukeiri. . ."

12:15 P.M.
A Mossad safehouse in the Golan
Israel

"We are slaughtering your husband." Ariel turned away from the map on the wall of the safehouse, glancing down once more at the photos of their target, splayed out across the table before him.

Had he been the one to take that call, his hands stained with Yossi Avrahami's blood as he mocked the man's wife? Or had he simply sanctioned the butchery?

No matter, the young man thought, his face darkening. There was no distinction to be made between the two, no moral one. The man who threw the stones, the man who told him to do it—both of them the same.

Morality. He had been raised to believe that there was no morality to be found in military service, in the conscription of the IDF. That the work of the *Yeshiva* student he'd been intended to be was just as important as that of a soldier in the preservation of the Jewish state.

But no scholars—no *prayers* delivered by phylactery-adorned men at the Western Wall—would serve to defend the way of life they had built in this country. To ensure their very *survival.*

So he fought.

40

12:16 P.M.
Hatraklin
Tel Aviv, Israel

"How did you get this?"

Shoham spread his hands in an expansive gesture. "You know how it is in our business, David. Some of these things are best left unsaid, yes?"

"He's a member of the Palestinian Legislative Council," Lay continued, tapping the photograph before him with a forefinger, "Arafat's man in the West Bank."

A friend of the Palestinian leader for decades, al-Shukeiri had been at Arafat's side in Beirut—gone into exile with him to Tunis.

"The same," Shoham replied, the look of steel never leaving his eyes.

"He's been extremely influential in the peace process, one of the Palestinian leaders present in Paris to meet with Albright in early October. What are you trying to say, Avi?"

"This photo was taken by a British journalist in Ramallah on the day of the lynchings. It shows al-Shukeiri placing a phone call which we were able to confirm was made to the officer in charge of the Ramallah police station."

My God, Lay thought, sensing what was to come. Struggling to keep his face from betraying his thoughts. This was bad. Worse than Shoham had any way of knowing.

"And?"

"And we have reason to believe," the Israeli continued, choosing his words carefully, "that he issued a stand-down order. Moments later, the Palestinian 'police' stood aside and let the mob flood into the station, inaction which resulted in the butchering of our men."

Lay shook his head in disbelief. The horror of it all. *This wasn't possible.*

"You are certain of this?" he asked, gauging carefully how far to press. It had long been suspected that Mossad was exploring technological measures to exploit signals intelligence similar to those used by the NSA's ECHELON program, targeting the Palestinian Authority and the rest of their Middle Eastern neighbors—but they had never been able to confirm it.

"I am," was the simple response, Shoham's dark eyes warning him to pursue it no further.

"Then what you're telling me is that you believe al-Shukeiri responsible for the death of your men? And you intend to see him brought to trial."

"David. . .David, David," Shoham whispered reproachfully, leaning back in his chair. "Let us both have done with these meaningless. . .pretensions—speak openly with one another. We both know a man of al-Shukeiri's prominence can never be made to stand trial. Such a media spectacle would fan the flames of this nascent *intifada* beyond anything we can begin to imagine."

"Then what are you suggesting?" He knew, all too well. But this was no time to be speaking in riddles. Time for all the cards to go out on the table, face up. Almost all of them, at any rate.

"Al-Shukeiri will not live to see the new year," the Israeli responded grimly, his dark eyes little more than slits as he stared across the table at Lay.

And there it was, out in the open. Now to deal with it as best as he could. "I understand," Lay replied noncommittally, "but what is it you want from the Agency?"

"Your help in finding him."

12:37 P.M.
A Mossad safehouse in the Golan

"We've been able to identify three residences owned by Mustafa al-Shukeiri in Europe," Ariel announced, spreading a series of satellite photographs out on the table before him. "A cottage in Somerset, an apartment on the eleventh floor of a Marseille high-rise—and an expansive villa along the sea near Marciana on the island of Elba."

"He's a wealthy man," Tzipporah observed, shaking her head. As was so much of the high-ranking Palestinian leadership.

Grown rich from decades of siphoning off international aid which had been intended for those suffering the depths of poverty in the camps—perpetual refugees.

Ze'ev cleared his throat, looking up from one of the photographs. "So how do we get in?"

"We don't, just yet," Ariel responded. He glanced around at his team before continuing. "The immediate problem is to pin al-Shukeiri down, establish his location. He accompanied Arafat to the summit at Sharm el-Sheikh and never returned. He might still be in Egypt—he may have flown to Europe to be with his second wife, Zainab, who is confirmed to be staying in Marseille. An officer from our embassy in Rome has been dispatched to Elba along with another of our officers posing as his spouse, under cover of taking a winter vacation. They will reconnoiter the villa and report on any activity observed there."

"And in the meantime?" Nadir asked, Ariel's head turning toward the youngest member of the team. American, born in Brooklyn to Jewish parents, the young man had made his *aliyah* at the age of eleven—but could still pass as easily for an American tourist as the IDF soldier he had become at seventeen.

"In the meantime," Ariel responded, sifting through a stack of folders before him, "we work up assault plans on each and every residence. Gathering intelligence on transportation. Means of approach and egress. Local security profiles. Everything we could possibly need. Nadir, you'll take Somerset. Ze'ev, Marseille. Tzipporah—you and I will go over Elba."

1:36 P.M.
The United States Embassy
Tel Aviv, Israel

"The situation in the PA," he had said, sitting back there in the restaurant, *"is extremely delicate, Avi—as you know better than I. President Clinton may be leaving the Oval Office in a month's time, but he has no intention of letting the door of MidEast peace hit him in the legacy on the way out."*

"That wasn't your stance on the rendition of Abu Yusuf." A statement, delivered in the tone of an accusation.

An accusation to which there could be no answer. Because there wasn't one.

The devastating attack on the USS *Cole* had sent an unprepared administration scrambling, clawing for something—anything—that could prove to the American people that there would be retribution.

Finding that a low-ranking official in the Palestinian Authority had been responsible for funneling funds to the bombers had been an opportunity too good to pass up. Not even the realization that the man was a distant cousin of Arafat had dissuaded the President from authorizing Operation RUMBLEWAY.

The Agency's plan had been quite simple, really—a joint operation with the Israelis to snatch him from the West Bank, put him on a plane to Egypt.

Let the *Mukhabarat* go over him for a few weeks. See what they could learn.

But like most "simple" plans handed down from on high, it had gone completely sideways. Until they'd finally ended up with the mutilated body of the asset who had been feeding them information dumped off in the street just in front of the embassy.

Return to sender.

And now there was this. Lay sighed, reaching over to the Motorola STU-III on his desk and lifting the secure telephone unit from its cradle before punching in a brief number.

A few moments went by as the call was connected over the Atlantic, the CIA station chief staring at the blank white wall of his spartanly-appointed office—drumming the fingers of his left hand nervously against the wood of his desk.

"Request to initiate secure transmission," he said abruptly when a voice came on the other end of the line, cutting them off before they could finish their sentence.

It was another moment before a tinny electronic *beep* sounded, assuring him that the encryption sequence had completed.

"Director," Lay began, choosing his next words carefully, "we have encountered. . .a major problem."

10:49 A.M., December 16ᵗʰ, 2000 (One week later)
The Golan safehouse

"Shukeiri's apartment is located just over two kilometers from the water," Ze'ev stated, using a pointer to trace the route he had marked on the map. "In the fifteen arrondissement."

"Eleven floors up."

"Right," the older man replied, acknowledging Ariel's observation with a nod. "Only two real access points, one of them restricted to maintenance. We'll need uniforms to get inside—I'm thinking a utility crew, electrical most likely."

It was a sound suggestion, Ariel thought, glancing over at Tzipporah. A stratagem they had used successfully in the past. "How do we get into the country to begin with?"

"The simplest way would be by air. Fly in commercial to Marseille Provence on Belgian passports—separate flights—bring in the weapons through the marina. A small sailing vessel or powerboat. Something inconspicuous, something that would fit in there in Marseille."

Water always had been Ze'ev's preference, given his past history with Israel's navy. And in this case, he couldn't have been more right.

"And where do the weapons come from?" Nadir asked skeptically, speaking up for the first time. "A container ship?"

Ariel smiled quietly, watching the interplay between the two men. Ze'ev had been running operations with *Shayetet-13* when his younger team member had still been in daycare back in the United States. . .but this was the nature of the *Kidon*. Of the IDF at large, truly.

Rank, seniority—none of it protected you from having your ideas challenged, taken apart. Analyzed as harshly as they would have been on your first day in the unit. No one got a pass.

And Nadir's question was a good one.

"No," Ze'ev responded after a moment. "We get them in Spain. There's a Russian in Manresa we've done business with before. Run them up the coast."

It was a solid plan, on the face of it. . .except for one small detail.

"What about the wife?" Ariel asked, clearing his throat.

A shadow passed across the older operator's face. "We must be prepared to do what needs to be done. *Whatever* needs to be done."

The phone in the corner of the room began to ring before Ariel could respond, and he went over to answer it, listening for a few moments. "Of course. I understand. It will be done."

He replaced the phone in its receiver, glancing back toward Ze'ev. "You called it—Marseille it is. Everyone, get your equipment packed for France."

11:09 A.M.
Mossad Headquarters
Tel Aviv

"What kind of help are you looking for from the Agency, Avi?" David Lay had asked, Avi ben Shoham remembered—going through the files on his desk. The two of them sitting back in that café, their lunch well-nigh forgotten as the two of them touched swords, fencers circling each other—looking for an opening. *"Specifically."*

"We possess a series of mobile cellular numbers used by al-Shukeiri over the last year," he'd replied simply, staring across at his counterpart. *"One of which was used to call the police station in Ramallah. We know the numbers, but we lack the capability to track them on a global scale. A capability you possess: ECHELON."*

Lay had just looked at him, shaking his head. *"ECHELON, that's Fort Meade's baby, Avi—not ours."*

"And in the United States, do you not. . .cooperate with these fellow agencies of yours?"

"Not so much as you might think." The American's laugh had been grim and mirthless.

"A promise was made, David. This is us coming to collect upon it."

"I'll see what can be done—you have to understand, even if I can get you what you need, it's not going to be direct access to the raw feeds. You're an ally, but that's strictly Five Eyes territory."

Australia, Canada, New Zealand, the United Kingdom, and the United States.

The pantheon of Western espionage, born out of the Anglo-American alliance of World War II and fostered through the darkest days of the Cold War. His own country had been birthed in the same fires, but this was one table they would never have a seat at.

"The only way this goes down is if we analyze the intel and then hand it over, Avi. It's the only way."

"We have a deal."

And that's exactly how it had gone, Shoham thought, reaching down and powering on his desktop computer—the machine coming to life with a wheezing groan. The Agency supplying them with location data on al-Shukeiri's most recently active number. Letting them know when he moved.

All very straightforward. So straightforward. . .he found it almost unnerving. But perhaps that was nothing more than the unwarranted suspicion of a man who had spent far too much of his life at war.

11:51 A.M. Western European Time
The Embassy of the United States
Paris, France

"You're asking me to do *what?*" Paul Renninger rose from his seat, taking the encrypted STU-III's handset with him, looping the cord over the CRT monitor as he paced around to the other side of his desk. His face betraying his agitation.

He'd spent nearly thirty years with the Agency—the last two as the chief of the prestigious and storied Paris Station. He'd run assets into East Germany—seen one of them executed a scant hundred meters from Checkpoint Charlie in Berlin. But this. . .

"Listen to me," he said, addressing his fellow station chief. "Do you understand the implications of what you're asking?"

But of course the man did. Because he was an old hand at this himself. And that meant he knew what he was doing in making the request, even if the infamous prerogatives of "need to know" made his reasons for doing so helplessly obscure.

Renninger listened silently for a few more minutes, before responding. "All right, Lay. I'll get a team in the field right away."

4:37 P.M. Israel Standard Time
An olive grove outside Beit Shemesh
Israel

"Is it done?" the man asked, not even glancing back as Shoham approached through the grove—his eyes fixed on the west, toward the setting sun, out across the fields now barren of grain.

Faint tendrils of smoke escaping from between his lips, a cigarette in his left hand.

Shoham nodded, stopping as he came abreast of Eli Gerstman, glancing over into the man's face.

Efraim's lieutenant was only a couple years his senior, but he looked far, far older—his face lined beyond his years. They had both seen far too much.

"It is," he replied, glancing back through the grove toward the road where Gerstman's personal vehicle was parked—the same battered old Citroen he'd had for. . .over a decade, maybe longer.

"I'm telling you, Avi," Gerstman had said on more than one occasion, *"the French are the only people in the world who know how to make a decent car."*

"Well, you have to admit. . .you haven't tried Volkswagen," he would always retort—a jocular response which ever evoked a sharp, bitter laugh, punctuated by a flurry of obscenities about a country that had cost both their families dear. Dark humor, the kind that had sustained the Jewish people through nearly two millennia of exile—scattered across the face of the earth.

But today was no time for jokes, dark or otherwise. "The *Kidon* team has received their orders. They'll depart for France in the morning."

"Good," Gerstman responded, taking a long, slow drag of the cigarette. "How long?"

Shoham shook his head, watching as the smoke drifted away on the cool evening breeze. "Impossible to say with any certainty, Eli, but I expect al-Shukeiri to be dead within the week."

"Our intelligence on his current location," Gerstman began, turning to look at him for the first time, "it came from the Americans. Do you consider it reliable?"

A challenging question, Shoham thought—thinking back to his meeting in Tel Aviv with David Lay—the CIA station chief's reaction to the news about al-Shukeiri.

There had been something there. . .something *off*, in the way he responded. As if he knew more than he was saying—more than he was *allowed* to say.

That had been their last face-to-face—the flow of intel on al-Shukeiri being passed along through subordinates in the days since.

"It's actionable," he responded slowly. "The CIA will. . .bear watching."

"Fair enough." Gerstman dropped his cigarette and ground it into the dirt beneath the heel of his old, scuffed dress shoes as he turned to leave. "See that you do."

3:49 P.M. Western European Time, December 17th
Av Jean Henri Fabre
Marignane, France

Ariel shrugged himself deeper into the folds of his light jacket, staring out across the wind-chopped waves of Étang de Berre. It wasn't his first time in France, but then it had been in the middle of the summer.

It had to be at least sixteen degrees Celsius—not bad for a December day in Europe, but the breeze coming in off the waters of the lagoon was making it feel at least ten degrees colder.

He heard the sound of jet engines growing steadily ever closer and glanced up to the horizon to see the form of an Airbus coming in for a landing at the nearby Marseille Provence Airport, its landing gear already down—visible against the sky even at this distance. With a member of his team aboard?

Impossible to say.

He'd flown out of Ben Gurion to Ankara, from Ankara to Budapest, from Budapest to Brussels—before driving across the border into France and catching a regional commuter flight from Paris to Marseille Provence.

The passport he was now traveling under bore no trace of ever having entered the nation of Israel, which was precisely how it was supposed to be.

By way of deception, thou shalt make war.

A form seemed to materialize at his side and he glanced over to see Tzipporah standing there only a few feet in the sand of the beach, silent as a ghost.

"Good flight?" he asked, glancing back toward the large rocks which lined the avenue to the east as if he expected to see more of their team members behind her.

She just looked at him. "Which one?"

That was a fair question. And Mossad wasn't exactly known for sending people first class. "Has anyone else been here?"

He shook his head. "You're the first. Go on ahead to the hotel and sleep off the jet lag. We conduct our first reconnaissance of the target at 0730 hours."

9:13 A.M., December 18th
Marseille, France

Surveillance. It was all about establishing patterns. Getting a feel for your surroundings. Your terrain.

Growing to understand what could be considered natural—and what wasn't.

And those two men. . .Ken Weathers grimaced, adjusting the focus of the binoculars in his hands as he stared through the tinted windshield of the surveillance van. They didn't belong.

He'd first noticed them nearly an hour before, on the street approaching the high-rise Marseille apartments. Just the two of them, clad in jeans and light jackets—the younger of the pair talking occasionally on a cellular phone. Swarthy skin, dark hair—very typical of the Mediterranean. Inconspicuous enough not to attract attention from any casual observer.

But try as he might, it was impossible to escape the conclusion that they were there for the exact same purpose he was.

Surveillance.

Quis custodiet ipsos custodies? He thought with a faint, ironic smile. Who watches the watchers?

In this case, that would be him. He'd joined the CIA straight out of college nine years before, in 1991—too late to have played any part in the Great Game that had once held sway in the rivalries between East and West. The intelligence services of NATO and the Warsaw Pact.

It was like volunteering to fight a war, only to have it end as you were finishing boot camp.

The Agency had been entering a new era back then. Downsizing, shifting focus to more asymmetric threats now that the great Russian bear was "vanquished."

And he'd found himself shunted from one station to the next, none of them exactly what could be viewed as career-enhancers. His college sweetheart had left him in the middle of a three-year stint in Kingston working against the narco-trade, dissolving their marriage and moving back home to Nebraska.

He smiled tightly at the memory. Liv should have stuck it out with him. . .she would have loved Paris, even if he didn't.

And that, he thought, lifting the binoculars back to his eyes, was the problem with surveillance—it gave you far too much time to think.

A third man came walking in from down the street, pausing for a moment to talk hurriedly with the pair before he continued on, glancing frequently back at the high-rise. He was young, but there was something unmistakable in the way he carried himself. An air of authority.

No doubt about it. "Get Paris Station on the phone," Weathers advised, reaching over to hit his dozing partner in the middle of the chest. "Tell them we have eyes on the Mossad team."

1:14 P.M.
The hotel
Marseille

"With due respect," Ariel began, his voice low as he gazed out over the lights of the city from the hotel balcony—the only place he'd been able to get cellular reception, "what you're asking unnecessarily complicates realities here on the ground."

There was a moment's pause before Shoham's reply came through, the edge in the general's voice clearly audible even through the static. "I assure you, this *is* necessary."

"Is there a problem with the information we received about the package?" Ariel asked, his mind racing. It wasn't an impossible request to fulfill, but it was going skew their timeline beyond anything they had made allowance for. Increasing the danger of something going wrong—as field operations tended to do, if given half a chance.

"Our information. . .was received from a third party," came the *aluf*'s unsettling response. "We need to be certain."

". . .no visible security at the service entrance," Tzipporah stated, laying the photograph on the low table between them. Taken with a telephoto lens, it showed the area around the door in sharp relief, down to the lock itself. "I think we can reasonably assume an alarm of one sort or another—that will need to be defeated before we can progress into the building itself."

Ze'ev leaned forward, his eyes scanning over the photo. "According to the blueprints, the service elevator is ten meters past the entrance. From there, it's a straight ride to the eleventh floor—maybe a minute, on the outside."

"And the weapons?" Nadir asked, speaking up from his position near the suite's door.

"It's been arranged," the older operator responded, glancing at his watch. "Our personnel in Spain should be acquiring them from Matveyev within the hour. They'll be delivered to the marina tomorrow evening."

Tzipporah nodded slowly, her fingers brushing lightly over the photos until they were fanned out before her like a deck of cards. Her dark eyes seemed to contract into glittering points, hard as obsidian. "Then we'll be able to strike on the night of the 20th."

"Not necessarily," her head jerked up at the sound of Ariel's voice, the glass door sliding shut behind their team leader as he stepped in off the suite's balcony—the phone in his hand. "Tel Aviv. . .wants independent verification of al-Shukeiri's presence. Eyes on. *Before* we go in for the kill."

5:56 P.M. Israel Standard Time
The United States Embassy
Tel Aviv, Israel

"I understand, Paul. Thanks for keeping me in the loop." David Lay replaced the STU-III in its cradle and leaned back in his office chair, musing over the words of his counterpart in Paris. If Renninger's people knew what they were talking about, the Kidon unit was already in France—nearly on al-Shukeiri's doorstep.

Shoham had moved fast, even faster than he had expected—but the Israelis weren't known for taking casualties lying down. Particularly when they had been inflicted in such a shockingly horrific manner.

An atrocity beyond words. And that only made what he had to do all the harder.

He slid open the desk drawer to one side of his chair, eyeing the unopened bottle of bourbon Vukovic had given him as a going-away present. Wild Turkey Rare Breed, distilled in the hills of Kentucky.

He'd intended to save it for his return to the States, to celebrate the end of three long years, but now he just needed the drink.

There was no black and white in this business, he had come to learn—just a haze gray the color of ash. No way to keep your hands clean of it, not if you stayed in.

He removed the cork and tilted the bottle forward, watching as the amber liquid splashed into his glass.

In the end, you traded the ability to look yourself in the mirror—for your service to your country.

And that. . .well, that was something he was just going to have to learn to live with.

4:51 P.M. Western European Time, December 19th
Marseille, France

"We have a woman approaching from the west," Nadir announced, adjusting the pair of binoculars to his eyes as he aimed through the windshield of the small Renault toward the entrance of the apartment building across the street.

Across from him in the passenger seat, Tzipporah operated the camera, her telephoto lens focused on their target through the trees.

Its shutter opening and closing with the speed of a semi-automatic weapon, the series of *clicks* clearly audible across in the quietness of the parked car.

"It's not her," she announced after a moment, glancing at the pair of photos taped to the dashboard, a clear note of disappointment in her voice.

That was becoming a theme. They'd been here for nearly ten hours, taking over from Ze'ev and their team leader. With no sign of al-Shukeiri's wife. Or the man himself.

The litter of fast food cartons from Brioche Dorée in the backseat serving as testament to the boredom that came with this work.

Tzipporah reached over, taking a once-warm leerdammer from the open box between them and biting into the small, breaded round of cheese. She shook her head, gesturing toward the apartments towering above them in the slowly gathering dusk. "I had expected something more. . .impressive, I guess."

As had he. Marseille's economy had seen brighter days.

"Apparently, she's not his favorite wife," he responded, shaking his head in dark amusement. The man had three, each one of them younger when he'd married her than her predecessor.

Moments like this were when the differences between the Mossad and his time in the IDF became the most apparent. A matter of gathering the intel, rather than simply acting upon it.

He winced, attempting without success to straighten his legs in the cramped quarters of the driver's seat. Remembering Ariel's words from the previous night. His relaying of the message which had up-ended all the mission plans they had laid out back in the Golan.

"*. . .need us to obtain independent verification of the target's presence.*"

It wasn't that plans didn't survive contact with the enemy, it was that your allies shredded them before they could even reach that point.

"Take a look at this," Tzipporah whispered urgently, gesturing briefly to the parking lot across the way from them before lifting her camera in one hand—the shutter clicking rapidly as Nadir followed the direction of her gaze toward the figure of a smartly-dressed woman in Western clothes stepping out of a Peugeot sedan, dark, nearly jet-black hair framing her face.

Zainab al-Shukeiri, he thought, hearing Tzipporah breathe, "*Got* you."

One down. . .one to go. Time to find her beloved husband.

6:29 P.M.
The marina
Marseille

"You said he'd be here." Ariel shook his head, glancing about them in the semi-darkness, the dusk held at bay by the marina lights. A forest of masts obscured the horizon, hundreds of sailboats riding at anchor.

"He will be," Ze'ev replied grimly, glancing about them. A few meters away down the pier, loud music poured from within a cabin cruiser, along with the sound of women laughing.

Americans. They were all over the marina, loud and boisterous, apparently celebrating Christmas early—tourists with enough money for a holiday abroad, and not enough to spend it on the actual Riviera.

A few police patrolling the piers, nothing out of the ordinary. None of them in sight at the moment. And then he spotted it, the glow of a pair of chemlights in the stern of a powerboat anchored about eighty meters off down a long pier. Red left, yellow right.

The signal.

"There," he said, inclining his head toward the lights. "We've got him."

The Russian had been thorough, Ariel thought, hoisting the heavily loaded duffel bag over his shoulder as they walked back toward the car, feeling the wrapped weapons within jostle against each other as the bag shifted.

Inside there were another pair of Beretta 92s like the one he now wore in an inside-the-waistband holster within his jacket, along with long, black can-style suppressors specially designed to be screwed into the semiautomatics' threaded barrels and spare magazines for both weapons.

A suppressed Russian *Bizon* submachine gun rounded out the armaments they had secured—all of them deniable, nothing that could be traced back to Israel, or their supplier in Spain.

Not unless they got caught.

He smiled grimly, glancing over at Ze'ev as they approached the car, parked thirty meters or so from the waterfront. That was the cardinal rule of their business, the only one that mattered, when it came right down to it.

Don't get caught.

"I'm driving," he announced, unlocking the car as the older man moved around to the passenger side.

He had opened the rear door and started to place the duffel on the back seat when a voice from behind him arrested his movements, speaking in rough, accented French.

His head jerked back, seeing three men standing there, spread out in a loose semi-circle—silhouetted against the marina lights in the distance. No weapons visible, but the men's openly aggressive posture indicated more clearly than words that they possessed them.

"They're Maghrebis," Ze'ev breathed in English, causing Ariel to glance over his way for a brief moment. "He says he knows we're smuggling in drugs—says this is their territory, wants you to hand over the bag."

It was always the scenario you *hadn't* planned for that came back to trip you up. They'd been on the lookout for the police, not Marseille's dominantly Algerian criminal element.

"You can tell him that's not going to happen," Ariel replied. Nothing could blow their mission more surely, the loss of the weapons—their very *existence* if they fell into the wrong hands—could lead to more questions than any of them cared to have asked. Or answered.

"You told me yourself," the man in the center announced in the same language, taking a step forward. His dark eyes never leaving Ze'ev's face. "But you're wrong—you *will* be giving me the bag. In exchange for the lives of you and your friend."

The Israeli shook his head, keeping his hands away from his sides as he faced the leader. No sudden movements. "You're making a serious mistake. We're not smugglers. There are no drugs in the bag."

"Then open it up," the man sneered, taking another step in close. *Just one more*, Ariel thought, forcing himself not to look Nadir's way—his partner's torso still largely hidden by the body of the Passat.

"That's simply not something I can do," he responded, putting out a hand in a gesture of non-aggression. "I'm sorry."

"You will be." The blow came fast, faster than he even expected, crashing into his stomach and driving the wind from his body.

He stumbled back against the open door of the car, trying to recover his balance—his hands out in front of him as if to beg mercy, feigning weakness. And then he felt the ice-cold muzzle of a pistol jammed against his temple. "I am not going to say this again, *imbécile*. You will give us—"

The Algerian's words were cut off by a muffled *crack* like that of two hands clapping together, a warm fluid spraying over Ariel's face.

His hands came up, a reaction born of instinct as he seized control of the man's gun hand—his eyes briefly registering the sight of blood spurting from a wound in his shoulder. Ze'ev, not two meters away, his suppressed Beretta recoiling back into his hands as he got off another shot.

The Algerian screamed out in pain as Ariel wrenched his arm backward, the semiautomatic clattering uselessly to the ground—his elbow slamming back into the man's throat, sending him reeling backward into the pavement.

He saw the body of another gang member collapsed lifeless on the asphalt—saw the third man catch a bullet from Ze'ev's pistol, but he didn't go down. His own weapon coming out, as if in slow motion. Unstoppable.

Ariel threw himself forward, his hand a blur as it flew into his jacket—fingers closing around the butt of his own Beretta as it slipped from its holster. But there was no time.

The Algerian got off a round, his bullet going wild in the dark, the unsuppressed gunshot reverberating across the water of the marina like a cannon blast.

Ze'ev's next shot caught the man between the eyes, the 9mm hollowpoint slug smashing through the hard bone of his skull and into the brain.

He stood there for what seemed like a long moment—swaying drunkenly. Then his feet went out from under him, crumpling like a broken doll.

His own weapon now in his hand, Ariel glanced over at his partner—the older man standing there on the other side of the Passat, breathing heavily, Beretta still leveled.

"We're going to need to clean up these bodies," Ze'ev announced after a long moment, seeming to collect himself. "Find a place to dump them out of sight. Get rid of the brass."

"No time for that," Ariel retorted grimly, his words startlingly punctuated by the distant wail of sirens. "We have to get out here."

He closed the open back door of the Passat, starting to open the driver's door when he heard a moan come from the man he had felled—the leader of the Algerians. Glancing back to see the man raising himself up on one elbow, trying to drag himself across the pavement. Toward his gun.

He withdrew the long suppressor from within his jacket, screwing it into the muzzle of the Beretta as he walked over, kicking the man's weapon out of reach.

The man's eyes lifted to meet his own, full of anger and fear. Ariel bent down, shaking his head sadly—the end of the pistol's suppressor scant inches from the Algerian's face. "I warned you that you were making a serious mistake."

And his finger tightened around the Beretta's trigger, taking up slack. . .

11:08 P.M. Israel Standard Time
A cottage in the Galilee
Israel

". . .Foreign Minister Shlomo Ben-Ami met with his Palestinian counterparts at Bolling Air Force Base in Washington, D.C. today, as peace talks continue. Negotiators maintain a grim outlook toward the prospect of any deal—with the leader of the Palestinian negotiating team, Saeb Erekat, maintaining that Israel must withdraw to the borders held prior to 1967 before any deal can be achieved."

Pre-'67, Shoham thought grimly, nursing his drink as he stared across the living room at his television set. What Israeli diplomat Abba Eban had once referred to as the "Auschwitz borders."

He'd been only a young teenager then, scarce past his *bar mitzvah*. His father, among Mordechai Gur's paratroopers as the IDF flooded into the Old City of Jerusalem that bright summer day, unstoppable as the incoming tide. Excitement in the *aluf*'s voice as he transmitted back over the army's military frequency, *"The Temple Mount is in our hands! I repeat, the Temple Mount is in our hands!"*

The trumpet blast of a shofar ringing off stones which had borne witness to millennia since the Jewish people had last controlled this holy ground.

Blood-stained, battle-hardened men lowering their weapons, tears streaking grimy cheeks as they strained forward to touch the stones. The fulfilment of centuries of yearning.

Next year in Jerusalem. The wistful prayer of thousands who had been herded aboard the trains in Europe, only to perish at the hands of the Nazi regime. *Dachau. Buchenwald. Auschwitz.*

"We have returned to all that is holy in our land," Moshe Dayan had said upon reaching the Wall, his single remaining eye shining with barely-restrained emotion. *"We have returned never to be parted from it again."*

Never again.

"Are you all right, Avi?" A woman's voice asked, breaking in upon his dark reverie.

He half-turned in his chair—rising to his feet as he saw his wife standing in the doorway, a warm, almost motherly concern in her eyes. When they had met in 1971, he had been a young lieutenant with the 188th Barak Brigade, stationed in the Golan. Rachel, a girl raised on a *kibbutz* in northern Galilee.

Neither of them yet out of their teens. Neither of them prepared for the darkness that would soon try to consume them.

The kind of darkness that had now dispatched Ariel's *Kidon* into the night, hunting the enemies of Israel before they could strike again.

"Of course, *neshama*," he said with far more assurance than he felt, kissing her lightly on the forehead as he took her into his arms, holding her close. *My soul.* "Everything is going to be all right."

6:13 A.M. Western European Time, December 20th
The hotel
Marseilles, France

"This operation has been compromised—there's no other way around it," Ze'ev said, the heat audible in his tone. "The chance we had of getting al-Shukeiri? It evaporated the moment that *Maghrebi* put his gun to your head. It's time to get out before they seal everything off."

"Not without doing what we came here to do," Ariel responded, glaring down to the end of the suite's dining table at his subordinate. "Running now is only going to alert the authorities. They don't know who we are or why we're here—so let's exert every effort to keep it that way."

"That you know of."

"That any of us know of," came the even response. He could have easily added that he had been a split-second away from seizing the Algerian's weapon and taking him hostage when Ze'ev had chosen instead to open fire. . .but recriminations were pointless now. Tzipporah entered from one of the bedrooms at that moment and Ariel looked over at her. "Has the incident at the marina made the news yet?"

She nodded. "A brief reference to a shooting involving 'criminal elements' during the top of the hour news. No details given."

That could be either good or bad. Good, if the killing of three gang members was being treated as ordinary, if unusually violent, crime. Bad, if the French authorities already had enough intel at their disposal to suspect otherwise and were simply keeping it away from the media.

And if they had involved GIGN, well, then Ze'ev's worst-case would be more than justified. And likely already far too late.

Ariel shook his head. *No matter.* "All right," he began, placing both hands on the flat wooden surface of the table, "here's what we're going to do."

7:49 A.M.

"They're on the move," Ken Weathers announced into his radio, watching as two of the Israelis—the man and the woman he had first seen together in the car near the apartments the previous night—entered the BMW rental, the car's engine revving to life moments later.

And if they were moving, then it was time to move with them. He glanced regretfully at the thermos of coffee on the van's console—forcing himself not to drink any more of it than he already had. Knowing all too well he was better off with the bottled water in the back, even if it wouldn't wake him up nearly as fast.

You walked a fine line with hydration on a stake-out. Too little, and you couldn't stay alert. Too much, and you found yourself having to take a leak at the wrong moment. Which was, after all, what the *other* bottle was for.

He waited until the BMW pulled out before he put the van in gear, aiming for a hole in the traffic about five cars back. A safe following distance, far enough to let the other members of his team cycle in.

So far, maintaining surveillance on the Israelis had been nothing more than glorified babysitting. If they were actually going to do anything. . .they hadn't given any sign of it yet.

7:51 A.M.
The hotel

"You need to come take a look at this." Ariel looked up from his work, the *Bizon* submachine gun field-stripped on the table before him—seeing Ze'ev standing by the window facing the street, the venetian blinds pulled to one side.

The former *Shayetet-13* operator hadn't said a great deal since their heated dispute over the path forward an hour before, but now there was an unusual urgency in his voice.

Ariel rose, moving to the window just in time to see a nondescript grey van pull out of a side street across from their hotel, merging with traffic. "What is it?"

"I don't know, precisely." Ze'ev shook his head, frowning. "It was as if it was just sitting there, waiting for the BMW to leave."

"When did you first see it?"

"I only looked out a couple minutes before they pulled away. It could have just rolled up, could have been sitting there. . .ever since before dawn. No way of knowing."

During an active operation, it was impossible to fully analyze and rule out everything that *could* be a threat. You had to learn to make quick assessments and act on them. "What are your instincts telling you?" he asked, gazing keenly at the older man.

"They're telling me we have a problem."

All right, then. Ariel moved back to the table, gesturing to his subordinate. "Tzipporah is driving—get Nadir on his mobile and warn them they may have a shadow."

"And you and I?" Ze'ev asked pointedly.

"We get to work. The utility uniforms—your contact has a way of obtaining them?"

"He does."

1:17 P.M. Israel Standard Time
Mossad Headquarters
Tel Aviv, Israel

"The latest intel from the Americans just came in over the telex five minutes ago—Mustafa al-Shukeiri is still in place in the apartment, hasn't moved."

"Hasn't moved" was relative, Avi realized. Even for the Americans, technology only got so precise. He could likely move a kilometer or more before anyone would notice, though the odds were against him making such a short "journey."

But even so, the inactivity was troubling. It was as though al-Shukeiri had already gone to ground. He turned, looking at the analyst for a long moment before asking, "Do you think he suspects he is being targeted?"

"No," the man replied slowly, "I don't think we can reasonably draw that conclusion. There's nothing in al-Shukeiri's psychological profile to indicate paranoia."

At least not beyond that normal for a high-ranking former PLO leader, Shoham thought with a snort.

After all, al-Shukeiri had been in Tunis back in '88 when Israeli commandos from *Sayeret Matkal* had waded ashore and shot Yasser Arafat's top aide, Abu Jihad, dead in his own home, in front of his wife and young son.

No doubt he still remembered that night—the panic that had swept through the exiled *Fatah* leadership in the days and weeks that followed. Bringing terror to the terrorists. . .well, that was the only way you won this kind of war.

"*Aluf*," a Mossad officer began, entering the war room behind them, a clipboard in his hand, "we just received this over the satellite uplink from Elba."

Shoham took the clipboard from him, scrawling his signature over the *Eyes Only* cover sheet before peeling it away to reveal the message beneath. "What. . ." he breathed, his eyes scanning down the sheet, the attached photo. Feeling every dark suspicion of the last week now racing once again to the fore. *How was this even possible?* But he knew all too well. "Has this intelligence been confirmed?"

"It has," the Mossad officer nodded. "It's him—Mustafa al-Shukeiri. In Elba, ninety minutes ago."

It was a moment before anyone spoke up, each of them looking at the others. The analyst clearing his throat, finally. "I can talk with the Americans, sort out what has been—"

"*No*," Shoham responded, cutting him off harshly. This was bad, worse than he'd even thought. "You say *nothing* to the CIA. Not a single word. Where they are concerned, you deviate not a wit from the operation as it has proceeded to this point."

"Of course, *aluf.*"

"Now," he began, turning on the Mossad officer, "I want you to establish comms with the *Kidon*. I need to speak with Ariel."

11:21 A.M. Western European Time
An empty lot
Marseille, France

"It's clean," Ze'ev observed, climbing out the back to the utility van to stand beside Ariel on the asphalt of the vacant lot. "Looks like exactly what we need."

"And you said you needed this for what?" the Frenchman piped up from a few feet away, his eyes darting from one man to the other.

Ariel shot him a dark look that warned him more clearly than words to press no farther along that line of questioning. "We didn't," he responded evenly, an edge of steel in his tone. "Now, about the uniforms—you have them?"

"Of course, of course," the man replied, seeming to quail beneath the Israeli officers' gaze, nervously stroking his mustache as he reached into the van and opened a duffel bag. Reaching inside, he pulled out a faded set of coveralls with the *Électricité de France* logo emblazoned on the left chest pocket—holding them up for inspection in the light of the morning sun. "There are another seven just like this."

They had deliberately overstated their numbers. If their source was actually playing another angle, might as well use him as a means of sowing disinformation.

If he was straight, well no harm done. There had been no signs of anyone following when they left the hotel through an employees entrance earlier in the morning, but it still paid to exercise caution.

"Now, *messieurs*," the man began hesitantly, "about the payment I am owed. I ran. . .great risk in obtaining these for you, and feel—"

Ariel's cellular phone vibrated from the pouch on his belt and he motioned for Ze'ev to deal with their source, moving across the lot back to their car, glancing at the phone's pulsing screen.

Tel Aviv. Something had to be wrong—this was well outside their normal comms window.

"Go for Ariel," he began, making sure he was out of earshot. "What's happening?"

"We have a problem," Shoham replied, surprising him even further. He hadn't expected to hear from the *aluf* himself. "The information provided by our third party has proven. . .unreliable."

It wasn't the first time intel had been bad—that was an uncomfortable staple of field operations. But there was a strange note of tension in the *aluf's* voice—as if there was something more there than a simple intelligence foul-up.

"What are you telling me?"

"The package is not there with you in Marseille. You are going to have to look for it at the tertiary location."

Elba. "Are you sure?" Ariel asked, too surprised to contain the outburst—glancing back to where Ze'ev was still haggling with the Frenchman. If it was true, well. . .the intel hadn't just been *off*, it had been flat-out *wrong*.

"Eyes on in the last three hours," came Shoham's response. "It's certain."

"Then I'll regroup my people and we'll head out for the pick-up." *The pick-up.* It was a cold, curiously detached way to refer to the thought of putting a bullet through a man's head, but dehumanization was part of this process.

"No," the *aluf's* voice came through an instant later. "Take one with you, leave the rest."

5:07 P.M. Israel Standard Time
The olive grove
Beit Shemesh, Israel

"We've had a complication," Shoham announced, placing his hand on the gnarly trunk of a centuries-old olive tree as he came up on Gerstman, the lit ember at the end of the senior Mossad officer's cigarette glowing in the gathering twilight.

He'd never asked Gerstman why he preferred the two of them to meet out here, but he suspected the solitude had much to do with it. The sense of. . .*peace*, so damnably hard to find in their world.

"I heard," the man responded finally, smoke billowing from his mouth into the evening sky—the sun a blood-red sliver off toward the Shephelah. "I trust you have already taken steps to redress these concerns?"

"I have. Half the team is on their way to Elba."

"And the other half?" Gerstman half-turned toward him, taking another long drag from his cigarette.

"They've been ordered to remain in Marseille. Serve as a diversion."

"A diversion for whom?"

It was a moment before Shoham responded, glancing up into the ancient boughs of the olive tree above his head. It had stood here long before he was born, and its branches would still be providing sustenance long after he had returned to the dust of this promised land. All of them naught but mere footnotes of history—if that.

But for this moment. . .he shook his head. For this moment, it was left to them to defend their own, best they could. He looked back over into Gerstman's eyes—knowing it was a question that had to be answered. "The Americans. . ."

8:05 P.M. Western European Time
A CIA safe house
Marseille, France

"They're back?" Ken Weathers asked, wrapping a towel around his body as he stepped out of the shower—water still dripping from the showerhead, his cellphone pinned between his ear and wet shoulder. "Good."

They had lost track of the Israeli team earlier in the day—a traffic jam in the 9th arrondissement turning their surveillance operation into a nightmare. He might have even thought it was a deliberate effort to shake them, but not with them returning to their base this way. No way they would have deliberately eluded surveillance only to walk straight back into it.

"Just the two men?" the CIA officer asked, padding out into the kitchen, his feet wet against the tile. Not even the hot shower had sufficed to work all the kinks out of his back. "All right, keep an eye on the building. I'll be back there in a few hours."

If the Israelis began moving in on the target, they had to be prepared to react quickly, alerting the French authorities. He thumbed the *END* button and threw the phone over onto the sofa. *No rest for the wicked. . .*

2:03 A.M. Central European Time, December 21ˢᵗ
Isola d'Elba, Tuscany

The jet-black Cessna 350 Corvalis came in from the south like a ghost out of the night, the roar of its flat-six Teledyne engine throbbing through the cabin as the plane swept over the Mediterranean, less than a thousand feet above the wave-tops.

Banking to the east as it lined up on a perfect heading for the runway at Elba's only airport, Marina di Campo.

Only a few minutes now, Ariel thought, hearing the pilot's voice in his headset. "Tower, this is Charlie two-three-two Zulu, from Turin. Request permission for approach."

Shoham had to have moved heaven and earth to stage aviation assets for something like this. . .that much was certain. He'd never laid eyes on their pilot before this night, but he knew him to be one of the *sayanim*—Jews of the Diaspora who, despite having never made *aliyah* still swore their ultimate allegiance to the Jewish state and volunteered themselves to aid her in any way possible.

As vital to Mossad's day-to-day operations overseas as any intelligence officer—or *katsa*, as they were known.

"Charlie two-three-two Zulu, this is Tower. You are cleared for approach, Runway 16."

Ariel glanced over to where Tzipporah sat bolt upright in the seat beside him, her dark eyes seemingly trying to pierce the night ahead of them—the dim glow of runway lights only now visible.

Time to do this.

"He went down and slew a lion in a pit on a snowy day," Ariel stated, his eyes searching the middle-aged man's face as he delivered the countersign, the pre-arranged response to the opening greeting.

"And rare it has been for Israel to see snow ever since," the Mossad *katsa* from Rome responded with a laugh, his smile visible in the glare of the airport lights as he reached out a hand. "Welcome to Italy."

5:07 A.M. Israeli Standard Time
Mossad Headquarters
Tel Aviv, Israel

"We've received confirmation from Nesher," the Mossad officer announced as Shoham stepped off the elevator—using the codename of the *katsa* on the ground in Elba. "The *Kidon* has arrived—landed early this morning."

"And the target?" Shoham asked, moving into the open office space, a maze of desks and CRT monitors—several televisions mounted across one wall.

"Still in place. The operation is planned for tonight. Last report from the remaining elements in Marseille has confirmed that they are, in fact, under surveillance—they succeeded in making a tail car last night."

The Agency. He swore under his breath, shaking his head. This was all on him, now—it had been his decision to enlist the CIA's "help" and he would ultimately bear the responsibility for everything that followed.

Everything.

And if the Americans even began to suspect that they were being conned—there was no way to reasonably estimate the resources they might throw at the problem. "Tell me," he began, a sudden thought striking him, "how many more comms windows do we have with Elba before the assault takes place?"

"Only two," came the reply. "One in five more hours. Then comms will be established again just prior to the assault, to receive final mission-go."

No. "Cancel it. Cancel them both. Tell Nesher to go dark, all Mossad elements on the ground are to observe communications silence until al-Shukeiri has been eliminated."

"Such measures will. . ." the Mossad officer paused, seeming to consider his words, "place a strain on the execution of the mission. Are you certain they are of absolute necessity, *aluf?*"

Shoham nodded. "If the Americans could use ECHELON to aid us. . .they can use it to track us. Shut it all down."

6:19 A.M. Central European Time
Marciana, Isola d'Elba

"The only direct access to al-Shukeiri's compound is a long, winding road up the side of the mountain to the promontory upon which the villa sits."

They knew that from the satellite imagery they had reviewed when assembling the original assault plans back in the Golan, but there had been less intel on the Elba location than either of the others. And you never ignored input from people who had spent time on the ground.

"We've estimated his security team at nine strong," Nesher went on, "possibly as many as thirteen. No long guns visible, but I wouldn't discount the possibility of their presence. All the guards we've observed thus far have been wearing holstered sidearms."

"And the villa itself?" Ariel asked, sliding a loaded magazine of 9mm into the butt of the H&K USP semiautomatic as he moved across the room to stand beside the middle-aged man, the metallic *click* assuring him that it was secured in place.

The shift of plans had forced them to leave the weapons they'd smuggled into France behind in Marseille. . .all the risks they'd run at the marina rendered worthless. But fortunately the *katsa* had been prepared for that eventuality.

"It's a large compound dating back to the early 18th century," Nesher responded, taking a long sip from the bottle of Pepsi in his hand, "with the main residence being erected by the Grand Duke of Tuscany, Gian Gastone de' Medici shortly before his death in 1737. There's a period stone wall nearly three meters high surrounding the compound on three sides."

Ariel nodded, glancing over to see Tzipporah screwing a suppressor into the barrel of an H&K identical to his own. "And on the fourth?"

"A thirty-meter sheer cliff climbing straight out of the sea, nearly a hundred meters from the back of the residence. There's a swimming pool and bathhouse there, overlooking the Mediterranean."

A hundred meters. That was a healthy amount of open ground to cover, even at night. The odds of covering it undetected didn't get any better if you were already winded. Still. . .

"What are you thinking?" Nesher asked, setting his drink aside as he marked the thoughtful expression in Ariel's eyes.

"I'm thinking we're going to need whatever mountain-climbing equipment you can lay your hands on. And a boat."

11:05 A.M.
The villa

"Of course, I will see that it's done. Thank you, General—I look forward to our meeting. *Wa alaykum salaam.*"

And upon you peace.

Mustafa al-Shukeiri closed the Motorola StarTAC without another word, handing the small flip phone back to one of his bodyguards and gesturing for the man to return the phone inside the residence.

Another two weeks, and it would be done. The future of Palestine assured. Palestine, and only Palestine. . .from the river to the sea.

The fifty-seven-year-old former PLO leader reached into the breast pocket of the military uniform he customarily wore, leaning back against one of the old, neo-classical columns that supported the back portico of the house as he fished out a cigar, along with a silver lighter engraved in flowing Arabic script.

His fingers trembled with an unaccustomed excitement as he touched flame to the end of the Cohiba, the smoke curling around his dark mustache.

To be this *close*. It seemed almost impossible for him to believe, even now. The uniform was an affectation he had borrowed from Arafat, dating back to their days together at the siege of Beirut. Dark days, when it seemed as if the flame of Palestinian statehood might be extinguished forever.

But here they yet were, as God had ordained.

He pushed himself away from the column and walked out into the courtyard of the compound, catching sight of his young wife laying out by the pool, tanning—her form displayed to effect in a black bikini she had bought three weeks previous in some Paris shop.

Or rather, that he had bought *for* her. . .as he did everything. And in return, well—he hadn't married her for her intellect, what little there was of it.

He smiled, taking another puff of the cigar as he looked out over the Mediterranean—the taste of salt in the air, along with the pungent aroma of burning tobacco.

The fires which would consume the Zionist state had been already lit in Ramallah, in the countless attacks and reprisals of the weeks that followed. And once this weapon was in their hands, not even the Jews' allies in America would be able to stop them.

He laughed as if at a private joke known only to him and God, his lips curling upward into something that was halfway between a smile and a sneer. *The Americans. . .*

11:17 A.M.

The cliff wasn't perfectly sheer, Ariel thought—cutting the engine back as the powerboat circled around the point, staying about a kilometer out. Far enough not to be thought suspicious in an island that was bustling with European and American tourists fleeing colder climates in time for the Christmas holiday.

Steep, yes—but not impossible, the stratified rock offering handholds to the experienced climber. Even in the dark.

He heard an obscenity explode from Tzipporah's lips and looked back to see her standing a few feet behind him—the high-powered binoculars in her hands aimed at the top of the cliffs. "It's him."

That seemed impossible, but there was no mistaking the look of darkness in her eyes. "Are you serious?"

"If only I had my rifle," she murmured, handing the binoculars over to him as he stepped back from the wheel. "I could end all of this, right here. Right *now.*"

It was no idle boast, he thought, adjusting the binoculars to his own eyes. He had seen her make shots well in excess of eight hundred meters. A boat rocking in the ocean swells didn't make for the most ideal of weapons platforms, but it would have been the simpler alternative. . .if only they'd been able to acquire a rifle.

Out of the question, given the circumstances.

And there he was. The magnification was great enough for Ariel to make out the cigar in the Palestinian leader's hand—the tendrils of smoke wafting from its tip. The dark, purplish scars pitting the man's right cheek from where he had been struck with shrapnel nearly twenty years before in Lebanon.

But it was his eyes, more than anything, staring out over the sea. Dark and hard, the way they had to have been the day he ordered the killing of the reservists in Ramallah.

"We are slaughtering your husband." He shuddered, a surge of anger seeming to swell up from deep within him. *They have been killing us for far too long.*

72

"What do you give as our odds?" Tzipporah asked quietly, her eyes resting on his face.

"Mustafa al-Shukeiri will be dead by the time tomorrow's sun rises," he responded, a cold certitude in his voice. They *would* reach their target—no matter what it took. There was no other choice.

She seemed to consider his words for a moment, reaching up to brush a strand of dark hair out of her eyes. "And what of us?"

At some level, it startled him how little thought he had given to that question—their own chances of survival. Perhaps because it had been a long time since he had cared.

He lowered the binoculars, returning her gaze. "Do you have family?"

It seemed strange that it was something he had never asked before, but personal matters were never really something that had come up.

"A father in Haifa," she said, seemingly lost in thought. "My mother left him years ago and moved to the United States. My younger brother is in Naora with the 36th Armor."

There was a moment's hesitation before she went on. "And what about you?"

"No," he responded simply, looking away from her—back toward the cliffs. *Their target.* "There is no one."

She closed her eyes, as if realizing she had crossed a line, an invisible boundary between the two of them. "Forgive me. . .I am sorry to hear of the death of your parents."

"They didn't die." He turned his attention back to the wheel, only too aware of the irony in his words. "I did."

Tzipporah shook her head. "I—I don't understand."

The boat's engine roared back to full power as he thrust the throttle forward, its prow cutting through the chop as wind-tossed salt spray filled the air around them.

"My parents," he began after a long moment, "are devout Haredis."

The ultra-Orthodox. She nodded, an understanding beginning to dawn in her eyes. Devoutly religious Jews known for their rejection of any and all elements of secular culture, the Haredis were exempted from military service.

"When I was thirteen, I told my father my intention to enlist rather than attend *yeshiva*," he continued, referencing the Jewish religious schools where many Haredi young men spent the years of what would have been their military service in the study of the Torah and Rabbinical literature. "He flew into a towering rage. . .threatened to disown me if I dared 'defile myself' with the world in such a way."

"And you did anyway."

"The day I turned seventeen," Ariel replied, a sad, bitter smile creeping across his face. "It's listed on my tombstone in *Har HaMenuchot* as the date of my death. Perhaps it was, after all. The day that 'David' died."

"You mean. . ."

"I do." He laughed despite himself, a sound empty of any genuine mirth. "You might have thought I had done something truly heinous—converted to Christianity, or something like that."

She shook her head, as if still incapable of believing his words. "I'm sorry."

"And I am. . .*not*." He glanced back at the rocky promontory, now receding in the distance. With any luck, the boat had gone unnoticed. "What's done is done—there's no taking back any of it. And that's why the only thing for me to focus on now is what's ahead. Those cliffs. And that man."

7:31 P.M. Israel Standard Time
The United States Embassy
Tel Aviv, Israel

"Look, John, I've been around this Agency for a long time. I know something like isn't going to be handled overnight." David Lay leaned back in his office chair, the cord of the STU-III looping around his wrist. "But I need to know that you all are taking this seriously and getting it *dealt* with. This is something that could blow up in our faces like nothing you or I have ever seen."

A moment's pause as he listened to his counterpart back in Virginia, then Lay added. "If we don't, the Israelis *will*—sooner or later. These delaying tactics are a smokescreen that's only going to last us so long. And then we're going to have a major problem on our hands."

There were a few more words of empty reassurance from the other end of the line before Lay said "goodbye", glaring at the phone as he replaced it in its cradle.

Just ten more days, that's what he kept telling himself. Ten more days and he'd be back in the States. But this was something that had the potential to undermine everything he'd spent the last three years building. Not to mention haunt his career for years to come.

And Langley was tying his hands. . .

11:49 P.M. Central European Time
Isola d'Elba

The light of the waning gibbous moon glistened off the waters of the Mediterranean as Ariel put the anchor over the side, lowering it into the water without so much as a splash.

They'd cut the engine well over two kilometers out, drifting in with the tide until they found themselves nestled in the small cove at the foot of the cliff. Sound carried over water at distances that were difficult for the uninitiated to fathom.

Last thing they needed was to blow this mission before it even got underway.

"Ready?" he asked, his voice nothing more than a whisper as he glanced over at his partner. She just nodded, her face blackened with camouflage paint like his own, her dark eyes almost invisible. He was going to lead the ascent, accomplishing it in a single "pitch" with her acting as belayer below.

They were carrying only the bare minimum when it came to weapons—their suppressed H&Ks with two spare mags for each pistol. Not enough to last them through a firefight. . .but the only way they got into a firefight was if things had already gone completely sideways.

"Go with God," Nesher whispered, reaching out to clasp Ariel's gloved hand. The older man would remain with the boat, awaiting their return—the *katsa*'s Beretta holstered within his jacket, insurance against any surprises.

Checking once again to make sure the rope was paying out smoothly, Ariel lowered himself over the side and into the shallow water, wading forward until his feet touched the rock forming the base of the cliff.

He brought his modified PVS-5 night vision goggles down over his face, his eyes adjusting as the landscape around him changed to dark green. They were going to play with his depth perception, but using them was unavoidable. There just wasn't enough moon to make the climb unaided.

Glancing upward to get his bearings, he reached above him, his gloved fingers searching for the first handhold and slipping a wedge into the crevice of the rock, securing the rope to it with a carabiner taken from off his harness—part of the equipment Nesher had secured from a store in Marciana catering to climbers seeking to conquer Monte Capanne, a few miles inland to the east.

He could still remember the first time he had gone climbing—mountain training with the *Duvdevan* on the Carmel, years before. The sickening feeling of a foothold giving way—swinging you back to smash against the face of the rock. Pinned there like a fly against the wall.

Some things you just never wanted to repeat.

Testing the anchor with a quick, sharp tug to ensure it was holding, he straightened—his body pressing against the rock as he levered himself up, his feet finding a hold on the same tiny ledge where his hands had been only moments before.

His heart pounding against his chest as he began to repeat the process. *Just keep moving.*

1:09 A.M. Israel Standard Time
Mossad Headquarters
Tel Aviv, Israel

No matter how old you became, Avi ben Shoham thought—or how many times you had done it—you never got used to the feeling of sending men and women to what could very possibly be their deaths.

Or at least he hoped you never did.

The small office was unbearably quiet, the only sound that of the clock ticking away on the wall behind his head. *Maddening*.

Even now, in his late forties, somehow he imagined himself still that young tank commander in the Golan. His Patton rolling forward, tracks grinding over the rough ground as the entire vehicle rocked from the recoil of its 105mm main gun.

Engaging the enemies of the Jewish state at close range—hot brass spewing from the ejection port of the coaxial machine gun to cover the floor of the cockpit as Syrian infantry rushed forward in support of their armor.

But now here he sat. Waiting to hear of the deeds of other men.

12:15 A.M., Central European Time, December 22nd
Isola d'Elba

Easy there. Lying prone against the cliff to reduce his profile against the sky, Ariel reached out, pulling the rope in as Tzipporah picked her way up the face of the cliff, the other end secured to her harness—removing the wedges as she came. *Not far now*.

With the rope now firmly secured to the summit with a carabiner, they'd be able to rappel their way back down after the neutralization of their target. With any luck, they wouldn't be doing it under fire.

He glanced back over his shoulder, scanning the grounds through the green haze of his Gen. II NVGs as he had been doing every couple minutes since reaching the summit. No guards, no sign that their ascent had drawn notice. *Yet*.

Another few moments, and she was close enough for him to reach down, seizing her right hand in his and pulling her the rest of the way to the top.

"You good?" he asked, taking a knee beside her as he checked the ropes one more time. Making sure they were holding fast.

She nodded wordlessly, unholstering her H&K and screwing the suppressor into its barrel. "Let's go."

He rose from his crouch, his pistol up as he led the way across the promontory toward the house, moving at a half-run.

Pausing every few moments, his eyes scanning the darkness for threats. *Nothing.*

Everything was silent.

The faint rays of the moon glistened off the water of the pool as they began to circle around its edge, a distracting iridescence in the glow of the NVGs.

And then he felt, rather than saw, a sudden movement off to the side— the goggles destroying his peripheral vision.

Heard Tzipporah's pistol cough twice even as he turned—catching sight of a guard who had just come around the corner of the bathhouse, flanking them and taking them off-guard.

Her rounds caught the man high in the chest even as she fired again, his legs going out from under him as he fell backward into the pool with a loud splash. His blood staining the water as silence fell once more over the courtyard.

"Good work," Ariel breathed, ripping off his night-vision goggles and stuffing them into a pocket of his assault vest. Combat was all about trade-offs, and they had nearly just cost him his life.

They just stood there for a moment, weapons up—waiting for a reaction, some sign that the suppressed shots had been heard.

Nothing.

The two of them reached the portico at the back of the villa without further incident, slipping between the ornate stone columns to reach the door. Tzipporah moving back to stand guard as he pulled a snap gun from his pocket, fitting it into the lock, his gloved index finger finding the trigger.

There. The gun "fired", striking all the bottom pins of the lock and transferring their kinetic energy upward, jamming them open.

And they were in.

12:21 A.M.

High mahogany bookcases filled with old volumes bound in Moroccan red rose from floor to ceiling around them as they made their way through what had to be the villa's library.

They hadn't been able to obtain floor plans for the 18th-century structure, so they were left groping in the darkness.

There was a light shining from the rooms ahead of them, along with the sound of. . .voices. Low and indistinct.

A television set, he realized after a moment—motioning for Tzipporah to cover him as he advanced—the muzzle of his pistol leading the way forward.

There was a guard sitting there on a couch only feet from the entryway, his holstered pistol lying on the endtable beside his drink—his attention focused on the television as the face of American action film star Steven Seagal appeared on-screen.

The guard was a big man, taller than either of them and heftily built. But he was distracted by his movie. *Unfocused.* Taking him would be easy enough.

Ariel had just begun to advance from the darkness of the library when the man rose, stretching his arms as he circled around the edge of the couch.

No going back.

He put his head down and charged across the few remaining feet, slamming into the man and knocking him back with the force of the collision—his free arm wrapping around the man's throat like a fleshy garrote. Cutting off the scream on his lips before it could be uttered.

The man's eyes went wide, struggling desperately against Ariel as his left hand clawed toward the endtable, and his weapon. And then it came back, suddenly and without warning, slamming into the Israeli's stomach with the force of a sledgehammer.

Pain. It felt as though every ounce of breath had been driven from his body—sending him staggering back, into Tzipporah's line of fire.

No shot. He saw the man reach the endtable, hands fumbling with the clasp of the retention holster.

His H&K came up even as he struggled to regain his balance, iron sights centering on the man's temple. His finger taking up the slack.

The suppressed shot echoed like a handclap in the tight, enclosed room—the 9mm hollowpoint entering the man's head just in front of the ear. He toppled sideways, crashing into the table and taking it down with him, his blood spilling out over the lush carpet.

Target down. Ariel just stood there for a moment, looking at the man's corpse as he struggled to regain his breath. They had to keep moving.

There was the sound of footsteps from down the hall before they could move, a man calling softly, "Ibrahim?" as he entered the room.

He looked up to see both Ariel and Tzipporah's pistols aimed at his head. Death staring him in the face, a scant few pounds of pressure away.

A moment passed, his eyes widening in fear and shock—then he raised his hands in a gesture of surrender.

"Your employer," Ariel began in fluent Arabic, keeping his weapon up as he circled the man, "Mustafa al-Shukeiri. Take us to him."

12:27 A.M.

Peace. The reward of God for those who had proved faithful to His struggle. Mustafa al-Shukeiri leaned back against the pillows, his arm curled around the soundly sleeping form of his wife—fingers idly caressing her soft skin.

Once, in Beirut so long ago—he could have never imagined such a feeling of tranquility. Artillery shells reducing buildings to rubble, Israeli tank columns moving inexorably up the Beirut-Damascus road, cutting off any hope of escape. Palestine's darkest hour.

But now. . .he smiled to himself in the semi-darkness, the soft glow of the lamp on the dresser providing the room's only illumination. Now, their future had never seemed more bright.

He heard a muffled sound from the hall without, sitting up in bed just as the door came crashing open—the body of one of his guards crumpling to the floor, rolling helplessly over on his back not five feet from the foot of the bed—the bloody, gaping hole of an exit wound swallowing up the space between his eyes.

The former PLO leader opened his mouth to scream, but no sound escaped—the words dying in his throat as a pair of figures stepped over the body and into the room, a man and a woman, their faces blackened beyond recognition. *Ghouls come for the dead.*

"Mustafa al-Shukeiri?" the man asked, the suppressed pistol coming up in his hand.

He had long envisioned how he would die, fighting bravely against the Jews—words of defiance on his lips, words which would be remembered down through history. Taught by Palestinian mothers to their children for as long as their people remained.

But he found it impossible to utter a single syllable now, sweat pouring down his face in rivulets, his hands trembling uncontrollably beneath the linen sheets. Incapable of even pleading for a mercy he knew would not be granted him.

"Vadim Novesche," Ariel pronounced simply, staring coldly into al-Shukeiri's eyes, his finger curling around the pistol's match trigger as he recited the names of the reservists lynched in Ramallah. "Yossi Avrahami. The Jewish people do not forget. We do not forgive."

1:31 A.M. Israel Standard Time
Mossad Headquarters
Tel Aviv, Israel

"Avi," the Mossad officer began, poking his head into Shoham's office. "We just received a microburst transmission from Elba."

"And?" Shoham demanded, turning back toward the door. He had spent most of the last half hour pacing, unable to calm himself enough to sit.

"Best that you hear it for yourself."

The thirty meters down the hall toward the operational hub were covered in a matter of moments, one of the analysts handing the general a pair of headphones.

He put them on, listening as the transmission began to play—Ariel's voice coming through the speakers, clearly distinct. "Sound the trumpet. Break the pitcher. The sword of the Lord and of Gideon. I say again, the sword of the Lord and of Gideon."

Success. Shoham slipped off the headphones and laid them to one side, allowing himself a grim smile.

Their dead were still dead. But their deaths had not gone unavenged.

And for this life. . .that would have to be enough.

81

1:34 A.M. Central European Time
The villa
Isola d'Elba

It was past time for them to be going—even if the sound of the suppressed shots hadn't been enough to bring the rest of the now dead Palestinian's security team. . .they would find the bodies of their slain team members soon enough.

They had left al-Shukeiri's wife tied to the bedposts of their bed beside his body—her face flecked with blood—a pair of lace underwear stuffed in her mouth as a rude gag to muffle her screams for help.

"Are you finding anything relevant?" Ariel asked quietly, glancing back to where Tzipporah sat behind al-Shukeiri's desktop computer in his small office, her fingers moving swiftly over the keyboard. The man's passwords had been written down in a notebook kept in the top drawer of his desk—the rough, nearly illiterate scrawl the only impediment to their search.

"I'm not sure," she replied, her brow furrowing. "There are a series of e-mails here. Between al-Shukeiri and an Iraqi general. . .Tahir Kamal Siddiqi."

"Siddiqi?" Ariel demanded, moving around behind her. "He's a member of the Revolutionary Command Council—Saddam's right hand. What are they saying?"

Tzipporah shook her head, gesturing to the Arabic on-screen. "It's all very cryptic. Something about a deal taking place in the next two weeks. After the new year. A deal between *Fatah* and the Iraqi government. A 'package' changing hands."

A chill ran through his body, all thoughts of haste forgotten as he leaned forward, looking over her shoulder. *This was important.*

"See what else you can find," he said, his eyes following her movements on-screen as she clicked from one window to the next, the computer responding with agonizing slowness.

There. His finger shot out, indicating a folder near the top of the screen. "What's that?"

"It appears to be financial records," she responded, opening it with a double-click of the mouse and beginning to work through the files within. "Money transfers, all of them to a numbered account in Bern. A series of payments from a company based in the Turks and Caicos, BRS Distributing, LLC."

That name. . .something about it was undeniably familiar, but it took him a moment to place it.

"BRS Distributing," he began slowly, "is a known front company used by the American intelligence community to launder funds for their overseas operations."

Tzipporah just looked at him, her dark eyes wide open in disbelief. "Are you saying. . .?"

The question trailed off, as if she couldn't bring herself to form the words.

He nodded, seeming only then to realize the import of his own words. "I'm saying that Mustafa al-Shukeiri is — no, *was* — a CIA asset."

Episode II

The sun was setting, at last nearing the end of its long march across the western sky. Its rays streaming in through the open blast door as Tahir Kamal Siddiqi entered, flanked by his bodyguards—the fading light bathing the interior of the hardened aircraft shelter in a blood-red hue.

Fitting, he thought, his eyes fixed on a group of soldiers clustered in the middle of the hangar. *A harbinger of all that was to come.*

The sound of his boots against the concrete marking each purposeful step as he strode toward them—the men snapping to attention at his approach. Fear visible in their eyes.

As well there should be.

"You've inspected the shells for any possible leakage, I presume?" he asked, brusquely returning the soldiers' salutes as he turned toward the foremost man, a scientist in the uniform of an Iraqi Army colonel.

"Of course, general," the man said, his voice trembling slightly, gesturing toward a container sitting on the floor beyond them—about twice the size of a normal footlocker, its dark paint faded and worn by the years. It was a question he hadn't needed to ask—it would have been as much as any of their lives were worth to have failed to take the necessary precautions prior to his

85

arrival. To have exposed a member of Saddam's Revolutionary Command Council to such danger.

"Then open it up," the general ordered, catching the eye of a muscled sergeant off to his right, a man with whom—like most of the men gathered here—he had served years previous in the Iran-Iraq War, they and their fellow Guardsmen driving the Iranian militias from the Al-Faw Peninsula in the operation of *Ramadan Mubarak*. Two days of bitter fighting, the kind of struggle that binds men to each other.

And then he had himself risen through the ranks in the wake of the purges which had followed the American invasion in 1991, as the Iraqi Army struggled to overcome the disgrace of defeat. The distrust of their President.

Gaining the confidence of Saddam Hussein himself. . .and through it all, maintaining a cadre of men like these—men whose loyalty was owed only to himself.

A dangerous path for a man to take in Saddam's Iraq, Siddiqi thought, watching as the sergeant stooped down—undoing the container's heavy locks. A path from which many a lesser man would have quailed.

But Allah had not ordained him a lesser man.

The sergeant threw back the lid, the sound of metal impacting against concrete ringing across the hangar as he rose, taking a step back so as to let the general approach.

A half-dozen 130mm artillery shells clearly visible in the dim light as Siddiqi stepped forward, the soldiers looking on as he took a knee by the container—his fingers brushing away the dust cloaking them. His breath catching in his throat despite himself as he made out the symbol inscribed into the metal of the shell's casing.

Nerve gas.

"*Alhamdullilah,*" he breathed, overcome by emotion. Praise be to God.

First developed by Iraqi scientists in the early '80s, all such stockpiles were supposed to have been destroyed under the terms of the United Nations Security Council Resolution 687, and indeed, even Saddam himself did not know of the existence of this one. One of many secrets he had kept. . .against a better day.

Chemical weapons had not decided the day at Al-Faw—a hundred thousand crack Guardsmen pitted against a mere fifteen thousand Iranian *Basij* militiamen had been a foregone conclusion from the outset—but he would never forget the sight of so many *safawi* fighters writhing in the dust of the street, helpless. Convulsed in the throes of death.

The sheer *power* of that moment. A power Iraq could never afford to give up, no matter the arrogant decree of the West. Or perhaps rather *because* of it.

"And the rest of the cache?" he asked, looking up into the face of the scientist.

"They are in equally good condition, General. As you had hoped. Sixty shells, just like this one."

"Then we can spare a few to fulfill our. . .obligations," Siddiqi said, rising to his feet. "And, if things come to the worst, to provide ourselves with a field test of the sarin's continued efficacy. Colonel Hadi, what have you learned?"

A man in his late forties stepped from the back of the group, the insignia on his uniform marking him as a lieutenant colonel of the Iraqi Army, the maroon beret of the Republican Guard poised securely atop his dark hair. His eyes meeting Siddiqi's with the calm, unrelenting gaze of a veteran.

"Our contact is dead, General—as we learned two days ago. A victim of an assassination, most likely carried out by the Jews. But I have been able to determine that there is still interest in our offer on the part of those he represented. With your leave, I will need to visit Gaza myself, meet with my contacts there. I am confident that al-Shukeiri's death will make little difference in the end."

"*Insh'allah,*" Siddiqi breathed, looking around him as he closed the locker with a reverent hand. As God wills. "Then we shall strike a blow for a free Palestine. From the river. . .to the sea."

8:04 P.M. Israel Standard Time, December 31ˢᵗ
A bar
Tel Aviv, Israel

One more day. That's what he kept telling himself. David Lay leaned back in his chair, letting the music wash over him as a young Ethiopian woman up on stage grasped the microphone firmly in her right hand, belting out a soulful blues rendition of Deborah Coleman's "I Found You."

Just one more day. He'd be turning over Station Tel Aviv to the incoming station chief in the morning and boarding a flight out of Ben Gurion hours later. Bound stateside. Back *home*.

Home? Where was that? It was strange how alien that concept seemed to him now. He'd spent nearly the last twenty years of his life in the CIA's employ, moving from one place to the next—a career that had cost him his marriage. His *family*. Everything he'd once thought precious.

And for what? And that was the most unanswerable question of them all. . .one that had kept him awake long nights in West Berlin back in the '80s, just after Trisha had left him. One that was costing him sleep now as he prepared to leave Israel behind for good.

They'd received confirmation of Mustafa al-Shukeiri's death eight days earlier, the former PLO leader found dead in his bed at his clifftop villa in Elba. His blood soaking the satin sheets, a pair of bullet holes in his upper chest, a third between his eyes.

Mozambique drill. The mark of a trained professional.

Al-Shukeiri's wife had been found lying beside her dead husband, still alive but bound to the headboard, a rude gag stuffed into her mouth according to the police report.

Eight days—and not a word from the Israelis, Lay thought, nursing his Jack Daniel's. And that. . .was probably the most troubling aspect of all this.

If they had found al-Shukeiri—and his death bore all the hallmarks of Mossad's *Kidon*—then Avi ben Shoham had to know that the CIA had spent most of the last month misleading its closest ally in the Middle East. Feeding them disinformation, leading them *away* from their target, not *to* him.

He had known it couldn't last forever—not that any of this had been his idea from the beginning. A plan passed down the chain of command from Langley's seventh floor, the lofty heights of Mount Olympus where the Gods of Good Intentions held eternal court.

In comparison to their grandeur, a Station Chief was a mere functionary. A cog in the wheel. Weren't they all?

He could still remember the words of one of his first instructors at the Farm, the Agency training facility in Camp Peary, Virginia—the man's eyes narrowing as he came to the front of the room, staring out at the trainees. *"The first thing you must learn if you are to pursue a career with the Company—we do not make policy here. We* execute *policy. If you're suffering from some grand delusion of saving the world, you've come to the wrong place."*

Perhaps there was some peace supposed to be found in that, he didn't know. He did know that after tomorrow, none of this was going to be his problem. *Like it or not.*

The Agency had never been big on closure.

8:16 P.M.
An olive grove outside Beit Shemesh

Betrayal. It was the reality of the spy business—a world where loyalties were bought and sold, subject to a thousand agendas as unknowable as the mind of God.

None of that made it any more forgivable.

The headlights of General Avi ben Shoham's SUV caught the familiar outline of the darkened Citroen sitting there by the side of the road—tapping the brakes as he slowed, pulling in just behind it and killing his own lights.

The lights of the Citroen flashed twice, then went dark once more. *The pre-arranged signal.*

He pushed open his door and stepped out onto the road, a chill night breeze rippling through his dark hair as he came up alongside the car. A hundred meetings like this one over the years since he had become a part of the Mossad in the late '80s, he thought, casting one last careful glance up and down the road before opening the passenger door.

A pungent wall of cigarette smoke hit him in the face as he slid onto the Citroen's threadbare seat, his eyes watering. "God, how do you *breathe* in this thing?"

"It's something you get used to," Eli Gerstman replied calmly, stubbing his cigarette out in an ashtray perched precariously on the dashboard. He was only a couple years older than Shoham, but the years had taken their toll on him.

Years spent defending the Jewish state. By whatever means necessary. "Any word from Dichter?"

Gerstman shook his head. "Nothing yet. If any of *Shin Bet*'s people in the Palestinian Authority know something about this. . .'Iraqi connection' your team uncovered in Elba, they're not talking."

And that was to be expected, Shoham mused, staring through the windshield into the darkness. Good intel was something that took time to develop.

Weeks, months—years, even. And those were under optimal conditions. . .with the continuing unrest of the *intifada*, the situation in the West Bank and Gaza could hardly have been less so.

It was time they didn't have. If the intelligence garnered from al-Shukeiri's computer was accurate—it was more like a question of *days*.

And there was no way to accurately calculate how much the death of the former PLO commander might have disrupted the "deal" in progress. Perhaps not at all. And if that was the case—they were faced with a serious problem. . .and left with only the most desperate of measures.

"Your operation," Gerstman began after a long moment, digging another cigarette out of the crumpled pack in his shirt pocket, "where are we at with it?"

"It's underway as we speak," Shoham replied, making a show of glancing his wristwatch. He knew perfectly well what time it was.

The senior officer shook his head, cigarette clenched between his teeth— a brief flash in the darkness as flame spurted from his lighter, the tip of the cigarette flaring for a moment before relapsing into a dull glow. "The Americans are going to be furious."

"Let them."

8:17 P.M.
The bar
Tel Aviv, Israel

"She has a beautiful voice, doesn't she?" Lay glanced up to see a young woman in a club dress standing there over his table, her hand on the back of the neighboring chair—her face shadowed in the semi-darkness of the bar.

"She does," the CIA station chief responded, taken by surprise at the woman's sudden appearance. "Truly talented. . .I only regret not having heard her before tonight."

"There will be other nights."

He shook his head, his gaze returning to the Ethiopian woman on stage, her voice low and husky as she leaned into the microphone. "I'm afraid not—not for me. I fly out of Ben Gurion tomorrow afternoon. Back to the States."

He wasn't sure exactly why he had just told her that, but there was an earnestness about her that was disarming—something in the way she carried herself. Perhaps it had something to do with the emptiness he felt this night. . .or perhaps it was just the Jack Daniel's talking.

"May I?" she asked, gesturing to the chair and he nodded quickly, watching her as she pulled it out to take her seat there at the table with him. She couldn't have been far out of her mid-twenties, a beauty about her that her clothes only served to accentuate—swarthy olive skin, black hair swept back over her shoulders in dark waves. High, prominent cheekbones highlighting a face a sculptor would have been proud to have been responsible for creating.

Something of a laughing challenge in her eyes as a waitress approached and she ordered a whiskey, neat. Introducing herself to him. *Amira.*

"The name's David," he responded, taking a sip of his Jack Daniel's. The best lies always began with a kernel of truth, and for some reason, despite the difference in their ages. . .he found himself wanting to make this a good one. "I work for the State Department."

He saw her eyes open wider at the statement, her attention taken from the stage for a moment. "Oh?"

A shrug. "It's nothing, really. . .I'm just a functionary, nothing more."

She laughed—a clear, ringing sound, her dark eyes dancing as she looked at him. "I have to say," she said, raising her glass, "you really know how to impress a woman."

Something in her eyes, catching him off-guard once more. *Did she mean she was. . .?*

He shook his head, managing a half-embarrassed smile in response. "Perhaps it's just been a long time since I tried."

8:24 P.M.
A surveillance van
Tel Aviv

". . .saw her in concert before I left the States. Has one of the best voices of any blues singer I've heard."

"You miss America?" The young man heard his partner ask, her voice coming through his headphones loud and clear, holding just the right note of sympathy—of concern.

He might have even believed it was sincere, he thought—his face tightening in the darkness of the vehicle. If he hadn't known exactly why they were all here.

What had led them to this point. *The Jewish people do not forget. We do not forgive.*

"She's good," he said, looking up into the eyes of the older man seated across from him in the back of the van, the glow of the electronics playing across his face—illuminating the Jericho 941 semiautomatic pistol sitting on the ledge next to him. A magazine in the man's weathered hands as he carefully fed one brass cartridge after another between its steel lips.

A nod served as the only reply. She was *trained* to be good.

"What do you think, Ze'ev. . .will he go for it?"

"Better men than him have before," the older man said finally, looking across at the screens showing the single surveillance camera, covering the entrance to the bar. "And the CIA's people, they've always enjoyed tomcatting around on foreign station. Last night in Israel. . .what does he have to lose?"

True enough. "Still, his jacket says he's been with them since the '80s." He shook his head. "Hasn't lasted that long in this business by being a fool."

The older man didn't smile, slamming the magazine into the Jericho's stock with an audible *click*. The slide running forward as he thumbed off the release. *Chambering a round.*

"We're prepared for that eventuality."

9:21 P.M.
The bar
Tel Aviv

". . .and that's how I came to work for the government," Lay said, leaning back in his chair, the last of his whiskey forgotten in the glass on the table, amidst the melting ice. "Didn't intend for it to work out that way, but it did. It's life. . .kinda funny, I suppose."

And all of it a lie, he thought, the music from the stage still swirling around them, unnoticed as he looked into the dark eyes of the woman sitting across from him.

Nothing more so than that last line. There were many words he could think of to describe life—funny didn't enter into it.

But this night. . .this had been something special. Somehow. Two lonely people sharing a moment in time. *Strangers in the night.*

"And I had no choice in the matter," she said, her glass poised delicately between long fingers. "But there's nothing else I would have chosen—nothing more important than the defense of the Jewish state against those who would seek to destroy it."

And they are many, he thought, hearing the passion in her voice. The passion of youth, of idealism. A passion he had once felt himself. . .where had it died? Berlin? *Here?* His own conscience no longer clear—stained by so much, actions he could never take back. Or undo. "I hope you succeed."

She drained her whiskey, eyeing him over the glass. Seeming to take his measure at a glance. "You're sympathetic to our cause? I find that surprising coming from someone in your position. . .the US State Department—well, you know what I mean."

He nodded. *All too well.* "My job demands 'neutrality' from me," he said finally, "but I have made many friends during my time in Israel and. . .not so many on the other side. I wouldn't be human if I didn't admit my sympathies lay with your people."

"Good," she responded, seeming to consider his words for a long moment, the light of the bar refracted in the crystal of her glass. "These days, Israel needs every friend she can get."

True enough. "I suppose I'd best be saying good-bye," he said, glancing at his wristwatch. Genuine regret in his voice as he pushed back his chair, rising to his feet. "New Year's Eve or no, it's an early morning tomorrow."

"Oh, I don't know—my apartment is only a few blocks from the airport," she said, a quiet smile playing around her lips as she looked slowly up into his face. "I'm sure you would enjoy. . .the view."

He just stood there for a moment, taken off-guard by her boldness. But hadn't he known this was where it was headed? Her words, the look in her eyes—making her intentions clear almost from the moment she had sat down.

The offer couldn't have been more tempting. She was so beautiful, and it had been so very long—yet he felt something of an alarm trigger deep within him.

He might have been lonely, but he wasn't delusional. Something wasn't right about any of this.

9:26 P.M.
The surveillance van

"No," he heard the American officer respond—his voice suddenly cold as ice, tension clearly audible in his tone. Somehow, something had alerted him. Perhaps nothing more than the instincts of an old spy rising to the fore.

No matter. He glanced across at his partner, nodding silently as the older man tucked his weapon into a holster inside his waistband—zipping up his jacket. He picked up a small syringe off the shelf and held it up to the dim light within the van, flicking it with a forefinger. A grim look passing across his face as he did so

Another moment, and the man had pushed open the back door of the vehicle, disappearing into the night. Leaving him alone, the glow of the screens washing over his bearded face.

The woman's voice coming over his headset. "Ariel, the target's on the move. Coming your way."

A taut, grim smile creased his lips as he toggled his mike to respond, his eyes on the street cameras. Lay's decision to leave. . .it wasn't going to change a thing, not in the end.

9:29 P.M.

David Lay cast a glance behind him as he exited the bar, unable to shake the feeling that something was wrong. That he was being targeted.

That woman. . .he found himself replaying her every word through his mind—every last thing *he* had said to her.

Cursing himself for a fool that he hadn't seen it earlier, that he had let his guard down.

You didn't get to make mistakes in this business, he thought, glancing down a street filled with partiers come to ring in the New Year, his eyes searching the crowd for any sign of a threat. Not on Mossad's turf, most of all.

Not without them costing you dearly.

He put his hand on a young woman's shoulder, excusing himself as he began to push his way through the crowd. It wasn't more than a few blocks to the small fifth-floor apartment he had called "home" ever since arriving in Tel Aviv—just a few blocks, and he was home free. So long as he wasn't tailed when he left for the Embassy in the morning, he should make his flight without incident. Would be back Stateside before the new year was a full day old.

He might been careless, but he hadn't given her anything operable. Anything that was even *true*.

This could be handled.

Twenty meters down the street, maybe more, and he felt someone jostle into him from behind.

Lay turned, catching a brief glimpse of a man in the crowd, already moving away from him—his face obscured by a hooded jacket.

A sharp, stinging pain suddenly shooting through his thigh—his eyes widening as he glanced down, searching in vain for a wound. Feeling suddenly disoriented, dizzy—unable to focus. He hadn't had *that* much to drink. There was no way. . .his mind consumed with self-recrimination. Memories of another time flashing before him. The Cold War, an assassination ordered from behind the Iron Curtain.

The Bulgarians had been masters at this sort of thing.

This. . .a reveler's angry shout ringing hollow in his ears as he staggered into her. Her face swimming before his eyes—his fingers digging into the pale flesh of her arm. *Struggling to stay aright.*

He saw a pair of men in paramedic uniform pushing their way intently through the crowd toward him, their faces blurry and unfocused. And then his legs seemed to give way—the ground rushing up to meet him as he went down hard against the pavement. Darkness, reaching out to enfold him.

And everything went black. . .

10:35 P.M.
Cairo International Airport
Egypt

Journey in Royalty, Lieutenant Colonel Umar Hadi thought as he descended the stairs of the Royal Jordanian Airways Airbus to the tarmac, glancing back up to see the airline's familiar dark livery resplendent under the runway lights—the Hashemite crown emblazoned upon the plane's tail.

A lofty thought.

Far too lofty for a soldier like him. He shook his head, running a hand across the dark mustache lining his upper lip—his maroon beret and uniform long gone, replaced by a dark, Western-style suit. A soldier—that's all he was, and after more than twenty years serving in the ranks of the Republican Guards, it was all he knew how to be.

Tahir Kamal Siddiqi, though. . .the general was another matter entirely. He had aspirations beyond the military, of that much Hadi was sure.

The kind of aspirations that placed a man in danger of coming under Saddam's scrutiny, or perhaps even worse, that of the President's son, Qusay.

It was dangerous even to swim close to such a man, let alone be counted among his inner circle. He knew that. . .but too many years had gone by for any of it to be altered now.

He could still remember the first time he had ever seen Siddiqi—only a colonel then—standing upright in the open hatch of his T-72 main battle tank as Iranian shells pounded Basra.

Furiously cursing young conscripts fleeing the midnight attack of 35,000 Iranian *Pasdaran* crossing the Fish Lake, rallying every man he could make stand and fight.

Service pistol drawn in his hand, shooting more than one who refused to fall in. Holding their part of the line as the Iraqi defenses crumbled all about them that night.

Truly a soldier's soldier, Hadi thought, walking through the concourse—his eyes searching the sea of faces in hopes of finding his contact. The young Palestinian who was to smuggle him across the Sinai and into Gaza.

A man like that. . .you'd follow him anywhere. To the very gates of Hell.

5:43 A.M., January 1st, 2001
The coast
South of Netanya, Israel

Avi ben Shoham could hear waves crashing against the beach scarce half a kilometer distant as he turned off the engine, pushing open the door of the SUV and stepping out onto the gravel. The dark shape of a warehouse looming in the night not fifty meters away—the sea breeze tugging at his suit jacket, exposing the Browning Hi-Power riding in a leather holster on the Mossad officer's hip.

It was too dark for him to be able to glimpse the Mediterranean, but he could *smell* it—the taste of salt on his lips as he stood there for a moment, gazing out into the night. Coming to terms once more with the reality of what he had done.

What he had ordered *done.*

He'd received the confirmation of "Mission Success" over Mossad's secure comms network hours before, but he knew all too well that this wasn't success. This wasn't the end.

This was only the beginning, the moment when the dice flew out over the table. Their fate yet to be decided. . .yet irretrievably cast.

Wars had been started over less.

His face hardened at the memory of those they had lost, his dark eyes gazing out toward the black of the sea.

For his country, this was a war which had already begun.

5:57 A.M.

Pain. It felt as though someone had taken an axe handle to the side of his head, Lay thought—coming awake slowly, his skull throbbing as if it had been split open—his eyes struggling to adjust themselves to the pitch darkness that surrounded him. Realizing only then that there was a hood over his face. His fingers reaching out, feeling *something*—like the fabric of a threadbare cot beneath him. The room was cool, but he was soaked with sweat all the same, his shirt clinging to his back.

He'd never known a hangover this intense, he thought, attempting to process what had happened—not even in the old days at Berlin Station.

Long nights in the dead of German winter he'd drunk himself into a stupor, trying to drown out the sorrow of a failed marriage.

A child half a world away.

But it had never been anything like *this*. This was—it hit him then, everything flooding back from the night before. The bar. The woman. *The man in the crowd. The paramedics.*

The feeling of a needle being stabbed into his thigh—he'd been taken out of play, but by *whom*?

He tried to push himself aright, a surge of unaccustomed panic seeming to flood through his body—his mind grasping too late that his hands were bound even as he lost his balance, crashing to the hard concrete of the floor.

Pain shooting through his shoulder as he rolled over onto to his back, biting deeply into his tongue in an effort to keep from crying out. Struggling to maneuver into a sitting position. He wasn't as young as he'd been in Berlin, either—the years of late nights and bad habits taking their toll.

The Agency, well it was hardly a place for health nuts.

The door opened without warning, the noise of his fall apparently having alerted someone without—booted footsteps against the concrete

Multiple men—at least two, maybe three. Hands grabbing him roughly under his arms, hauling him upright. "What's going on? What's—"

A sharp blow to the ribs silenced him as he felt himself hustled out the door and down a hall, his feet seeming to move sluggishly. As though the effects of the drug were still wearing off, dulling his reaction time.

He heard the harsh scrape of metal against concrete, even as his captors thrust him into a folding chair—ripping the hood away from his head, slicing away the zip-ties from his hands.

Leaving him sitting there blinking in the bright glare of utility lights surrounding his chair and the small table before him. *Disoriented.* Rubbing his wrists to restore the circulation, still struggling to find his bearings as a figure walked in from the darkness beyond the lights. A voice, so *familiar.* Chilling him to the very bone.

"So, David. . .why don't you tell me what we're both doing here?"

6:08 A.M.
The desert
Sinai Peninsula, west of Al-Arīsh

A barren land, Lieutenant Colonel Hadi mused, gazing out over the Sinai— the desert veiled in pre-dawn darkness as the battered old Renault flew down the road, seeming to threaten to shake itself apart more violently with every passing mile, its engine murmuring in protest.

All of which seemed to be of no concern to his driver, a young Palestinian in his early twenties who hadn't stopped talking since they'd left Cairo—seven long hours and nearly two hundred miles before. An endless stream of excited and angry commentary on the state of the *intifada*, his people's ongoing struggle against the Zionist state.

". . .and that day the tanks rolled into Jenin—I was standing right there, looking at one of those Jews through a pair of binoculars, standing in the hatch of his tank. Looking right at him—him looking back. If only I'd had a rifle, I would have. . ."

Been cut in two by the tank's machine gun, the soldier thought, shaking his head as he listened. As he would have done if it he had been the tanker.

Young men like this—this. . .*boy*, seated there across from him in the driver's seat of the Renault. They thought they had seen war. Thought they knew what it was.

They had no idea.

For all the talk of brutality and oppression current in the Arab world concerning the Israeli occupation of Palestine, few of them could have imagined what it would look like to see a modern army truly unleashed against a civilian populace.

Crushing an uprising. . .the way Saddam would have done it, Hadi reflected—his dark eyes shadowed at the memory.

Rolling into Basra back in '91 at the head of a column of Republican Guard loyalists. Iraqi Army deserters crushed beneath the treads of his T-72—the massive tank recoiling on its chassis as its main gun fired, sending a 125mm shell through the upper floors of an apartment building. Outnumbered and outgunned, the rebels hadn't stood a chance as Guardsmen moved street to street, killing anyone who resisted—executing many who surrendered.

It had all been over in a month, leaving thousands dead. Thousands more living only in fear of their lives.

That was war. The kind of war the Jewish state might find itself employing against the Palestinians if they were to learn the details of his own mission, he realized, glancing out through the dusty glass of the Renault's windshield into the first rays of the dawn—only too aware of the repercussions that could result from the deployment of this kind of weapon.

But he was a soldier, and he had his orders. *Just as he had back then.*

6:10 A.M.

"Avi!" David Lay exclaimed in surprise, the familiar face of his Israeli counterpart coming into view as the man emerged from the darkness surrounding the table. "What is the meaning of all this—what's going on?"

"That's what I was hoping you would be able to tell me, David," the Mossad officer said slowly, pausing with his hand on the back of the opposite chair. His eyes still veiled in shadow.

He knew, Lay thought, the instincts of a career intelligence officer rushing to the fore—even through the drugged haze. Everything becoming clear to him in that moment. *Deny.* Deny everything.

The stratagem of the spy, every bit as much as it was that of the politician.

"I have no idea what you're talking about," Lay responded, anger in his voice as he pushed himself to his feet—swaying slightly as he put a hand on the table to steady himself. *Anger.* Righteous indignation. Not to have displayed it would have as much as admitted he was lying. "I was kidnapped and brought here—"

"On my orders," Avi ben Shoham returned evenly, his eyes never leaving Lay's face. A dangerous calm pervading the Israeli's features.

"Oh, for God's sake, Avi." Lay shook his head, glaring across the table. "Have you absolutely lost your mind?"

"Sit back down, David."

It wasn't a suggestion.

Defeat. The CIA officer collapsed into the folding chair, feeling the cold metal through his thin, sweat-soaked dress shirt as he leaned back.

"Mustafa al-Shukeiri," Shoham began, placing a folder on the table between them, "what can you tell me about him?"

Lay shrugged. "He is—or rather *was*—a member of the Palestinian Legislative Council. Served by Arafat's side all the way back in Beirut, one of his closest advisers. And he was—"

"A CIA asset."

6:14 A.M.
The warehouse

He was standing on-guard outside the door of the warehouse, listening to the waves of the Mediterranean break against the beach when a pair of headlights swept across the entry road.

His eyes narrowed, his body straightening as the vehicle turned in—his hand closing around the butt of the Jericho 941 holstered on his hip.

A blue Toyota coming to a stop twenty meters away, a woman emerging from the driver's seat, the club dress she had worn into the bar long since exchanged for old *Madei Aleph* service fatigues—the kind she had worn during her years with the Israeli Defense Forces. "Ariel," she began, coming up to him, "is the general inside?"

He nodded, stepping aside to let her pass. "Ariel" wasn't his name, but it might as well have been, given how long it had been since anyone had used his real one.

David Shafron, dead and buried long ago—a name chiseled into the granite of a tombstone in *Har HaMenuchot.* Dead, disowned by his ultra-Orthodox parents the day he'd enlisted in the IDF. Long before he had become a member of a Mossad *Kidon. An assassin.*

"I would give him a moment, Tzippi," he said, using the diminutive of her codename, 'Tzipporah.' "He's still interrogating our man."

Interrogating might have been a little strong. Their orders had been to handle the CIA officer with care. They weren't, after all, actually trying to start a war here.

She shook her head, holding up a cellular phone. "Eli Gerstman wants to speak with him. At once. *Shin Bet* came through for us, one of Dichter's informants in the PA reporting that there's a man coming through the tunnels from the Sinai this morning—perhaps even within the next few hours. They're calling him 'the Iraqi.'"

6:17 A.M.

It was all here, David Lay realized, sifting through the papers before him—cursing once more the day the good idea fairy had paid a visit to Langley's seventh floor. Good intentions, so ever out of place in this business.

He had argued strongly against recruiting Mustafa al-Shukeiri, warned that the risks of him playing them were far too high. That the potential for blowback was real, should anyone—on either side—realize they had been running him.

As they just had. All of it here in black and white. Scarce even worth the trouble of denying. And he had been playing them. . .from the very beginning.

Lay swore softly beneath his breath. Even he couldn't have predicted it ending this badly, proving that not even cynicism sufficed in the Middle East.

"So," he began, looking up to meet Avi ben Shoham's gaze, "where do we go from here?"

"There is no *we*, David," the Israeli responded, finally taking his seat across from him. "Not any longer. We're both professionals—we know how this game is played—so I'm going to spare you the outrage. What you did. . .I have no doubt you did in the belief that it was in your country's best interests."

He paused, shaking his head as if incredulous that anyone could have thought such a thing. "Americans have always been hopelessly optimistic in their dealings with Arafat and those of his inner circle. But none of that changes the reality that, if you hadn't already served out your term as chief of station. . .we'd be revoking your diplomatic status. Declaring you *persona non grata*."

A thunderous finish to what had once been a promising career, Lay reflected bitterly, staring across the table at his counterpart. And so much of it due to decisions which had been made *for* him.

Out of his control.

He could have said as much to Shoham—could have protested—but doing so would have displayed weakness. The one thing you could never do.

103

"Then what was your purpose in all. . .this?" he asked, glancing around him into the empty darkness of the deserted warehouse. "You don't think you could have accomplished the same thing with a phone call—lunch at *Hatraklin*?"

"Bringing you here, David, was about sending a message. Making clear to your government just how seriously Israel takes such a threat to her security. The administration is in office a mere nineteen more days—they need to start deciding just how fraught with scandal they want those final days to be."

You're talking about a President who got it on with an intern young enough to have been his daughter, Lay thought, keeping his face studiously neutral. The bar for scandal was rather. . .high.

But this—the summary destruction of everything they had tried to achieve in the Middle East, already jeopardized by the unrest of the *intifada*—this was something different entirely. "So, what do you want?"

"We want the CIA to turn over its files on al-Shukeiri to Mossad. *Everything* they have. Anything that could enable us to further establish the connections between him and this Iraqi general."

"I don't know if that's going to be possible. The kind of files you're talking about are strictly NOFORN, Avi," the CIA station chief said, holding up a hand. *No foreign nationals.* "Highly classified stuff."

"I am *talking* about the preservation of the Jewish state!" Shoham spat, his eyes flashing as he leaned forward. "I—"

"General," a familiar voice interrupted—Lay's head snapping up just in time to see a woman in IDF service dress enter the circle of light surrounding the table. "My apologies, but we have a situation developing."

The woman from the bar, Lay realized, anger flooding across his face as he watched her lean down, speaking to Shoham in a hushed voice. ". . .coming in from the Sinai. . .an Iraqi. . ."

"This morning?" he heard the Mossad officer demand, and she nodded, continuing, "Gerstman is asking that you to call him immediately, wants the *Kidon* team to stage for the operation."

"All right," Shoham said finally, pressing both hands against the table as he rose to his feet. "I'm going to have to cut this short, David. Something has. . .come up. Do we understand each other?"

Lay nodded, still unsure how to play this. What Langley would *agree* to. "We do."

"I should hope so," the Israeli replied, his dark eyes hard and unrelenting as he stood there, staring at Lay. "If not, the repercussions will be serious."

He turned to leave, glancing at the woman as he did so. "You'll see that Mr. Lay receives an escort back to Tel Aviv. . ."

7:09 A.M.
Rafah
On the border between Egypt and Gaza

"Come in, come in," the man whispered urgently from the doorway, placing his hand on the shoulder of Hadi's driver and pulling him inside.

Hadi took a final look around him before heeding the man's admonition, taking in the dusty pavement of the street—Arabic graffiti sprayed on a nearby wall. The rising sun filtering across the rooftops from the east past lines of clothing hung out to dry, intermingled with the looming, incongruous shadows of satellite dishes.

He had hoped to be across the border and inside Gaza before the breaking of dawn, but that had proven an impossibility.

With the ever-increasing unrest, Mubarak's soldiers had stepped up their patrols near the border, one such unit passing them only a few blocks back— a squad of soldiers in the back of a Toyota pick-up truck, a Russian-made DShK machine gun mounted in the bed.

His presence in Egypt might have been perfectly legal, but that didn't mean he wanted to be answering any more questions as to the reasons for his trip than were absolutely necessary.

He wouldn't be the first visitor to Egypt to find himself "disappeared" by the *Mukhabarat*.

His eyes adjusted slowly to the gloom as they followed their host deeper into the dwelling, the man not turning on any lights—as if himself afraid to attract attention. He saw a young boy, no more than four or five years old, peering out the door of a side room—seeming to regard his father's visitors with a curiosity not unmixed with fear.

"Here," the man said, pushing open a door and letting them into a small storeroom—dust flying everywhere as he cast aside a rug which had been spread across the floor, exposing a square outline in the center.

His fingers digging under the slab of concrete and heaving it aside to reveal a hole, opening up into the darkness beneath.

A tunnel, Hadi thought, eyeing the man as he took a step back. One of literally hundreds which had honeycombed the border between Egypt and Gaza since the '80s—used to smuggle in everything from medicine and spare parts to the weapons need to carry on the fight against the Jews.

The Palestinian moved over to a low shelf mounted near the wall, fumbling briefly through assorted detritus before his fingers closed around a small flashlight, handing it over to the lieutenant colonel.

Hadi flicked it on, the beam of light playing around the darkened room as he knelt by the edge of the hole—glancing up into the eyes of his young guide. "Well then, let's be going."

7:14 A.M.
Mossad Headquarters
Tel Aviv

". . .there's no certainty as to his identity or whether he's even connected with al-Shukeiri. To describe the intel provided by *Shin Bet's* informant as 'vague' would be an act of charity. We—"

"Have to make a decision on whether to take him or not," Avi ben Shoham interjected, cutting his fellow Mossad officer off. "My officers are already on their way into the Strip along with Dichter's man and the informant. We're coordinating with the IDF to move a quick reaction force into Ein HaBesor to stage in the event of needing to rapidly extract the team from Rafah."

"You've certainly not wasted any time, Avi," Efraim Halevy observed from the head of the table, the first time the Mossad director had spoken since taking his seat.

"There was no time to be lost," Shoham responded evenly, meeting

Halevy's gaze. The older man's face as unreadable as ever. "If *Shin Bet's* intelligence was accurate, the Iraqi will arrive in Gaza within the hour."

"And when he does?"

"You know where I stand on this, Efraim. Giving this man the opportunity to slip through our hands if he makes it all the way into Rafah," Shoham shook his head, "it's a risk we don't *need* to take."

And this was no time to be taking unnecessary risks, he didn't add. Not with their relations with the Americans strained to the breaking point. Not with the Iraqi military involved in. . .whatever this was. "We can take him down there at the crossing point, bring him back here for interrogation. Find out what he knows."

"And if he doesn't talk?"

Shoham just looked at him, his face cold and expressionless. The odds of that were vanishingly small.

Halevy broke eye contact after a moment, glancing over to where Gerstman sat on the other side of the conference table, the senior officer's face wreathed by a haze of cigarette smoke. "Eli?"

Gerstman took another long drag of his cigarette before responding.

"Avi makes a strong case," he said heavily, stubbing it out in the ashtray at his left hand before continuing, "but it's not one I agree with. These last few months of this so-called 'intifada'—we're balancing on a razor's edge there in the Authority, one incident away from the kind of violence we won't be able to control. I'm uncomfortable with the idea of launching a full-scale raid into Rafah until we have a better grasp of what we're up against. Some idea, at least, of who our Iraqi is in contact with there in the PA. Who he's meeting."

Madness. "I'm not proposing a full-scale raid, just the *Kidon* team," he said, favoring Gerstman with a hard look. "They make the snatch, get him out of the Strip before anyone's the wiser."

"And if they don't?" Gerstman asked calmly, turning to look at him. "What if something goes wrong with the grab—if the IDF has to be called in to pull your people out? What then?"

What if? Nothing ever went according to plan out there, that uncertainty the only rock-solid guarantee of field work. Of HUMINT.

It was a risk all of his people understood. A risk they were *prepared* to take. But Gerstman wasn't done, his voice even and calculated as he continued, "I think we have to remember how this all began—with a pair of soldiers in an old Ford Sierra, driving into a Palestinian city."

A day that had ended in death and fire, Shoham thought, the images of that lynching in Ramallah still all-too-fresh in his memory. The sight of a young Arab shouting jubilantly from an upper window, his hands stained red with Jewish blood.

"I have to concur," he heard Halevy say, looking up to meet the old man's eyes. "Keep your people back. . .for now."

7:32 A.M.
Rafah
The Gaza Strip

"Are you sure that's the house?" Ariel heard the *Shin Bet* officer, a middle-aged man identified to them only as "Omri", ask—dark sunglasses shielding his eyes as he glanced over at the Palestinian man sitting in the passenger seat of the sedan.

Their informant.

A quick, anxious nod—the man's eyes darting all about like those of a trapped animal, seeming to anxiously scan the dusty street around their vehicle, the bright rays of morning sun filtering through the vehicle's heavily tinted windows. Sweat staining the collar of his dress shirt.

"Yes, it—it is," he said, gulping even as he spoke the words. He was either a terrible liar or frightened half out of his mind, Ariel thought as he watched both of them from the rear seat. *Perhaps both.*

He had a bad feeling about this, one that had been building ever since Shoham's call five minutes prior. *Shadow the Iraqi, don't take him. Not yet.*

That hadn't been the plan, and changing plans in the middle of an operation made him uneasy, his fingers tightening around the pistol grip of the Kalashnikov assault rifle laying across his lap. The variables of this operation, already far too many to be accounted for.

"You're certain," Omri pressed, his hand closing around the informant's wrist—forcing him to look at him. Clearly he was fully cognizant of their danger, as well he should be. He'd been running assets in and out of Gaza ever since the early '90s.

"Yes, yes. . .this has to be the end, I'm telling you." The man swallowed hard, his face twisting into an agonized grimace, tears of fear streaming down his cheeks, the words pouring out of him like the breaking of a dam. "If they even *suspect* that I've been passing information to you. . .they'll kill my wife and I—they'll take my little girl and rape her in front of me. She's only five, I beg of you—you have to get me out."

"You know I've been working on doing just that, Daoud," his handler replied, his eyes invisible behind the shades. His face impassive. "These things take time."

And we need more from you, Ariel added silently, turning his face away. Knowing all too well that the *Shin Bet* officer was lying to the man—that they had no intention of pulling him out.

Assets in the Palestinian Authority were too valuable—too difficult to cultivate—to waste by pulling them out before you had gotten everything you could from them. *Every last drop.*

Those were the realities of the intelligence business. Cold and brutal. It made him glad to be out on the sharp end, charged with *acting* upon the intelligence gathered by other men.

Removed from it, somehow. *Look away.*

The door of the target dwelling came open in that moment, a bearded man in jeans and a faded t-shirt emerging from its shadow into the street. Followed by a second. And a third. Their heads up, alert. Eyes searching the street.

He felt Ze'ev tense in the seat beside him, heard Omri turn to his informant, demanding, "The Iraqi—is he there?"

"I don't know," the man replied, his voice trembling. "I've never seen the man before in my life."

Great. Ariel shook his head as he watched the first man approach a faded

109

white Chevrolet, swearing softly beneath his breath. It was the kind of information that would have been useful an hour earlier—*before* they placed themselves in this kind of jeopardy. Human intelligence. . .in all its glory.

"But *these* men," the *Shin Bet* officer pressed, "they are smugglers, yes? Locals?"

"Yes, yes—part of a gang. They. . ." Ariel heard the man's voice trail off as a fourth man stepped from the doorway, behind the others. A tall man, in street clothes like all the rest, but his bearing. . .it was unmistakably that of a soldier.

He saw the informant's face and knew without even hearing him say the words. *This* man wasn't one of the locals.

"Keilah-2," he announced, toggling the mike of his two-way radio, "we have eyes on our target. Be prepared to take up following positions."

7:39 A.M.
The United States Embassy
Tel Aviv, Israel

It was a strange feeling being back here. . .like *this,* David Lay thought, still rubbing his chafed wrists as he moved through the halls of the diplomatic mission.

He had intended to arrive early on this morning—hold the final transition meeting with his successor.

Clear out his desk. *Move on.*

Put it all behind him. Leave this part of his life forever in the past, once and for all.

That was the funny thing about the past—it had a way of coming back to haunt you. Again and again.

A black Marine NCO in desert combat fatigues stood guard before the door that led to the CIA station, his M-16 carried at patrol ready.

"Sergeant Rutherford," Lay greeted, nodding to the man as he approached. Only too aware of how he must look—his suit rumpled from having been slept in, his shirt only now drying from the cold sweat which had soaked his body.

He could feel the man's eyes on him—but the Marine simply nodded, a terse "Good morning, sir" escaping his lips as he took a step back, allowing Lay to pass.

The room Lay found himself in as the door closed behind him could have passed without mention in most any corporate office the Western world over—bland white cubicles occupying the body of the space, bulky CRT monitors and fax machines perched on desks groaning from the weight of stacks of print-outs. A few conference rooms off to one side, larger offices encircling the room.

Bearing no resemblance whatsoever to the kind of thing seen in one of Pierce Brosnan's Bond films.

Nothing nearly so high-tech, the station chief thought with a wry grimace. He spotted Daniel Vukovic, his deputy chief of station, standing by a cubicle talking with one of the Agency analysts and made his way over to them.

"David!" Vukovic exclaimed, looking up as he approached. He put his hand on Lay's shoulder, both of them turning away from the analyst as he lowered his voice. "Where have you been? You were supposed to be here an hour ago—I called your apartment, tried your mobile."

"I was. . .unavoidably detained," he replied, only too aware of the irony in his words. No humor in any of this.

"Fournier is in Conference Room #3," Vukovic said, going on as if he hadn't spoken. "I had to go ahead and start the transition meeting already without you. We need—"

"And you're just going to have to continue without me," Lay said grimly, cutting him off. "I'll be in my office—on the secure line to Langley."

7:47 A.M.
Rafah
The Gaza Strip

The contrast between these men and the boy who had picked him up in Cairo couldn't have been more stark, Hadi thought, looking into the grim eyes of the smuggler to his left in the cramped backseat of the Chevrolet Corsica—

glimpsing the old, weathered Makarov he was clutching in his lap, the pistol's bluing long since worn off.

They might have lacked the professionalism which made good soldiers, but they had been operating under the nose of the Zionist state for years—and that made them good at what they did.

The kind of men they would no doubt utilize to bring the shipment across once the deal was reached.

"Abu Awad," he began slowly, looking out the window as the car navigated the narrow streets—stone buildings a century old seamlessly intermixed with modern concrete. Graffiti in flowing Arabic script spray-painted haphazardly on the walls. Electric wires criss-crossing above their heads, seeming to tie everything together like a spider's web. "He's been informed of my arrival?"

"He's waiting for you."

8:01 A.M.
The United States Embassy
Tel Aviv, Israel

"I understand, sir," David Lay said, the television droning on in the background as he leaned back into his office chair, staring at the photograph on his desk, the last thing he hadn't packed—all the rest of his personal effects, what there were of them, stuffed into the cardboard box sitting on the table across the room. A woman standing outside a hotel in Miami Beach—the wind playing with her blonde hair. Sunglasses hiding her bright blue eyes. Eyes which had enchanted him from the moment he'd first met her.

Trisha.

He shook his head, still listening to the voice on the other end of the line. His third call, each successive one growing more strained as he explained to the powers that be the extent to which their brilliant plan had gone completely sideways. As their initial surprise and anger over the brazenness of Mossad's actions faded away, to be replaced with a bitter knowledge of their own peril.

"If that's the way you're wanting me to play this," he interjected finally,

"I'm going to need something I can give the Israelis. Something substantive."

His ex-wife was looking down in the picture, away from the camera, a bright smile creasing her face. Their daughter's tiny hand gripping her finger, her dress a splash of color against the background.

Carol had been nothing more than a toddler then, scarce past her second birthday. They had come down to visit him that week—a week together in the Florida sun, just the three of them.

One of the last times he could remember that they'd been happy—*truly* happy. *Before the fall.* Before everything he'd once thought certain began to irrevocably fall apart.

The Miami operation he'd been a part of had been shut down six months after the divorce went through—the CIA cutting its losses. *Moving on.* Like they always did.

"No," he responded, cutting his superior off, "that's not going to work. You want this circle kept tight, you want me to stay here and run this—under Fournier's nose—you're going to have to work with me on this. Give me something I can use."

The Iraqi, he thought, his ex-wife's face drifting out of focus as his mind flashed back to the warehouse. The woman's whispered conversation with Shoham. Someone coming across the border from the Sinai. . .

The general mentioned in the files Avi had showed him from al-Shukeiri's computer had been an Iraqi, a member of Saddam's inner circle.

Could it. . .it was a thin lead to go on, but it was something. More importantly, it was all he had. "*ECHELON*," he said abruptly, scarce even realizing he had spoken aloud. "I'm going to need you to put me in touch with Mike Hayden's boys up at Fort Meade. As soon as possible."

8:23 A.M.
The Gaza Strip

"They've turned north now, along the road to Khan Yunis," Tzipporah said, her voice coming loud and clear over Ariel's radio from the other car. "We're entering an open stretch, falling farther back now."

"Roger that, Keilah-2," he acknowledged, gesturing to get the attention of the *Shin Bet* officer. *Move up.*

Time for them to trade off once more, taking up the tailing position and allowing the second Mossad vehicle with Tzipporah and Nadir, the youngest member of his *Kidon* team, to turn off.

Leapfrogging their way across the Gaza Strip—like they had been doing for the better part of the last hour, Ariel thought, wondering for the hundredth time where precisely the Iraqi was being taken. Or whether this was all an elaborate ruse to throw them off the track, a surveillance detection run to check for tails.

He felt the car speed up, jockeying through the narrow side streets past pedestrians and the occasional animal—Omri certifying himself as a genuine Arab driver in his liberal use of the Mazda's horn.

The grimmest of smiles touching Ariel's lips as he adjusted the folds of the *keffiyeh* around his neck, nothing about it—like the rest of his clothing—distinguishing him from the average Palestinian in the street. One way or another, they were going to finish this. End everything al-Shukeiri set in motion, just like they had ended *him* there on Elba. Dead in his own bed, his blood and brains staining the sheets. *Retribution.*

"We have the car," he announced finally as they swept out onto the main road less than forty meters behind the white Chevrolet. "Keilah-2, pull back, prepare to stage for the next rotation."

We're going to get you.

8:57 A.M.
The United States Embassy
Tel Aviv, Israel

"And I think that about wraps it up," David Lay said finally, glancing from Vukovic back to his successor. "Daniel can fill in any details I've left blank."

Except for the things even he doesn't know about, Lay thought. He cleared his throat. "It feels strange, leaving here like this. With everything suddenly thrust into the throes of chaos after three years of hard work. Almost seems like I should stay and help pick up the pieces."

Fournier chuckled. "That's the Middle East for you, David. Picking up the pieces. . .it's something we'll be doing for years—all the way up until the next madman knocks it all apart again. I call it job security."

That was one way to look at it. *Perhaps the only way.* Lay forced a smile, extending his hand. "Well, I'm glad at least to know that I've leaving it in good hands."

That much was true enough, he thought, hearing the man's reply as he reached out, clasping Lay's hand in his own. Evan Fournier might not have been his first choice to take over Station Tel Aviv upon his departure, but he was a good choice all the same—having spent four years in Damascus in the early '90s as assistant station chief before being rotated back to the States.

He knew the region, understood its complexities about as well as anyone Langley might have chosen. A solid pick.

"I'll be here a few more days, as it happens. Finalizing things with Langley, procedural stuff—nothing important," Lay lied, feeling Vukovic's eyes on him as he looked Fournier straight in the eye. "I'll do my best to stay out of your way."

The new station chief smiled, a smile that seemed at once sincere and wary. Jealous of his newly acquired turf. "Not a problem, David. Be sure to let me know if you need anything."

"Of course. Daniel?" Lay said, motioning for Vukovic to follow as he turned, crossing the CIA station toward a small side office which had been vacated a few weeks earlier—a female analyst returning Stateside for the birth of her child.

He flicked on the light switch and walked across the room, setting the box containing his personal effects down on the edge of the flimsy metal desk.

"I'm going to need a secure line run in here, Daniel," he said, glancing back to where Vukovic stood by the open door. "And a computer with access to our network. As soon as it can be set up. Can you arrange that?"

"I can," the assistant station chief replied, his gaze unwavering as he stared at Lay. "But first, you're going to have to tell me what you're actually doing. Why you're really still here."

Lay pushed brusquely past his shoulder, shutting the door to the station without before turning to face his former deputy. "I'm cleaning up a mess, that's what I'm doing. And you're going to help me."

9:12 A.M.
The Gaza Strip

"It's there again," Hadi heard one of the smugglers announce, his voice filled with tension as he glanced back along the open highway as they sped north toward Gaza City itself

The same dark brown Toyota that had been following them ever since Khan Yunis, disappearing occasionally only to reappear once more in their rear-view mirror.

An uncanny, ever-constant presence—no matter how many side roads they took, criss-crossing the Strip as they worked their way north. Jinking like a fighter pilot avoiding a SAM. *They had a tail.*

But *how?* That was the question burning through the lieutenant colonel's mind, again and again.

Could the Zionists' intelligence network have somehow picked them up coming across the border? The odds seemed fantastical, and yet. . .the alternative was far, far worse.

That the Palestinian leadership was itself compromised. That they *knew* he was coming.

And if they knew. . .

He didn't even finish that thought, seeing the smuggler's fingers tighten around the butt of his Makarov, knuckles whitening—his bearded face betraying nothing but grim resolution.

"Firas," he heard, snatches of low, urgent conversation filtering back to him from the front seat. ". . .vehicle. . .the market, lose them there. . ."

It felt like he was going into combat once more, that old familiar feeling. Adrenaline flooding through his veins. Everything riding on the outcome of the next few minutes.

Everything.

9:21 A.M.
Mossad Headquarters
Tel Aviv, Israel

". . .report that the target vehicle has entered the Firas Market there in Gaza City," the communications officer announced, taking off his headphones and glancing up at Shoham.

The general swore under his breath, running a hand across his chin as he stared across the room at the large map on the opposite wall. This had been meant as a grab operation, in and out before the Palestinians even knew they were there.

The kind of mission at which the *Kidon* teams excelled.

But a two-car surveillance op was possible, or had been—in Rafah, and along the roads coming north. Sufficient, as long as they'd had reason to expect that the smugglers were going to ferry their target straight to his contacts in Gaza.

Now, entering the congested environment of the market. . .all bets were off.

"The team is still on them?" he asked, glancing over at the officer.

"They are," the man replied, seeming to consult his notes before continuing. "Keilah-1 is currently in position as the chase vehicle, approx hundred meters following distance."

As close as they dared. And yet so much that could go wrong in the time it would take Ariel's people to close that gap. "And the IDF?"

"*Duvdevan* has restaged north as per your orders, just outside of Nahal Oz."

A kibbutz just east of the Strip, Shoham thought, his attention returning to the map. Less than six kilometers from the heart of Gaza itself.

If anything went wrong and they needed to pull his officers out, they'd be able to deploy quickly. Very quickly. *If. . .*

9:25 A.M.
Firas Market, Gaza City
The Gaza Strip

"They're pulling off to the side," Tzipporah heard Ariel say, his voice crackling with static over the radio connection. "Stopping. The Iraqi is out of the vehicle, I say again, our target has exited the vehicle. What's your ETA, Keilah-2?"

"Two minutes," she replied tersely, glancing over to where Nadir sat, his face drawn and tense. Hands gripping the steering wheel of the Toyota tightly as the young Mossad officer tapped the gas, sending women scattering as he accelerated around a produce stall

"Easy," she whispered, looking over at her younger partner as she reached into her light denim jacket for the pistol, assuring herself it was ready. Knowing just how delicate of a balance presented itself to them—too fast, and they risked drawing far more attention to themselves than they could afford.

Too slow, and the Iraqi would have rabbited before they could arrive, Ariel's vehicle already having moved on—unable to maintain surveillance at such close quarters.

"Coming up on the target," she announced a moment later, glimpsing the vehicle perhaps another thirty meters north along the crowded street. "Pull over—right *here*."

She had pushed open her door almost before the vehicle came to a stop, pulling the dark cloth of the hijab more closely around her face as she stepped out.

Only too aware of how dangerous this was. How quickly things could go so very wrong.

Her eyes scanning the crowd, searching for men matching the descriptions Ariel had given over the radio. The white Chevrolet just sitting there at the mouth of a side street choked with stalls selling fruits, vegetables, and merchandise. *Abandoned.*

Pushing past a Palestinian woman in dark, voluminous clothing haggling with a street vendor over the price of limes—glancing back to see Nadir emerging from the Toyota, his eyes on her.

And then she saw them—three men in a group, moving among the stalls, pushing their way through the crowd of shoppers. Moving in the opposite direction down the street—the man in the center taller than either of his companions.

"Keilah-1, I have eyes on the target," Tzipporah announced, her voice low, shielded from being overheard by a dozen other voices, the ever-present bustling hum of the market. "Moving through the souks on foot, just east of the target vehicle. In pursuit."

Had to keep him in line of sight, she thought, her eyes briefly meeting those of a young Palestinian man bagging up sweets for a customer. They couldn't lose the Iraqi, not now.

"Be careful, Keilah-2," she heard Ariel warn, her earpiece hidden by the fabric of the hijab. "Maintain your following distance—we're coming back around."

She opened her mouth to respond, but the words hadn't even left her lips when a firm hand descended upon her wrist, seizing it in a tight grasp. A man's face, close to her own. His eyes flashing in anger. "Who are you—what are you doing here?"

9:31 A.M.
The United States Embassy
Tel Aviv, Israel

"My God," Vukovic breathed, looking across the small office at Lay, "how did we get to this place?"

Lay shook his head, recognizing the look in his former deputy's eyes. *Disbelief.* Sometimes, not even the cynicism of a career intelligence officer was sufficient.

"Good intentions," he shrugged. "How ever else?"

"I just don't understand—why wasn't I read in on this operation? Why—"

"It was being handled as an SAP," Lay replied evenly. A Special Access

Program, run directly from the top. "They knew that if things went right, al-Shukeiri could be their ace-in-the-hole in the negotiations. But if the Israelis found out the way they'd been back-channeling, it could kill the peace talks completely. Limiting access was their way of minimizing risk, or at least that was the concept. I was the only senior officer at the station who was briefed, with Doug Peters brought in to run al-Shukeiri."

A light seemed to dawn across Vukovic's face. "Then that's why. . ."

"He came in unannounced and then left in mid-December." He nodded. "Langley recalled him once al-Shukeiri's involvement in the Ramallah lynchings came to light, once we realized Mossad was gunning for him. Damage control. Too little, too late. And now we're left to pick up the pieces."

"And we don't even know what they all are," Vukovic mused, his brow furrowing. "This deal with Saddam's general. . .have the Israelis been able to establish the nature of it?"

"If they have, they're not saying. My money's on them being as much in the dark as we are."

"Except for this Iraqi."

"Right," Lay responded, rising from his seat on the edge of the metal desk and circling around to the rear, his big hand resting on the back of the office chair. "Except for this Iraqi. A slim lead, but it's all we have to go on. Langley had an aneurysm over the thought of giving Mossad access to their files on al-Shukeiri, so we're left with having to find a substitute."

"Or be shut out entirely."

"Precisely. And if that happens, our chances of keeping the circle close on this become. . .non-existent." The former station chief pulled back his chair, sinking into it. "Let's get to work. I need you to reach out to General Suleiman, see what he's able to give us."

"The head of the Egyptian *Mukhabarat*?"

Lay nodded. "If he's coming in from the Sinai, he may have crossed their radar on his way into the country. Time to find out what we don't know."

9:32 A.M.
Firas Market, Gaza City
The Gaza Strip

"*Answer* me! Why were you following us?" Tzipporah felt the smuggler's foul breath hot against her face as he pushed her back against the table, wrapped sweets cascading to the dirt of the street. His hand still gripping her wrist, another pair of men visible behind him.

It took everything within her not to react, to respond in accordance with her training—using his body weight and momentum against him, sending him crashing into the stall. *Her own weapon drawn in the space of a moment.*

And their covers blown in the same time. The thin line they walked out here—your own safety subordinated to the *success* of the mission.

"I don't know what you're saying!" she protested, shaking her head in apparent distress, only too aware that the Iraqi was getting farther away by the moment. Unless Ariel was already on him.

She caught sight of Nadir approaching through the crowd in that moment, a circle already gathering around them there in the market.

No weapon in his hand. *Good man.*

"Let go of my sister," she heard him call out angrily in Arabic as he pushed a Palestinian businessman to the side, punctuating his words with a string of curses. "Let her go *now.*"

"Or else. . .tell me, boy, just what will you do?" one of the men demanded, his face just visible over her assailant's shoulder—an old Makarov pistol suddenly materializing in the man's hand.

Aimed straight at Nadir's head. She saw him recoil, indecision written in his eyes, clearly debating whether to draw his weapon.

Her own right hand pushed back against her chest by the weight of the smuggler's body, fingers only inches away from the stock of her Beretta.

And then she heard a woman's scream, people scattering as another pair of armed men pushed their way through the crowd toward where they stood.

Their faces obscured by checkered *keffiyehs*. . .secured with the green headbands of Hamas' *al-Qassam* Brigades.

A Kalashnikov assault rifle in the foremost man's hands as he raised it—aiming at the smuggler with the pistol.

"Let them go," he ordered in Arabic, an icy calm pervading his voice. *So familiar.* "They're ours."

She felt the smuggler slowly release her arm, taking a step back—his hands held carefully out from his sides, glancing at his companions as if to see whether they would back him up.

"Move," the newcomer ordered impatiently, gesturing with the muzzle of his rifle. "*Yalla, yalla!*"

Quickly.

"But they followed us here from Rafah!" the smuggler exclaimed, finally finding his voice. "They—"

"Stay here another moment and you'll answer to either my rifle or the mercy of Salah Shehade," the *keffiyeh*-masked man warned, using the name of the leader of the Brigades as he cut the smuggler off. "Your choice."

The man took another look at his companions, both of them already backing away as if hoping to lose themselves in the crowd—anger distorting his face as he spat in the dirt.

Turning his back on them wordlessly, shoving a woman out of the way before vanishing among the stalls of the souk. *Gone.*

"Are you all right?" Ariel asked, scanning the street for a long moment before turning to them—his voice low, his eyes just visible beneath the *keffiyeh.* She nodded quickly, trading glances with Nadir as Ze'ev motioned them forward, back toward the vehicles.

Hearing the *Kidon* leader curse as he ducked his head away from the crowd, keying his mic. "Base, this is Keilah-1. We have lost the target. I say again, we do not have the target. Mission abort, mission abort."

12:49 P.M.
Mossad Headquarters
Tel Aviv, Israel

"Three hours, and there have been no further reported sightings of the Iraqi. *Shin Bet* has alerted their network of informants in the Strip, but thus far," Eli Gerstman finished, looking up from his notes, "he has yet to resurface."

Halevy shook his head, glancing over at Avi ben Shoham as he closed the briefing folder. "So essentially, we have nothing."

Precisely. The cruel irony of an operation that had been doomed from the very outset.

"That's correct," Shoham replied slowly, struggling to repress his growing anger in the presence of the Mossad chief, "just as I warned could be the result when the decision was made to completely alter our operational plans at the last moment."

"Avi—" Gerstman began, but Shoham cut him off, tapping his index finger roughly against the hard wood of the conference table. Raising his voice as he continued.

"We had the people in position. We could have pulled it off. We could have had the Iraqi, *here.* Instead, as you say. . .we have nothing."

He leaned back in his chair, his eyes locked with Gerstman's as the senior officer paused, seeming to choose his words carefully.

"*Could* have," Gerstman said finally, placing both of his hands on the table. "Or we could have just easily ended up with our assets caught in the middle of a street riot. Your man took a huge risk, going into the market like that."

The kind of risk we used to take every day of our lives, Shoham thought, his eyes narrowing as he looked across the table into the eyes of his old friend. "A risk he wouldn't have *had* to take if we hadn't decided to change horses in mid-stream, as I believe our American friends would put it."

Something had changed Gerstman. Had it been Ramallah? The horror of that day, searing itself into their memories as if with a brand. Perhaps it had changed all of them.

"Speaking of the Americans," Halevy interjected, clearing his throat as he glanced at Shoham, "have you heard anything further from our counterparts at the CIA, Avi?"

"No, nothing," he replied, caught off-guard by the older man's sudden change of tack. "I'll be meeting Evan Fournier, the Agency's new station chief, tomorrow for lunch at *Hatraklin*. It's something I'll bring up with him then."

The Mossad chief nodded. They both knew how such meetings went, the awkward dance of two spies meeting for the first time. And this time complicated all the more by the gravity of the situation they were now facing.

"With the Iraqi once more in the wind, the intelligence the Americans can give us on al-Shukeiri has become all the more vital." Halevy paused. "You're *certain* that they received the message?"

"I'm certain."

1:23 P.M.
A Fatah *compound*
The Gaza Strip

"Spread your legs apart," the bodyguard ordered, running his hands up Umar Hadi's inner thigh as he frisked him for weapons, lingering for a moment before passing back up and over his buttocks.

Too long, the lieutenant colonel thought, an uncomfortable grimace passing across his face as the man's hands ran across his body. If the rumors about Arafat were true. . .well, perhaps he sought out others of similar inclinations to protect both himself and other members of his inner circle.

There was something of genius in it, surrounding yourself with protectors who were themselves pariahs in your own society. Owing their very existence to the continuance of your own.

Much as the later emperors of Rome had done, surrounding themselves with barbarians from beyond the Rhine.

"Clear," the man announced finally, rising and taking a step back. The smile on his face as he looked Hadi in the eye only confirming his suspicions. *Sodomite.* "You can go on in. Abu Awad is waiting."

A large man stood in the far corner of the windowless room as Hadi entered, his back turned toward the lieutenant colonel's entrance—appearing intent on studying a large map spread out over the opposite wall.

"Colonel Damra," Hadi said quietly after a moment, knowing the man knew he was there.

"Tell me. . .what do you see when you look at this map, colonel?" Mahmoud Damra asked, still not turning to greet him. Hadi paused before advancing across the room, regarding the man carefully. Known popularly in the occupied territories by the *kunya* "Abu Awad", Damra was the commander of the feared Force 17, a small commando unit which had once been responsible for Arafat's personal security.

A dangerous man. And an unpredictable one.

"I see Palestine," Hadi replied quietly, stopping just short of the colonel's shoulder. It wasn't a particularly profound comment, just a statement of fact. The map on the wall, like most of those in the Authority, bore no reference whatsoever to the Zionist state anywhere across its face. It simply didn't. . .*exist.*

"Yes," Damra responded, a strange intensity in his voice as he turned to face Hadi. "Palestine. Not as it is, but as it should be. As it *will* one day be, *insh'allah*. From the river to the sea."

His dark eyes seemed to change in that moment, a smile breaking across his face as he clapped the Iraqi soldier on the shoulder—gesturing toward one of the chairs. "Sit—sit! You've come a long way and there is much we need to discuss."

1:37 P.M.
The United States Embassy
Tel Aviv, Israel

". . .Nasrallah has remained largely quiet thus far in the course of the *intifada*," Daniel Vukovic said, glancing up from his briefing folder to look over at the new station chief. "The usual anti-Israeli rhetoric we see from all top Hezbollah leaders on a routine basis, of course, but very little more. No escalation, shall we say."

"We can't count on that holding, long-term," Evan Fournier mused, running a hand across the lower half of his face as he leafed through the notes. He cleared his throat. "My years in Damascus, the Secretary-General was never far off our radar. And if he does make a move. . .then Israel will be faced with growing unrest on their northern border, in addition to Gaza and the West Bank. It could derail the upcoming summit at Taba."

It wasn't as though that would be difficult to do, Vukovic thought. The talks at Bolling Air Force Base outside D.C. had fallen apart completely scarce more than a week before—and a last-ditch attempt to establish a follow-up summit at Sharm el-Sheikh on the 28th of December had failed after the Palestinians balked at accepting the so-called "Clinton parameters" put forth by the American administration and Prime Minister Barak elected not to attend.

Not hard to "derail" something that already so far off the tracks as to make recovery well-nigh impossible.

Irreconcilable differences. A wry grimace passed across the deputy station chief's face. Kind of like his first marriage.

But Taba. . that was in the Sinai, at the tip of the Gulf of Aqaba. The *Sinai*, he realized, Lay's intel about 'the Iraqi' flickering back across his mind. *Could it. . .*

"But even if Hezbollah does decide to get involved," he said, forcing himself to refocus on the briefing, "our analysis doesn't necessarily indicate that they will do so in coordination with Arafat's government. After all, it wasn't that many years ago that Hassan Nasrallah was publicly calling for a modern-day 'Khaled Islambouli'—Sadat's killer—to rise up and assassinate the Palestinian leadership."

Which wasn't the same as saying it *couldn't* happen, as both he and Fournier knew. The term "strange bedfellows" had, he was certain, been coined with the Middle East in mind.

"Task a few of your people to it," the station chief said finally. "Make sure we're up on any communications between Hezbollah and the Arafat government."

"Of course," he nodded, closing the folder and rising to his feet. The briefing over. "I'll be certain to flag anything that comes up and bring it to your attention."

"Tell me, Daniel. . ." Fournier began, his voice arresting Vukovic just as he turned to leave. "This with David Lay—is there something going on that I should know about?"

"Not that I know of," Vukovic responded, keeping his voice neutral with a mighty effort. "Why?"

What they were doing—keeping a chief of station in the dark on an ongoing op—was as dangerous as it was unprecedented. All of their careers on the line if this went wrong, Langley's orders notwithstanding.

It wouldn't be the first time CIA officers had followed orders straight into the underside of a bus.

"Lay's an old hand," Fournier said, pushing back his chair. His eyes never leaving Vukovic's face as he rose. "Knows the ins and outs of Agency bureaucracy as well as any officer I've ever known. No way he'd let 'paperwork' tie him down here. Do me a favor and poke around a bit. . .see what you can find."

"Of course."

2:01 P.M.
Mahmoud Damra's compound
The Gaza Strip

". . .at the rendezvous point—here, in the desert fifteen kilometers southeast of al-Karameh," Hadi said, spreading out the map on the colonel's desk—marking the spot with the tip of his pencil. A single mark, seemingly only inches from the border crossing with Jordan. Surrounded by blank space representing the Syrian Desert, the small Iraqi village of Turaibil not even labeled on the map.

Forbidding terrain, as he remembered it—the westernmost part of Iraq's Al Anbar Governate. A wild, desolate expanse.

"You have a way of getting it back across the border?" he asked, watching Mahmoud Damra carefully. That was critical—there was no way they could risk it falling into the wrong hands, not so close to home. Not with the risks so high.

The gallows for all of them if Saddam learned of what they had done.

"Of course. We have made. . .arrangements with the border guards," the colonel replied, gesturing with his hand. "Both there and on the border with Palestine. There will be no problems."

No problems. It was a confidence he wished he could share. But it would have to be enough. "And this will all take place on the night of the 8th?"

"As previously arranged with al-Shukeiri, yes." *Before Jewish assassins killed him*, Hadi didn't add. The possibility that their operation could have been penetrated with his death never far from his mind.

That car, following them from Rafah this very morning. *Hamas?* Perhaps, but none of it made sense.

"That should be in sufficient time," Damra said, still studying the map. Something in his voice sending a chill down the Iraqi's spine.

For what?

"What do you mean?" he asked, only too aware that he was treading on dangerous ground.

"The summit at Taba, of course." The man looked at him, a dark smile spreading across his face. "That's what this has been all about, from the beginning."

6:23 P.M.
A cottage in the Galilee
Israel

Home, Avi ben Shoham thought, hearing the sound of music coming from the kitchen as he shrugged off his jacket and hung it in the closet. The lilting voice of a woman singing along to the radio in Hebrew—ever so slightly off-key, but he found himself smiling all the same.

Remembering the first time he had heard his wife sing. Back when they had first met, long ago on a *kibbutz* not far to the northwest of where their cottage now stood.

Scarce two years before the Syrian Army washed over the Golan Heights on the afternoon of Yom Kippur like an incoming sea, finding Shoham's unit waiting squarely in its path, an immovable rock of men and tanks amidst the tide. Over a hundred of his fellow tankers dying in the hard fighting that followed, giving their blood as an atonement on that most holy of days.

The 188th Barak Armored Brigade nearly wiped out to a man before they were reinforced by reservists rushed up from the south with scarce time to boresight their main guns.

To this very day, he could still hear the chatter of machine-gun fire lashing the heights, smell the burning. . .he shuddered, pushing the memories aside with an effort. Memories of darkness, like that which hung over them once more. As it so often had.

He nearly hadn't returned home this night, had considered remaining there at the headquarters of Mossad—sleeping on the couch in his office. *Ever at hand.* Like he had so many nights before when the security of the Jewish state had been threatened.

But there was only so much any of them could do. The Iraqi, gone to ground since his disappearance in the market, no sign of him in the hours following—not even any whispers from *Shin Bet*'s network of informants in the Authority.

Nothing for it but to wait. And get what sleep he could. This storm would break upon them, soon enough.

He removed the Browning Hi-Power from his belt, placing the still-holstered weapon on the small endtable by the closet. Reaching to place his cellular phone beside it—the phone beginning to ring even as he took it out of its pouch.

Every fiber of his body suffused with tension, an unfamiliar number displayed on its small screen. "Yes?"

"Avi," a familiar voice replied simply, Shoham's face darkening at the sound of his name. *David Lay.*

"How did you get this number?" he demanded, casting a glance back toward the kitchen as he walked into the living room—away from his wife. Glancing out the window into the darkness of the night.

"That doesn't matter," Lay responded, his voice even. *Certain.* "What matters is that we meet, as soon as possible."

The Mossad officer shook his head, struggling to keep the anger out of his voice. "I thought I made myself quite clear, David. You're out."

"Nothing would make me happier. But Langley had different ideas. They want to keep the circle of knowledge on this close, so you'll deal with me or you won't deal at all. And you *need* to see what I've uncovered, Avi."

"Listen to me," Shoham began. *Time to put an end to the games.* "You—"

"It's about your Iraqi."

6:31 P.M.
Mossad Headquarters
Tel Aviv

"Someone has to have seen him," Ariel said, shaking his head in frustration as he tossed the just-developed photograph back on the desk, running a finger along his upper lip as he leaned back in his chair.

It was one of a dozen pictures taken of the Iraqi that morning by a *Shin Bet* undercover officer—one of Omri's colleagues—in the moments before the *Kidon* team took up pursuit.

Before they lost him.

"It's not your fault," Tzipporah said quietly, seeming to read his thoughts. "If I hadn't been made there in the market, we could have—"

"*No.*" He brought his fist down solidly onto the desktop, cutting her off. Its metal frame vibrating under the impact. "They wouldn't have diverted into Firas in the first place if they hadn't suspected something. *What*, we don't know. All we know is he's still in Gaza."

"And given how much time has passed," Ze'ev observed, standing there in the doorway, "we can assume that he's already met with. . .whomever he came to meet."

Likely enough, Ariel thought, closing his eyes. Remembering that night on Elba. The look in Mustafa al-Shukeiri's eyes when he'd glanced up to see them enter in his bedroom.

Fear, raw and naked.

His own voice cold as ice as he'd circled the bed, reciting the names of the reservists butchered in Ramallah. The muzzle of his pistol never leaving the Palestinian's head. *"Vadim Novesche, Yossi Avrahami. The Jewish people do not forgive. We do not forget."*

The suppressed *cough* of the Beretta punctuating his words. Followed by the screams of a woman wakened from her sleep by her husband's death.

And that had been the end of it, or so he'd thought. He'd been wrong. That night, only the beginning. The end, still nowhere in sight.

The phone on his desk rang a moment later, its insistent buzz breaking through the silence that had fallen over him and his team.

"Yes?" he answered, bringing the receiver to his ear—his body coming to full attention as he heard the voice on the other end of the line. Listening for the space of a couple minutes. "Of course, sir. We'll leave immediately."

8:02 P.M.
The shores of Galilee

Galilee. The waters upon which once Christ had walked, the hills which had once borne witness to His ministry on earth.

David Lay killed the engine and removed the key from the ignition, the lights of the Agency Crown Victoria going out as he sat silently there in the darkness, staring out over the waters of the sea toward the glittering lights of Tiberias in the distance. The only sound that of light rain spattering against the car's windshield. *Peace be still.*

But his business here tonight. . .it couldn't possibly have less to do with peace. *Or God.* A grim shadow passing across his face as he pushed open the door of the sedan—stepping out onto the gravel.

His eyes searching the night as he moved toward the boathouse, the waters of the Galilee lapping against the lake shore. Making out a dark figure standing by the water's edge, the visibility hampered by the rain.

"It looks peaceful, doesn't it?" Avi ben Shoham asked as he approached, coming up to stand alongside the Israeli in the shadow of the rusting hull of a fishing trawler. He went on without waiting for an answer. "In ancient times, my people called it 'the abyss.' A place of darkness. . .waiting to swallow us all. Sometimes I think they were right. That the Jewish state—*Zion*—is still right there, on the edge of the abyss. There was another bombing earlier tonight, southwest of here in Netanya. A car rigged with improvised explosives, next to a bus stop. Dozens injured, no final casualty report as of yet—won't be one for hours."

A grim shadow passed across Lay's face, no words seeming sufficient in such a moment. He had seen the emergency vehicles on the drive north from Tel Aviv, heard the news bulletins on the radio—his Hebrew still rough after three years in-country, but enough to make it out. *Tragedy*.

Shoham turned toward him then, his face unreadable in the darkness. "Peace is a beautiful dream, but we won't see it. Not in your lifetime or mine. So, what do you have for me?"

"Your Iraqi," the former station chief said, pulling a folder from within his coat and passing it over. "We know who he is, and most likely *where* he is. He's—"

His voice broke off suddenly, movement out of the corner of his eye as he glanced up to see the woman from the bar standing there not fifteen feet away, her face masked in the shadows of the night. Her right hand shoved deep into the pocket of her jacket, clearly holding a weapon. "I thought I made it clear that we were to meet alone."

"And I thought I made it clear that you weren't the one making the rules here, David," Shoham returned evenly, inclining his head toward where Ariel stood at the opposite corner of the boathouse, just under the eaves. "So I took. . .precautions. You were saying?"

Lay just looked at him for a long moment, clearly weighing his options. Then he shook his head, seeming to think better of it. "Your man," he said finally, gesturing toward the folder in the Israeli's hands, "is Lieutenant Colonel Umar Hadi, of the Iraqi Army. He's a decorated veteran of the Iran-Iraq War and a member of Siddiqi's inner circle. He flew into Cairo International aboard a Royal Jordanian Airways flight from Amman last night, according to what information we were able to obtain from the *Mukhabarat*."

Shoham opened the folder, the hulk of the fishing trawler looming above him shielding it from the rain as he leafed through its contents. Taking in the file photos of Hadi. Younger, the pictures dated half a decade or more—but without doubt the same man who had crossed over the border into Gaza. But even yet. . .

"And what makes you think this is our man?" he asked, glancing shrewdly up into his counterpart's eyes. "An Iraqi Army officer flying into Egypt—it's not so very uncommon."

"You want to talk of rules, Avi," David Lay said, Shoham reacting almost imperceptibly as the American reached into his jacket, bringing something out in his fingers. "You don't even want to know how many of them I had to bend to receive authorization to hand these over to you."

He reached out, pressing a pair of compact discs into Shoham's hand. His voice low and earnest. "These are recordings of ECHELON intercepts from a few days ago—telephone conversations between senior members of the *Fatah* leadership. They're talking about the arrangement of a meeting between Hadi and Abu Awad. . .to discuss the delivery of a 'weapon.'"

8:16 P.M.
Mahmoud Damra's compound
The Gaza Strip

"My meeting with our friends here in Palestine has gone well," Hadi replied in answer to General Siddiqi's question, the phone pressed close against his ear as he glanced across the room to where Mahmoud Damra stood, a few feet away from the desk. "I believe we have sorted through any possible misunderstandings or miscommunication which might have proceeded from the unexpected departure of our colleague."

"Good, good, and just in time for planting," he heard the general respond, something of a chill running through his body at the words. *Colonel Damra had been telling the truth.* The strike against Taba had been a part of the plan, ever since the beginning. *Madness.* "Everything is now back on schedule?"

"It is," Hadi answered, struggling to keep his face neutral. Knowing that the Palestinian was watching him closely. "They will take delivery of the agricultural equipment as previously arranged."

"I'm not surprised," Siddiqi said after a moment. "I've always been able to depend on you. May you have a safe flight home."

"*Insh'allah*," the soldier responded as he began to sign off, the words devoid of feeling. *As God wills*. But what *did* God will? *This?* It was impossible to believe.

He replaced the phone in its cradle, looking up as he heard Damra begin to laugh. "Agricultural equipment? I love it."

"You can never be too careful, Colonel," Hadi warned, an unintentionally sharp edge to his voice. "It's impossible to know who might be listening."

"Listening?" The Force 13 commander laughed again, approaching the desk and taking out a bottle of brandy and a pair of glasses. "You worry too much."

And you, far too little, the Iraqi thought, watching the man as Damra opened the bottle, liquor splashing into the glasses. He still couldn't shake the feeling that the incident in the market had been more than it seemed—that his mission had been compromised even before it began.

"So," the Palestinian began, taking one glass for himself and extending the other in an outstretched hand—his sharp eyes searching Hadi's face. "We have a deal?"

"We do," Hadi replied slowly, accepting the drink. "I'll leave within the next few hours, before morning light."

8:21 P.M.
The shores of Galilee

". . .would lead us to believe that Hadi will be going back across the border into the Sinai sometime tomorrow morning, most likely before dawn."

"And this 'weapon'," Avi ben Shoham began, searching his counterpart's face for any sign of dissimulation, "you have no idea what it might be."

"None," came the even response as Lay looked him in the eye. Not even the faintest trace of deception in his voice.

Not that there would have been, Shoham thought, the cynicism that came with this job rising as ever to the fore. He'd read Lay's jacket years prior—when the American had first arrived to take over Station Tel Aviv—had found himself reviewing it once again these last few days.

The man was good. He had to have been to have done what he'd done in Germany back in the day, and that was only what they knew about. *Always far more below the surface than above.*

And what *did* lie below the surface on this night?

"Then I guess we're going to have to take Hadi out of play," Shoham said calmly, turning and beginning to walk back toward the Mossad vehicles. *Time to get out of the rain.* "Find out what he knows."

Lay didn't react, not right away—he gave him credit for that. His voice only rising to answer him after he'd already taken six steps away from the shoreline.

"Do that, and you run the risk of spooking them, forcing them to go to ground. That happens, you're going to lose control of this altogether."

"Lose control, David? Is this what you think control of a situation looks like?" The Israeli demanded, turning back toward Lay, his words coming out in a low hiss. "If you want us to stay our hand, you'd better have an alternative. Because right now, I'm not seeing one. And I *will* do what needs to be done, that I promise you."

"Give me a few hours, Avi. Let me see what I can do. Before we all find ourselves in deeper than we can well afford to be."

"If your intelligence is right, a few hours is all any of us have, David. I make no promises."

Lay closed the door of the Crown Vic on the rain outside, its gentle tap against the windshield breaking the quiet as he sat there, his exchange with Avi ben Shoham still running over and again through his head. Watching the taillights of the Mossad vehicles fade in the distance.

It shouldn't have happened this way. None of this should have happened, and yet. . .here they were.

No help for it. And no end in sight. He shook his head, a curse escaping his lips as he slammed the heel of his hand into the steering wheel. Forcing himself to calm down.

Get a grip.

He dug the cellular phone from its pouch on his belt after a long moment, flipping it open and keying in a number. "Daniel," he said when the other end was picked up, "I just parted with our friends the Israelis."

"And?" There was a peculiar note of strain in Vukovic's voice. *Impatience.*

"And what we have right now isn't enough," Lay replied, gazing out the windshield into the darkness. "Not nearly enough to prevent this from blowing sky-high. What can you give me?"

"Right now, David. . .not a thing." There was a distinct and awkward pause on the other end of the line before the deputy station chief continued. "You're calling at a bad time."

9:43 P.M.
Mossad Headquarters
Tel Aviv

". . .according to our best analysis this 'weapon', whatever it may be, has not yet been delivered. I think one could reasonably infer that the removal of al-Shukeiri created difficulties on the Palestinian side of the deal, and this Iraqi officer was dispatched in person in an effort to clear them up."

"So, this new intelligence from the Americans. . .you're telling me you believe it can be trusted?" Efraim Halevy asked finally, his eyes gazing wearily into Shoham's own as he looked up from the briefing notes.

As compared to the intelligence the CIA had given them on al-Shukeiri, he didn't add, but he didn't need to. They were all thinking it.

Disinformation designed to throw them off balance—keep them looking in all the wrong places. *Could it be happening again?*

Of course it could. Ever the risk you ran in this business, and the Agency's alliances in the region had always been questionable, going back decades.

"Our analysts are going over the tapes now," he responded, choosing his words carefully. "They appear to be legitimate. I am of the opinion that our

136

message was received in Washington. Loudly and clearly."

Halevy's gaze shifted across to Gerstman. "Would you concur, Eli?"

The senior Mossad officer cleared his throat, his elbows resting on the table as he leaned forward, glancing from one to the other. "Dichter's network was able to confirm a heavy increase of activity in the area of Mahmoud Damra's compound only a few hours after our *Kidon* team lost the Iraqi in Firas. As reluctant as I am to say it. . .it checks out."

"And since?"

"Nothing." Gerstman spread his hands. "If Umar Hadi went in, he hasn't come back out."

"Damra's compound is located near Beit Hanun," Shoham observed, watching the Mossad director closely, "nearly four kilometers to the southeast. Out in the countryside. A single access road."

He paused, letting the implications of his words sink in, the look in the older man's eyes showing he clearly understood what was being suggested.

The Iraqi had to leave sometime. And when he did. . .

"You're suggesting that we intercept his vehicle," he heard Gerstman say, turning to look down the table at his old friend. "Have you honestly thought this through, Avi?"

"I am, and I have."

The man just looked at him, shaking his head. "Then you know that as soon as we take Hadi, all bets are off. Any intelligence we can extract, useless almost from the moment the grab goes down. And we'll be left with nothing."

It was Lay's point, made an hour earlier in the Galilee. A grab like this, so close to Gaza—it was going to be impossible to conceal. And it was unlikely that the Palestinians were going to stay the course once they realized their go-between was in Israeli hands. But they would at least have a better grasp of what they were dealing with, and that was *something*. "Nothing is what we have right now, Eli. And it's all that we'll have if we just let him go. The Americans—if we can trust them—have agreed to keep supplying us with operational intelligence as this continues to unfold, but that only takes us so far. So, what is *your* plan?"

Silence hung over the conference room for a long moment before

Gerstman responded. "From the evidence you've presented us," he began, seeming to choose his words with utmost of care, "it would appear that the Egyptians are already aware of the interest being expressed in Colonel Hadi. I say we reach out to the *Mukhabarat*, have them hold him at the airport on some. . .pretext. They've always known boundless creativity in such regards."

No. Their situation with the Americans was tenuous enough. Bringing in a third intelligence service—an *Arab* intelligence service—could be the undoing of them all. "Let's be realistic here—Egypt isn't going to 'disappear' an Iraqi Army officer. Not at our behest. And if they should find out the nature of the weapon transfer he was arranging before we do. . ."

Shoham let his voice trail off, his dark eyes hard and glittering as he glanced around the table. They *all* knew the realities that were facing them. In a part of the world where you only trusted "allies" as far as you could throw them. . .this wasn't a risk worth taking.

"Your concerns are not without validity, Eli," Halevy said finally, a heavy sigh escaping the old man's lips as he leaned forward, his elbows resting on the table's surface, "but Avi is right. Allowing Colonel Hadi to leave Gaza is unacceptable, and should we—together with the Americans—be unable to ascertain the details of the plan by other means in the next few hours. . .we will be left with no choice but to take him in."

"Efraim, duty compels me to—" Gerstman began, but the Mossad chief cut him off, taking off his glasses as he turned his attention toward Shoham.

"Enough," he said, laying them deliberately on the table. "I will brief the Prime Minister. How soon can your teams be in position?"

9:47 P.M.
The United States Embassy
Tel Aviv, Israel

Station Tel Aviv was alive with activity as David Lay came through the doors, spotting Vukovic in the far corner of the room—leaning over an analyst's desk as he gestured at the screen of his monitor.

". . .get me everything you can from our assets in the area. And I mean *everything*," he heard his former deputy say, pushing himself away as he spotted Lay's approach. "I told you this wasn't a good time, David."

"Looks like it," Lay observed, glancing around the station, "But we don't have the luxury of awaiting a better one. We—"

His voice broke off suddenly, seeing Vukovic's eyes flash a warning only moments before he heard Fournier's voice from behind him.

"David," the station chief said, Lay turning to see him standing there a couple cubicles away, a folder in his hand. "What are you doing here?"

It was a question that could have easily cut both ways. He hadn't expected to find Fournier still in the office at this late hour. Might not have come in person if he had. Not that he'd been left with much choice.

"I heard about the bombing in Netanya. Thought I'd come in and see if I could offer any help," he lied, using what he suspected was the reason for Fournier's own presence. Attacks in Israel were coming with distressingly greater frequency of late, most of them not large enough to warrant the presence of the chief of station. But it *was* his first day.

And reason enough for him to be jealous of his turf if he chose to be, Lay thought, watching his face. Knowing only too well how this could backfire.

"Then I'm sure we can find a way to make use of you," Fournier replied finally, his smile only too obviously forced. "Vukovic, take care of this, will you? Make sure he gets set up."

"He knows something is going on, David," the deputy station chief said, flipping on the light as he ushered Lay into the corner office. Casting a glance back over his shoulder as if to assure himself of Fournier's location. "He's known, and you showing up here tonight has only confirms his suspicions. He's already asked me to keep an eye on you."

"Then by all means. . .keep an eye on me, Daniel," Lay replied calmly, keeping his face neutral, unperturbed as he turned to face his former deputy. "And while you're at it, reach out to Fort Meade. See if you can get them to task an analyst or two to us for the night—Arabic-speakers, preferably. We're going to need all hands on deck for this one."

Vukovic just looked at him, shaking his head. He took a step closer to Lay, lowering his voice as he glanced back out at the station. "This is insane. We are running an op under the nose of the *chief* of freaking station. Do you understand the gravity of that? Do you?"

"I do," he replied, measuring his words carefully. Vukovic always had been the voice of caution, the legacy of a career spent in the Intelligence Directorate. He wasn't comfortable with field operations under the most optimal of conditions, and no one was going to describe this day as anything close to "optimal."

"I don't think you do, David," the deputy station chief shot back, his eyes flashing. "Or maybe you just don't care. You've got your orders straight from Langley, you're covered no matter how this goes down. My orders? They're coming from someone who no longer has the authority to give them, so I'm the one whose butt is left hanging out in the wind."

It wasn't an unreasonable concern, one he might even have given voice to himself if their situation had been reversed. Chain of command, authorization. . .accountability, it was everything in their business. *Never more murky than now.*

But he didn't have time for trepidation. No time to think about what could happen if they failed, because Vukovic wasn't the only one going to be left holding the bag.

"Just make the call, Dan," he said after a long moment, staring into his former deputy's eyes. "Do it now."

10:27 P.M.
The reservoir outside Nir Am
Israel

"Comms check, all units," Ariel breathed into the lip mic of his radio set—gazing across the still waters of the reservoir toward the scattered lights of the Gazan city of Beit Hanun, visible not even four kilometers distant.

Just across the border.

"Have you loud and clear, Keilah," a man's deep voice responded over his earpiece. "We're two minutes out."

"There they are," he heard Ze'ev say, glancing back toward the dark shadows of the kibbutz nestled on the low hill to the west, just then seeing headlights sweep across the night sky as they crested the rise—rolling down the access road toward the reservoir.

A pair of dark SUVs pulling to a stop maybe twenty meters away, just alongside the cement escarpment leading down into the reservoir.

The lights going out as a short, stockily-built man in civilian clothes pushed open the driver's side door and stepped out—the familiar sight of an AKM assault rifle slung across his chest, its metal stock folded back along the receiver.

Chaim Silbermann, Ariel thought, recognizing the figure of the IDF colonel as he advanced across the gravel, his right hand extended. More armed men disembarking from the vehicles behind him.

"David," Silbermann greeted warmly, an unnoticed shadow passing across Ariel's face at the use of his birth name. It had been so long since anyone had used it. . .its very sound reminiscent of memories. None of them good.

But that was how Silbermann had known him, long before, back in those days when they'd served together in *Sayeret Duvdevan*.

Then, as this night, hunting the enemies of the Jewish state. "It's been a long time, my old friend," he responded, forcing a smile to his face as he clasped Silbermann's hand in his own. "Too long."

"It has," the man responded, a tight smile creasing his own lips as he glanced past Ariel, acknowledging Tzipporah's presence with a nod. "Do you have a location for our target?"

"It's not that simple, I'm afraid," Ariel replied, turning to lead the way to the back of the vehicle—the rear door raised, weapons and clothing bearing the distinctive insignia of Hamas spread out on the floor. "Have your men put these on. I'll explain en route."

10:52 P.M.
Mossad Headquarters
Tel Aviv

As of ten minutes before, the *Kidon* team was across the border, Shoham thought, bringing the cup of coffee to his lips as his eyes shifted across the map table. Re-acquainting himself with the terrain his men were going to be traversing.

Open ground. Naked and bare. There wasn't much cover there, on the very border of the Negev. It was only one of the factors that was going to make their lingering in the vicinity the more hazardous. Even with the *Duvdevan* team backing their play. It seemed only a few months before that Israeli television stations had spoken hopefully of peace. That newspaper headlines had borne the promise of an end to the violence which had consumed this land for so many decades.

And now it all lay in ashes. As he had known it would, he thought—his eyes shadowed as he gazed at the map. Peace was a dream for those who knew nothing of man. And he knew far too much.

"Sir," he heard a voice exclaim from behind him, looking back to see a communications officer approach, taking off his headphones as he came, "we've intercepted radio communications between Damra's compound and *Fatah* headquarters in Gaza City."

"And?"

"The language they use is veiled, but as far as we can determine, they seem to be requesting official authorization for passage back across the border. A car to be sent to the compound to pick up a 'guest.'"

"How soon?"

"Within the next ninety minutes."

He swore softly, shaking his head. That was going to move their timeline up beyond anything they had anticipated. *Force their hand.*

"Red-flash the *Kidon* team," he said finally. "Make sure Ariel is made aware of these developments."

11:08 P.M.
The United States Embassy
Tel Aviv, Israel

"Look, I understand the concerns the State Department has expressed about reading the Israelis in on any further such intercepts," Lay replied, keeping his voice level with a mighty effort as he glared at the blank wall—the receiver of the Secure Telephone Unit pressed against his ear, "but this is why we have

ECHELON in the first place. To give us an edge."

An edge the State Department themselves had been none too loathe to exploit over the years when it suited them, he thought ironically, a strange, bitter smile playing around the corners of his mouth. But now, with the peace process remaining little more than a cruel joke, State's people were getting skittish.

"You've seen my authorization," he continued, not giving the NSA officer time to butt in. "You know this is coming from the highest levels at Langley. The *very* highest. So are you going to give me what I need, or do I have to trouble my boss to speak to yours?"

It would have been a more effective threat a few hours later, with both Tenet and General Hayden home with their families. Or, possibly, out to dinner.

But those were hours he didn't have. So you rolled with what you had. *Watched the dice tumble through the air.*

"All right," the man said finally, seeming to let out a heavy sigh. "I'll authorize on-site access to our listening station in Haifa, brief them on what you're looking for so they can prepare for your arrival."

"I'll leave at once."

11:35 P.M.
Near Beit Hanun
The Gaza Strip

This was going to have to be timed so precisely, Ariel thought, Shoham's words running over and again through his mind as he stood there beside the vehicle—his binoculars trained over open fields toward the *Fatah* compound not three kilometers distant.

"You understand, taking Hadi is a last resort. I'm going to need you to hold off as long as possible before making the grab. Give our people time."

Time to come up with an alternative. Time to gather the intelligence they so desperately needed, some other way—he didn't know how.

And knowing. . .that wasn't the job of him or his team. Their role in all of this confined to this moment, this road.

Just another cog in the machine that stood watch over the Jewish state. The *final* cog, he realized grimly, hearing the door open behind him— glancing back to see Tzipporah emerge into the night, her face shrouded, like his, by a *keffiyeh*. A Kalashnikov assault rifle in her hands.

They were always the last resort.

11:58 P.M.
The Fatah *compound*

Palestine, Umar Hadi thought, staring out the second-story window into the night—out over the compound's wall over the flat, open fields stretching toward the lights of Beit Hanun to the northwest, visible in the faint moonlight.

It reminded him of home, growing up along the banks of the Tigris. The son of a farmer. Impossible even for himself to conceive then what he would become.

The things he would *do*.

"Colonel Hadi, the car has arrived," he heard a voice from behind him announce, turning to see one of Mahmoud Damra's subordinates standing in the doorway of the room. A heavy weight seeming to descend upon his shoulders in that moment.

The knowledge of his duty. Ever the burden of the soldier.

Mahmoud Damra was waiting without, near the vehicle. Flanked by his bodyguards as Hadi stepped from the door—his eyes searching the Palestinian's face.

"Is everything as I requested?"

A nod served as his reply, Damra's look telling more plainly than words what he thought of the precautions the Iraqi had insisted upon. His opinion of this kind of ruse.

But it didn't really matter what he thought.

"All right," Hadi replied, nodding slowly as he stared at the vehicle, its driver obscured by tinted windows—the darkness of the night. "Time we set this in motion."

12:01 A.M., January 2ⁿᵈ
South of Haifa

The Crown Victoria's lights went dark as Lay pushed open his door and stepped out onto the rain-slick concrete, staring at the building looming large in the darkness before him, a forest of antennas and large aerials sprouting from its roof.

The regional headquarters of a nascent American telecommunications corporation out of San Francisco. A company which functioned, in its nearly non-existent day-to-day operations, as a wholly owned subsidiary of Fort Meade.

He had known of the listening station's existence ever since it had come first on-line two years before, but he'd never once set foot on the premises—although the signals intelligence garnered from the intercepts processed by the building had doubtless crossed his desk more than once.

The wall between agencies as high as it ever had been, he grimaced, forcing those thoughts away with an effort. One of these days, it was going to cost them dearly.

But not this night. Not if he had anything to say about it.

An armed security officer—an ex-military type with a Beretta 92 holstered in the waistband of his Levis—ushered Lay inside, escorting him down a long hallway and into a large room sub-divided into cubicles. Men and women in attire that would have passed muster at the offices of the corporation this building was supposed to belong to, hunched over computers. Headphones almost universally covering their ears.

The throaty hum of circulation fans vibrating the walls, the lights themselves lowered in an effort to keep the electronics cool.

"Mr. Lay," he heard someone say, turning to see a black man perhaps a few years his junior standing there a few feet away, the sleeves of his dress shirt rolled up beyond his elbows. He made no motion to extend his hand. "Josiah Galvin, the duty officer in charge of this station. I was told to expect your arrival."

He clearly was even less happy with the CIA officer's presence than Lay was to be here, but no matter. "Where are your people at with the intercepts?"

"Still filtering through archives of recorded audio from the last week. It's going to take time."

The one thing they didn't have. But there was no help for it.

"Narrow the search parameters to conversations between Damra and the Palestinian upper echelon—the people he discussed Hadi's arrival with—if you haven't already," Lay instructed, shrugging off his windbreaker and dropping it unceremoniously over a nearby office chair. "We'll work from there. Put every Arabic-speaker you have on it."

"We're dealing with more threats than just yours here tonight. Our allies were bombed not forty miles south of this building just a matter of a few hours ago," Warren responded coolly, his dark eyes locking with Lay's. "On whose authority?"

"Mine."

12:08 A.M.
The Gaza Strip

And there it was. Headlights flashing briefly across the flat open fields toward them, a car just visible exiting through the compound's gates. Dust kicking up into the night, a haze in the moonlight.

"Netzach-1, we have movement," Ariel announced, keying his radio's microphone. "I say again, we have movement from the target location. They're on their way out."

"Copy that, Keilah," Silbermann's gruff voice acknowledged over his earpiece. The *Duvdevan* unit staged another seven kilometers down the road, lying in ambush. "We'll wait for your order."

The plan was straightforward—allow Hadi's vehicle to pass their first position, then use the *Duvdevan* team to cut him off further down the road. Block the car, distract his driver.

Ram into him from behind with the reinforced bumper of the *Kidon* SUV, force him off the road.

Take out his guards, take *him* before anyone could react. *A simple enough plan.*

Time to execute it. Ariel took a final look through his binoculars before hoisting himself into the passenger seat of the SUV, glancing over to where Ze'ev sat behind the wheel. The older man's face shrouded in shadow, his eyes impassive.

"Let's do this."

12:11 A.M.
The NSA listening station
Haifa, Israel

It had been less than ten minutes since he had walked through the doors of the station, David Lay thought. Far too soon to expect results from anything short of a miracle, and he no longer believed in those.

If he ever had.

He took off his headphones, staring at the opposite wall. It seemed hard to believe that this had all started this very *morning*—waking up from a drug-induced stupor to the sight of Avi ben Shoham's face. The first domino, tumbling down in what had become a cascade. Unstoppable as a mountain avalanche.

And he wasn't helping—his own Arabic just barely passable enough to facilitate conversations on the street. Nowhere near the fluency needed to help process the kind of audio they were sifting through.

He put a hand on the edge of the metal desk, pushing himself aright. Feeling suddenly dizzy, a lingering after-effect of the drugs and lack of sleep.

A water-cooler stood in one corner of the room and he made his way over to it, his hand trembling ever so slightly as he filled the paper cup. He glimpsed the NSA duty officer making his way over and turned to meet him, willing the momentary weakness to go away.

"Anything?" he asked, taking a sip of the water. Coffee would have been more welcome.

Galvin shook his head. "Nothing yet. I've tasked everyone I can spare, but I can't guarantee—"

A shout from the far corner of the room cut him off, an analyst waving his hand over the border of one of the cubicles. "Galvin, over here! I think we may have found something."

12:13 A.M.
The Gaza Strip

"We are maintaining visual on target vehicle, Netzach-1. He's turning south, on the road toward you. Should reach your position in the next few minutes."

Everything going according to plan, Ariel thought, his eyes focused on the tail-lights of the moving car maybe five hundred meters ahead of their blacked-out SUV. Almost *too* according to plan, his palm slick with sweat where it met the wooden grip of the Kalashnikov assault rifle lying across his lap.

It made him nervous.

"What are your orders, Keilah?" Silbermann asked, the tension only too audible in the *Duvdevan* officer's voice. *Impatience.* "Do you want us to intercept?"

Ariel grimaced, staring into the night ahead, feeling their own vehicle surge into the turn as Ze'ev tapped the accelerator. Staying just close enough to maintain a following position, just far enough not to be made.

They could close the distance in a heartbeat once Silbermann's vehicles blocked the road, but that decision was going to have to be made and made soon. Shoham's words echoing tortuously again and again through his mind.

"Maintain your position."

12:15 A.M.
The NSA listening station
Haifa, Israel

". . .we were searching for keywords, 'Iraq' or 'Iraqi' being one of them. And that's how we got this."

"And what *did* we get, precisely?" David Lay demanded, trying unsuccessfully to keep the impatience out of his voice.

"It's Mahmoud Damra," the analyst replied, glancing at Lay before returning his attention to his own boss, "on the phone with another a man whose voice we've not yet been able to identify. But the call Damra received was placed from Arafat's personal compound in Gaza City. He makes a passing reference to the upcoming summit in Taba, to which his friend replies with something about the 'judgment of God.' Whatever that is supposed to mean."

A cold chill seemed to crawl slowly up the former station chief's spine, a premonition of danger. "And?"

"And then a few minutes later, Damra references Iraq—an upcoming meet in the Anbar Governate, out in the desert. A dozen kilometers, give or take, from the al-Karameh border crossing with Jordan. He didn't give an exact date, but it sounded as though it's about a week away."

"That's it." *Got you*, Lay thought, unable to keep from feeling a sense of triumph, quickly replaced by gnawing fear as the analyst continued.

"There's a reference to the passage of trucks back across the Jordanian border," the man said, his brow furrowing, "and Damra's contact mentions artillery shells."

Lay shook his head. That didn't make any sense. *None* of this made any sense. Palestinian fighters had never had any problem getting their hands on rockets and mortars in plenty over the years.

Getting more wouldn't require machinations of this scale. No. . .something was wrong.

"Is that all there is?"

"We're still working to translate the rest of the call. We—"

The man's voice broke off as one of his colleagues reached over to grip his arm. Headphones still covering the analyst's ears, his face suddenly pale in the glow of the computer screens surrounding them in the darkness of the room.

"*Kimiayi*," he said, looking up at Lay—the blood draining from the station chief's own face as he heard the Arabic. Every fear confirmed in that moment. *And more.* "They're talking about chemical weapons."

12:19 A.M.
The Gaza Strip

"We're inbound on your location, Netzach-1," Ariel said, keying his mike as he shifted position in his seat, making it easier to bring his weapon to bear. "No more than two minutes out."

A moment's silence, and then a burst of static in his ear as Silbermann's voice came over the radio network. "And your orders, Keilah? I say again, what are your orders?"

Indecision. It was death in a field operation, and yet he felt himself hesitate, the lights of the vehicle ahead of them drifting in and out of focus. Remembering Shoham's final orders. The look on the general's face when he'd given them, so clear in his mind's eye. *"Give us time."*

"Hold where you are," he responded grimly, hearing a string of curses explode in his ear.

"If we're going to be effective, we have to move *now*, Keilah," his old *Duvdevan* comrade insisted angrily. "Requesting authorization to engage."

"Request denied," he responded, shaking his head as the radio fell silent once more. This wasn't making it any easier.

Ariel caught a glimpse of Ze'ev's face out of the corner of his eye. His expression sphinx-like, betraying not the slightest reaction to the soldier's outburst. Or his own decision.

The former *Shayetet-13* operator might have argued him to the death during the planning of a mission—but he was too professional to second-guess him now.

"He's right, you know that," he heard Tzipporah say from behind him, giving voice to his self-doubt.

I know, he thought, cursing silently. Feeling the weight of responsibility bearing down more heavily upon him as the road flashed by. The SUV already accelerating as Ze'ev gently increased the pressure of his foot on the gas, preparing to ram.

Every passing second bringing them closer to the moment of final decision. *Give us time.*

Time they no longer had, his earpiece crackling with static once more. Silbermann's voice, once again. "I have visual on the target vehicle, Keilah. They're less than a klick out and closing. We have to do this *now*."

12:21 A.M.
Mossad Headquarters
Tel Aviv, Israel

"My God. . ." Avi ben Shoham breathed, uncharacteristically taken off guard. His mind still struggling to process Lay's words. The *enormity* of what they portended. "Are you certain?"

"Our best intelligence would indicate that—"

"*No*," Shoham hissed, cutting his CIA counterpart off, "you're not listening to me, David. I have men in the field, and with every moment that passes, our odds of having chosen an irrevocable course increase exponentially. So I don't need to hear what your 'best intelligence' *indicates*. You've been in this game for a long time, you're a professional. I need to tell me what *you* believe. Is your intel rock-solid? Is this *real*?"

There was a long, painful moment of silence from the other end of the line. Almost impossible to know whether the American was weighing out the truth. . .or coming up with his best lie. Then, finally:

"It is."

The Gaza Strip

This wasn't like him. He knew the order he needed to give, the order he *had* to give—and yet somehow he found himself incapable of giving it. Unable to escape the feeling that to do so would be making a terrible mistake.

"Stand down," he said instead, the words coming out with the force of an explosion. "Do not, I say again, do *not* cut them off."

"That wasn't the plan, Keilah," he heard his old friend respond, the tension all too audible in the man's voice. "We have to—"

"Those are your orders, colonel," he responded, more firmly this time.

"*Stand down.* Take up a following position behind us, prepare for the hand-off."

Silence fell over the line once more, the only sound in Ariel's ears that of their vehicle's engine as they continued to roll south, lights out—maintaining their distance. Even as the *Duvdevan* vehicles moved into position behind them. A dark oppressive silence, his own doubts weighing down upon him.

Another twenty kilometers to the border with Egypt—with three vehicles, they shouldn't have a problem staying on him, even at night. Could even yet take him down, if it came to that.

But it wouldn't be nearly as easy as it *could* have been. Nearly as bloodless. He was gambling with the lives of his team.

His radio crackled once more with static and he felt himself brace for the sound of Silbermann's voice.

"All elements," he heard, startled to hear the voice of Avi ben Shoham instead, "stand down. You are not, repeat, are *not* to interdict the target vehicle. Break contact and return to base immediately."

12:53 A.M.
The Fatah *compound*

"Our men report that they arrived at the border safely," Mahmoud Damra said, a satisfied smile creasing his lips as he rose from the table. "No one followed them, no one tried to stop them. No sign of the Jews whatsoever. See, what did I tell you? You worry too much."

Perhaps, Hadi thought. Perhaps he *was* paranoid, but it was hard not to be—not with the stakes this high for all of them.

It was at his insistence that they'd sent the decoy vehicle out ahead, hoping to draw out Mossad—provoke them into action if they indeed did lie in wait.

And nothing. It still did little to ease the nagging unrest in the back of his mind, the prickle of danger which had saved him so many times during the war. That something was wrong, that the slightest misstep could end in his death.

"Then I'll be leaving here in a few hours," he said finally, forcing a smile to his own face. A mask for all that lay beneath. "It's time for me to be returning to Baghdad."

"And may you know a safe return to your homeland, Colonel," Damra said, taking a step into him, his dark eyes hard in the light of the lamp on the table. He seized the lieutenant colonel's hand, drawing him into a close embrace. "For all that you have done for Palestine."

Hadi nodded, gazing expressionlessly into Damra's eyes. *Palestine.* The ideal to which every Arab paid token obeisance. A façade. . .for so much *else.* But he was a soldier, and he would do his duty.

"For Palestine."

4:07 A.M.
Mossad Headquarters
Tel Aviv, Israel

"The audio is genuine," Eli Gerstman announced, closing the folder before him. "It's Damra. . .we've verified his voice."

"And the references to the summit at Taba?" Halevy asked, glancing from one man to the other. Still in his shirtsleeves, his customary suit having been left behind when he'd been roused from his bed.

Shoham watched as Gerstman spread his hands, shaking his head. "Unclear, at best, but I think we have to assume that they mean to launch an attack on the summit—with a chemical weapon."

Killing American, Israeli, and Palestinian diplomats, all together. It was the kind of ruthless treachery Damra had always been known for.

"Have we heard anything from our other sources?" Halevy went on, seeming to digest that assessment. "Any other chatter, any details of exactly how this attack might be executed?"

"Nothing." The lack of chatter was itself worrisome, an indication of just how closely this plan was being held to the vest.

"Then we can't let it proceed that far," the Mossad director said, a note of finality in his voice. "The site of the exchange itself, have we been able to determine it?"

"The hand-off will take in the desert of Anbar," Shoham responded, "just across the border from Jordan, on the night of the 8th. The exact spot was not given in the course of the call—at least not the portion we received from the Americans—but we believe we've worked it out. It's just off a mining road roughly fifteen kilometers southeast of the border crossing, one of the few transit points through the region that could support this kind of movement."

"And they're going to bring it back across the border—through Jordan—into the Palestinian Authority?"

"Yes."

The Mossad director shook his head, swearing softly beneath his breath. Seemingly overcome by the insanity of it all. As were they all. "Can we get a team on the ground? Hit them at the rendezvous point, take it out before these chemical weapons can even leave Iraqi soil."

"We possess the capability, Efraim," Gerstman answered, moving in before Shoham could respond, "but the risks of such a course of action. . ."

His voice trailed off as he leaned back in his chair at the conference table, the implication of what he was saying only too clear. *Long odds.* "We might be better off reaching out to the Jordanians," he continued after a moment. "Seek their cooperation, have them stop the trucks as they cross the border."

Halevy just looked at him. "All these years, Eli. . .have we learned nothing? If the security of the Jewish state is to be assured, we can depend only upon *ourselves* to do it. There is no one coming to save us, no one who can be entrusted with our defense. There is only *us*—and we will have to be enough. Have your people put together a team. Take these weapons out of play."

"There *is* one problem, Efraim," Shoham said slowly, choosing his words with care. "The meeting point. . .it's within the southern NFZ."

The no-fly zone.

Gerstman's head came up from the papers before him, alarm spreading across his face. "Then any air operations. . ."

"Would have to be cleared in advance by NATO authority." Shoham nodded. "Or else we run the risk of being blown out of the sky by our 'allies.'"

Silence fell over the room, the only sound that of the clock ticking on the wall. Rhythmic, unnaturally loud in the stillness. Then Halevy looked over, meeting Shoham's eyes.

"Get David Lay on the phone."

Episode III

Going into battle. It was an old familiar feeling, Ariel thought, ducking his head as he returned to his seat, the vibration of the Beechcraft King Air's twin turboprops filling the plane's cabin, their sound dampened by the insulation of the fuselage.

Rays of the late afternoon sun entering through the windows, casting eerie shadows across his face.

To war, once again. As he had so many times through the years, carrying the fight to the enemies of Israel across the Middle East. And Europe. First as a member of *Sayeret Duvdevan*, then these last few years with the Mossad. Fighting the enemies of his nation. Fighting and *killing* them, for that was what he was. *An assassin.*

"We'll be entering Turkish airspace in five minutes," he said, looking over into the dark eyes of the older man seated across the aircraft aisle from him. "Barring delays, we should be on the ground in fifteen."

A nod served as his only reply as he took his seat, glancing around at the faces of the rest of his *Kidon* team. They all knew the truth.

Getting on the ground. . .that was only the beginning.

5:03 P.M. Incirlik Air Base
Adana, Turkey

The roar of a fighter jet passing by overhead washed over David Lay as the CIA officer walked out across the runway of the air base, the sleeves of his white dress shirt rolled up past the elbow, worn blue Levis completing the informality of his attire. Might as well enjoy the Middle East while he could—it was bound to be snowing back in Virginia by the time he got home. *Whenever that was.*

He felt the turbulence buffet his dark hair as he glanced up and back over his right shoulder just in time to see the familiar shape of an RAF Jaguar flash past, outlined against the darkening sky. Circling around to the north as the strike fighter prepared to come in for a landing.

Part of the NATO force deployed to Incirlik as part of Operation Northern Watch, enforcing the "no-fly zone" over the north of Saddam's Iraq.

And that was why they were here, after all—his gaze falling upon the unmarked black Beechcraft light transport which had just landed not fifty meters away, its propellers still turning as it taxied to a stop. *The no-fly zones.*

Just another in a long chain of events which had led them to this place, he thought—his face darkening as he reflected on the role he himself had played in them.

A part he'd thought was behind him. Over and done with. But the Agency. . .they'd had other ideas.

The door of the Beechcraft was already down on the tarmac as he circled around the tail of the plane, a man in a suit emerging from its darkened interior.

"Avi," Lay began, extending his hand as he advanced, raising his voice to be heard over the roar of the engines, "welcome to Incirlik."

"David," the Israeli general replied simply, his eyes hidden behind dark sunglasses. A faint chill audible in his voice, something more than his customary reserve. He didn't take Lay's hand.

All right. So that's how it was going to be.

Lay withdrew his hand after an awkward moment—forcing a grim, unfelt smile to his lips. His relationship with Avi ben Shoham had always been strained throughout his years as Station Chief Tel Aviv, their respective positions in the CIA and Israeli Mossad enforcing a healthy degree of professional distrust.

But these last few months—well, perhaps it *was* unreasonable to expect someone to still trust you after you'd deceived them. And that's exactly what he had done, lying to his counterparts in Israeli intelligence—covering up, deliberately leading them away from their target. Until the whole house of cards came tumbling down about them.

That he had done it all on orders from his superiors—a directive emanating directly from Langley's seventh floor—didn't really matter in the end. *Not when it came to trust.*

He looked past the Israeli's shoulder to see more Mossad personnel disembarking from the transport—a young man who couldn't have been far out of his early twenties leading the way.

Something strangely familiar about his eyes as they fell on Lay, the eyes of a man who had already seen far too much. A man old before his time.

And then it hit him. *Galilee.* His meeting with Shoham only a few nights before, passing over the ECHELON files on Umar Hadi. It was him—the man standing under the eaves of the boathouse on the shores of the sea. *Standing guard.*

Movement caught his attention and he glanced up to see a young woman in nondescript military fatigues descending from the plane behind an older man. Her hair pulled back into a tight bun, revealing the face of the girl from the bar on New Year's Eve.

The girl who had tried to *seduce* him. No doubt on Shoham's orders.

And just like that. . .the band's back together, Lay thought, a wry grimace twisting at the corners of his mouth. The realities of the intelligence game. Enemies one day, allies the next. The day after that?

God only knew. And like any intelligence collector worth his salt, the Almighty could be stingy about sharing.

"If your people want to go ahead and secure their equipment, Avi," he began, forcing himself to refocus on the present—the road that lay ahead of them both, "I can show you to the operations tent."

6:47 P.M. Arabia Time
Tikrit, Iraq

"General Siddiqi is waiting for you."

The soldier's words, ringing again and again in Umar Hadi's ears as the Iraqi lieutenant colonel made his way down the ornately appointed halls of the presidential palace, his every footstep echoing off the walls of the corridor—a rhythmic, purposeful sound.

He had been to the compound in Tikrit only a few times in the course of his military career, and now—as ever—he found himself well-nigh overwhelmed by the opulence of the place.

It was like being transported back in time. *The kings of Babylon.* Reigning over the known world from beside the banks of the Tigris.

Perhaps that was how Saddam envisioned himself, in truth. Perhaps. . .well, even having such thoughts was to place oneself in danger, Hadi thought, finding the visage of the dictator himself staring down upon him from a painting hung upon the wall as he passed through a doorway and into the large atrium beyond.

And all the more reason why he had found the general's choice of meeting place disconcerting. *Like placing one's head in the maw of a lion.*

6:03 P.M. Eastern European Time
Incirlik Air Base
Adana, Turkey

". . .second detachment will arrive from Tel Aviv in the morning, before dawn. A unit from the *Duvdevan*."

"*Sayeret Duvdevan?*" David Lay asked, looking sharply up from the maps spread over the large table in the middle of the operations tent which had been requisitioned for their purposes in Hodja Village, the tent city which had sprung up around Incirlik to house NATO personnel supporting Northern Watch. Its USAF personnel finding themselves temporarily evicted to make room for the needs of their mission. "I thought you used them for more. . .'domestic' operations, Avi."

Raids into the Palestinian Authority, to be more specific, Lay thought.

The kind of missions that the US State Department had been lodging complaints about for the entirety of his time in the region, claiming that such actions were "unwarranted" and detrimental to the peace process. Whether they were or not, well that was an issue so far above his paygrade as to not even merit consideration.

The "peace process" wasn't looking healthy of late for reasons that had little to do with the Israelis, and that brought them back around to where they were this night. Implementing measures that would have been considered unthinkable not five months before.

Desperate times.

"That is our normal practice," the Israeli said deliberately, meeting Lay's gaze, "but as Ariel can explain, we used these men in the aborted interdiction of Umar Hadi a few nights ago in Gaza, and they were briefed on the situation at that time. We share your concern for keeping the knowledge of this. . .'sale' of chemical weapons to the Palestinian Authority as tightly controlled as possible, David."

Good. Because if they didn't, things could easily. . .he didn't finish the thought, the arrival of another American in the operations tent distracting him in that moment.

He was dressed casually, in civilian clothes like Lay, his appearance nondescript—but there was something about him that was different. Something of suppressed violence lurking behind those coal-black eyes.

Or perhaps he only saw it because he knew who the man was. More accurately, *what* he was—having worked with him once before, in Gaza, during the abortive Operation RUMBLEWAY the preceding fall.

"Avi, I'd like you and your m—personnel," he amended, catching the eye of the Israeli woman at the end of the table just in time to catch himself, "to meet the man who will be heading up our end of the operation—

accompanying your teams on the ground in Iraq and acting as liaison between your people and our planes. Sergeant Michael Black, United States Army."

1ˢᵗ Special Forces Operational Detachment-Delta, Lay didn't add, watching his counterpart's eyes closely. The unit known in popular culture as "Delta Force."

Shoham cleared his throat, seeming to choose his words carefully before speaking. "I believe I had made myself clear, David. My men are professionals, but they are trained to operate as a *team*. Bringing in an outsider, no matter how skilled, threatens that stability. It's a risk I refuse to accept."

"It's a risk you'll have to accept if you're going to have the use of NATO air assets," Lay replied evenly, not giving an inch, "and we both know that's the only way we handle this without running the risk of a war. A war none of us can easily afford."

He shoved both hands in the pockets of his jeans, leaning back against the table as he watched Shoham wrestle with the realities of their situation, that they were going to have to work together once more to get through this.

Despite all which had gone before, despite the distrust.

"All right," the Israeli said finally, trading glances with his people before returning his attention to the Americans, "then tell me, Sergeant. . .'Black', what is the plan?"

7:23 P.M. Arabia Time
The Presidential Palace
Tikrit, Iraq

"So, colonel. . .our plan, everything is in place?" He heard Siddiqi ask as he emerged from the doorway into an expansive courtyard, finding the general standing there beneath a looming statue of the Iraqi President—looking out over the blue-green waters of the lagoon to the east of the palace complex. *And the Tigris beyond.*

The last few rays of the setting sun glinting off the water.

"It is," Umar Hadi responded hesitantly, removing the maroon beret which denoted his service in the Republican Guards as he moved to Siddiqi's side. Standing there for a long moment of awkward silence in the shadow of Saddam before adding, "The trucks will roll out for Anbar within the next three hours. They are to reach the rally point under the cover of darkness, go to ground for the day."

"Good, good," the general said, a smile crossing his face as he turned to greet Hadi. Seemingly as unconcerned by their surroundings as if he had been sitting in the comfort of his own home.

Or standing erect in the turret of a T-72 as he had that dark night in Basra as the Iranians broke through their defenses, bullets filling the air around his head. His pistol drawn, as if he could rally the line by nothing more than his own example.

And rally them Siddiqi had, heedless of his own danger. Holding the sector as many others crumbled around him. He had always seemed possessed by a belief in his own immortality, a quality which made it almost impossible not to be drawn to the man.

Or aware of the dangers that came with associating oneself with him. Dangers which could never have been more apparent than they were this night.

"And our friends, the Palestinians?" Siddiqi went on after a moment, seeming to sense Hadi's discomfort and reaching out to clap him on the shoulder. "You can speak freely, my old friend. We are alone here. . .the President is in Baghdad, and the staff, the guards who remain fear me almost as much as they do him."

And would inform on us both in an instant should they chance to hear us speaking, the lieutenant colonel thought, knowing the realities of their situation all too well. Even if Siddiqi somehow felt himself immune.

"As of last report, they've already crossed the border into Jordan. They should make it the rest of the way tomorrow night, arriving at the rendezvous shortly before midnight."

"Another day," the general said, seemingly overcome in the moment. The *reality* of it all overwhelming him. "Another day, and we shall have played our part in the struggle of God. For Palestine."

Hadi nodded, unable to suppress the sense of disquiet that still rose within him at the thought of what that "part" would mean. But it was too late for such second thoughts, such *doubt*. They were committed.

For Palestine.

5:43 A.M. Eastern European Time, January 8th
Incirlik Air Base
Adana, Turkey

Another twenty minutes, Ariel told himself, gazing out through the early morning darkness toward the runway lights. Smoke curling up through the twilight from the cigarette between the fingers of his left hand. And then the rest of their team would be on the ground, the first phase of their mission complete.

But only the first. So much more to come before the end—whatever that looked like.

From somewhere off in the distance, he could hear the whine of an incoming jet as he lifted the cigarette to his lips, taking a long drag and feeling a sense of calm flood through his body as the nicotine washed over him.

He couldn't remember just when he'd first started smoking before operations, but it had to have been during his time with the *Duvdevan*, long before he'd joined Mossad.

He'd come home from an op and shove the cigarettes into a drawer, to be forgotten until the next time he found himself preparing to go back into enemy territory. *Back into the war.*

But Iraq—this was going to be something different than ever before. The CIA's plan was bold, audacious, and. . .not theirs, which he knew rankled Shoham as much as it did him, if not more so.

Finding themselves essentially forced to play by the Agency's rules after all they had done in France—on Elba—was a bitter pill. But that was how it ever was, dealing with the Americans.

The new Colossus, he snorted, the thought bitter with irony. Standing astride the globe, attempting to enforce its will—its sense of *right*—on a world it didn't even begin to understand.

He didn't hear the man approach, just looked over to see him standing there a few feet away, materializing like a ghost out of the night. His face still half-masked in the shadows of the hangar, but Ariel recognized him all the same. The soldier from the operations tent.

"Sergeant Michael Black, United States Army," he thought, remembering how the CIA officer had introduced him. *And Special Forces*, of that there wasn't much doubt.

Not with the beard, and a haircut that would have never passed muster with the regular US military.

And not after watching him in the briefing, laying out their routes of ingress and egress from the drop zone. He knew what he was doing, no question about it.

Which didn't help to reconcile him any further to his presence on the mission.

"Plane should be here soon," he heard the soldier observe, his eyes focused out on the runway. Digging a packet of Marlboros out of his pocket as he advanced. "Got a light?"

5:47 A.M.
A Fatah *compound*
The Gaza Strip

"Thank you, Colonel," the man replied, leaning out of bed as he held the phone to his ear, the silk sheets falling away from his bare, flabby chest. He'd been expecting the call, but its arrival had caught him asleep all the same. "I am glad to hear of your safe. . .arrival, and will relay your message to our brothers in Jordan."

He listened for a few more moments as the Iraqi continued, his words veiled and cryptic as ever, as though he believed someone was listening to their every word. The Republican Guard officer was obsessed with security to the point of paranoia.

"Good, good," he said finally, a smile crossing his face in the darkness of his bedroom. "Let us tread them down until the strong are humbled."

"Until the spoils are divided," the Iraqi replied after a moment's pause, the pre-planned exchange serving as a final assurance that neither party had been compromised.

The call ended with a *click*, dead silence falling once more over the bedroom as Mahmoud Damra reached over, replacing the phone in its cradle. There would be no spoils at the end of this day, but now—as then—this morning would mark the dawn of a Jewish defeat.

The Palestinian colonel pushed back the sheets, casting a glance back at the outline of the young woman laying in his bed as he padded barefoot into the bathroom and turned on the light—pausing, as ever, to admire himself in the mirror.

He was no longer the young man he had been when he'd first assumed command of Arafat's personal security, he thought, running a hand through his black hair—his growing paunch more than testament to that. But with age had come power, and power. . .well, that was far more effective than looks or charm had ever been.

And after today, he would be on the cusp of achieving power like none he had known before. Like no one in *Palestine* had ever known. . .

5:48 A.M.
Incirlik Air Base
Adana, Turkey

Ariel nodded wordlessly, passing his Zippo over. Watching out of the corner of his eye as a small gout of flame spurted from the tip, the man cupping a big hand around it to shield it from the night breeze.

"Iraq," the American began after a long moment, smoke wafting away from his lips. "Ever been there?"

Ariel just shook his head slowly. He hadn't, but it was the way he would have answered no matter the truth. The intelligence business wasn't one you survived in by trusting your allies. "You?"

"Missed it by two weeks," was the reply, something almost of regret in the man's voice. He had to be close to a decade Ariel's senior, maybe more. "War was over before my unit could get there."

Of course. Over in weeks. That's the way war was for Americans. Neat, tidy. *Just.*

"Made it to Somalia, though," the man went on after a reflective pause. "And Kosovo. That was bad business, all the way around."

Like the Gaza Strip on a normal day. Or at least what this "intifada" had made normal.

"Why did you come out here," Ariel asked sharply, looking over at his counterpart, "really?"

The American met his eyes with a keen glance, his black eyes unreadable in the night. Taking another long drag of his cigarette before he replied.

Finally, "I'm going into battle alongside a man, I like to get a read on him. See what makes him tick. Figure out how best I can be of help."

There was something in the man's demeanor that nettled him, or perhaps it was more the reality of all that had gone before. The betrayal they had known at the hands of the Agency, the lives of his own people put at risk in France.

"You really want to know how you can be of help?" Ariel asked, throwing the butt of his own cigarette to the ground and extinguishing it brutally beneath his heel. "Call your planes and stay out of the way."

The man watched as the Israeli turned, walking out across the air base, his figure silhouetted by the runway lights. A quiet smile creasing the American's face as he replaced the cigarette between his lips.

That could have gone better.

He shook his head, his eyes drifting over to the pair of looming C-130 Hercules transports parked a hundred meters down the runway. At the end of the day, he supposed there was a reason he was a door-kicker and not a diplomat.

They'd be on one of those planes by the end of the day, the man thought, headed into the air like he had so many times before over the years. *Back to Iraq.*

He smiled. Been a long time.

8:43 A.M.
An NSA listening station
Haifa, Israel

"What are we looking at?" Josiah Galvin asked, bringing a steaming cup of coffee to his lips as he came around the wall of the cubicle.

"We got this," his analyst began, taking off his headphones, "a couple hours ago—just finished getting it translated. It's an intercept of a call between Mahmoud Damra and someone in Iraq."

Galvin cursed softly beneath his breath. Being in charge of the NSA's listening station in Israel—one of only two in the region—could be a thankless job on the best of days.

And ever since the CIA had come knocking six days earlier—well, "best of days" wasn't how he would describe any of it. And now they had found themselves tasked in support of. . .some Agency mission, he didn't know the details and suspected he never would.

Just as well.

"Give me the transcript," he said, setting aside his coffee with reluctance. God knew he would need all the caffeine he could get before this day was over. "I'm going to need to kick this upstairs."

9:27 A.M.
Incirlik Air Base
Adana, Turkey

". . .we're showing anti-aircraft positions here, here, and—here," Sergeant Black said, using his pointer to indicate the respective positions on the map of Al-Anbar Governate spread across the table, "as of our last recon flights out of Prince Sultan twenty-four hours ago."

Prince Sultan Air Base, Ariel thought, watching the man closely. Roughly eighty kilometers south of Riyadh, the base of operations for Operation Southern Watch, enforcing the no-fly zone over the south of Iraq.

The logical place to have launched *this* operation, in fact, if one wished to entertain for a moment the ludicrous thought of the Kingdom permitting Mossad to operate within its borders.

He suspected just getting the Turks on side had required more than sufficient "creativity" on the CIA's part.

But the soldier wasn't done. "Photo analysis of the imagery obtained reveals the sites to be SA-6 'Gainful' mobile launchers, presumably manned by Iraqi regular Army. Our flightpath to the drop zone should take us well away from their positions."

"What's your recent history of 'engagement' with the Iraqis?" he heard Ze'ev ask, lifting his head to see his second-in-command standing a few feet further down the table.

A former member of *Shayetet-13*, Israel's maritime special-ops unit, before coming to Mossad, the man was more than a few years Ariel's senior. An invaluable source of counsel on the *Kidon*, and a dear friend.

"Down from what it was in the spring of last year," David Lay responded after a moment, stepping forward to the table following an exchange of looks between the Americans. "But the Iraqis continue to challenge the no-fly zone regularly enough to keep us on our toes. They've learned not to turn on the fire-control radars of anything they don't want to lose, but that hasn't stopped them from launching missiles ballistically anyway, without radar assistance. Not too difficult to avoid."

No doubt. *In a fighter jet.* Ariel shook his head, trading a glance with Ze'ev. Knowing what they both were thinking.

A pair of lumbering C-130s were going to be another story entirely.

"And as far as air encounters?" he asked, turning toward the American.

"They send a few Foxbats up every now and again," Lay responded, using the NATO codename for the MiG-25. "Takes them time to scramble—you'll have dropped by the time they can get airborne and over the target area. And your exfil by helicopter following the mission will be covered by our customary Southern Watch assets."

There was nothing like American confidence, though he had to admit distance lent enchantment to the view. Having to *rely* on it was another question entirely.

"As for our plans to deal with the target itself," Lay began, motioning to the soldier, "Sergeant Black will explain—"

The former station chief broke off abruptly as another CIA officer entered the tent, taking him by the arm and pulling him to one side.

The Israelis looking on as the Americans exchanged a few hushed words off to the side, the officer placing a folder in Lay's hand, running his finger down the page as Lay opened it, seeming to whisper a question.

"Something we should know about, David?" Shoham asked finally, clearing his throat.

"My apologies, Avi," Lay said with a smile, gesturing with the folder as he turned back to the table. "It's an intercept just in from Fort Meade—Mahmoud Damra's residence."

"And?"

"And it's a call between Damra and Colonel Hadi, made earlier this morning. Their language is veiled, but we believe the call to be final confirmation of our targets' presence at the rendezvous. Damra references Hadi's 'safe arrival' and speaks of notifying 'brothers in Jordan.'"

Yes. Ariel felt a surge of adrenaline rise within him at the words. They were doing this.

"Was that all?" he heard Shoham ask, watching Lay's brow furrow as he scanned further down the sheet.

"That seems to be the substance of it," the American said after a moment's pause. "There's an exchange between them at the very end, a reference to the dividing of 'spoils.' I don't understand what they're trying to say."

A cold chill seemed to run through Ariel's body at the words. *A premonition of evil.*

"May I?" he asked, extending his hand for the folder. Lay nodded, handing it over and exchanging a glance with Shoham as Ariel opened it, his eyes falling upon the final lines.

"Let us tread them down until the strong are humbled. Until the spoils are divided."

Never again. "It's a reference to Islamic history," he announced finally, looking up from the folder. "Specifically, the Battle of Khaybar in 629."

"What does it mean?"

Ariel just looked at him for a moment, as if not comprehending his question. *Americans*. They truly knew *nothing* of this world.

"Khaybar was fought between the forces of Muhammad and the Jewish tribes of Arabia," he said, looking around at the faces gathered at the table. "It means they're going to kill some Jews."

As it ever had been.

An awkward silence fell over the table for a long moment, broken only as Black cleared his throat, a quiet, determined smile crossing the American's face.

"Then let's go kill them first."

10:36 A.M. Arabia Time
Prince Sultan Air Base
Al Kharj, Saudi Arabia

"Think it's the booze?"

Lieutenant Luke Capano considered his friend's question in silence for a long moment, the back of the young pilot's uniform shirt damp with sweat as he leaned back into the hard metal of the folding chair in the small office.

"Could be," he responded finally, glancing over at Ty Garrison, his Combat Systems Officer and the backseater of his F-15 Strike Eagle. They had both graduated from the University of South Carolina before joining the Air National Guard a couple years prior. And now they were half a world away from Columbia, flying fighter jets out of the desert.

In the middle of a country far "drier" than the driest town in the Bible Belt during Prohibition.

They'd been on leave in Kuwait two weeks earlier along with other pilots from their outfit, managed to smuggle back a case of Heineken to the barracks.

Breaking more rules than you could count. And now. . .

"No," Capano said with sudden conviction, shaking his head. "Something like that, our own CO would handle it. Not this."

Not a summons that was rumored to have emanated from CENTCOM itself, the headquarters of Joint Task Force-Southwest Asia back in Riyadh.

The door came open suddenly, both of the young officers coming to their feet and half-way to attention before they realized the middle-aged man standing in the doorway wasn't in uniform.

"Please, gentlemen, have a seat," the man said, a quiet smile of amusement crossing his face at their instinctive reaction.

He closed the door behind him—placing a thin folder on the table before them as he pulled up a chair. The smile seeming to vanish from his eyes even as he did so.

"What I am about to tell you," he began, his voice taking on a hard edge as he glanced between the two National Guardsmen, "does not leave this room. You don't tell your parents, your girlfriend, your bunkmate, or your chaplain at confession."

I'm Southern Baptist, Capano thought, his quick sense of humor returning along with the overwhelming sense of relief washing over him. *This isn't about the booze.*

A sense of relief that was gone with the man's next words.

"Who I am, my name—none of that matters to you. What matters is that what we are discussing has been authorized by your command authority at the very *highest* levels."

"And what *are* we discussing exactly?" Capano asked, nonplussed by the man's demeanor.

The civilian simply glared at him, adjusting his glasses on the bridge of his nose as he opened the folder, spinning it around on the tabletop to face them. "Tonight, the two of you are going to drop a pair of GBU-16 Paveways on a target in the western end of Iraq's Anbar Governate near the Jordan border, a target 'painted' for your identification by an asset on the ground with a laser designator."

"What's the target?"

"Sorry, son," the man replied, his tone of voice belying his words, "you don't have need to know."

1:06 P.M.
Seventeen kilometers southeast of the border crossing
Al-Anbar Governate, Iraq

The scorching noonday sun beat down hot on the maroon beret covering Umar Hadi's head as the Iraqi lieutenant colonel wiped a thick coating of dust from the lens of his binoculars, lifting them to his eyes and aiming them toward the west. *Toward Jordan.*

It was a barren landscape, rocks and sand as far as the eye could see, the monotony of the terrain broken only by rare pockets of low scrub brush—a rocky ridgeline rising from the earth three hundred meters to the north of their position, running westward for perhaps a kilometer before sinking back into the earth from whence it had come.

Heat visibly shimmering off the desert, distorting his view through the binoculars as he slowly brought them back around in an arc to the east. His eyes following the road from the border crossing, itself little more than a desolate track in the earth.

Another twelve hours and this would all be over, he thought. This. . .*weapon* out of their possession, once and for all.

And he could wash his hands from all of it. *Or could he?*

The Republican Guard officer shook his head. He had done far worse things in his life, for that was the lot of the soldier.

And he would do worse yet. Of that he had no doubt.

He didn't know what Siddiqi was planning, but something deep inside warned him that this was only the beginning.

And that many more would die before this was all over.

"I don't think you truly need to be concerned about visitors, sir," he heard a voice announce from behind him, looking back to find a man in the uniform of a Republican Guard captain standing there. "The likelihood of someone coming to investigate us. . ."

He smiled. The captain was a good man. The two of them had served together for a long time, ever since their days as enlisted men. Fighting against Iran.

"I want to share your confidence, Raffi," he said, turning his attention back to the horizon, "and yet I fear I won't rest easy until we all wake up once more in our own beds tomorrow. You said that you saw an Army unit moving along the roads to the west of here on your way in this morning?"

"A pair of mobile surface-to-air launchers along with their support personnel," Captain Thamir replied, the ends of his dusty black mustache twisting up into a contemptuous scowl. "It's the regular Army, sir—they're like a beaten dog which cowers at the mere sight of its master's hand. We both know they would never dare challenge us."

It was an apt simile, but he seemed incapable of finding the comfort in it.

"Yet even the most beaten of dogs will bite if they find an unguarded moment," Hadi said after a pause. "These launchers, how far away were they, exactly?"

"Five, maybe six kilometers to the north-west."

6:12 P.M. Eastern European Time
Incirlik Air Base
Adana, Turkey

The operations tent was quiet once more, mission personnel already dispersed to ready their gear for the jump—the only noise the steady hum of activity that never seemed to go away in Hodja Village. *A tent city that never sleeps.*

David Lay picked up his open can of Coca-Cola off the table as he moved over to the maps of Anbar Governate, making a face as he tasted it. It had gone flat hours before, in the midst of another of their interminable planning sessions.

This was going to have to be executed so *precisely* if it were to work. So many variables, so many things which could go so very wrong.

"Do you think this is actually going to work?" a voice asked, echoing his thoughts, and he looked up to see Avi ben Shoham standing in the doorway of the tent, the Israeli's suit jacket discarded long ago, his tie gone and the sleeves of his dress shirt rolled up past his elbows.

"At this point, Avi," he said wearily, taking another sip of the lukewarm soda before spitting it out in disgust, "what I think really doesn't matter. We don't have another alternative."

He took a step away from the table, his eyes never leaving Shoham's face. "We both know the stakes here, the consequences if they're able to launch an attack on the Taba Summit. With a chemical weapon. . ."

Lay just shook his head, the results almost too ghastly to even contemplate.

"Delaying the summit would buy us precious time," the Mossad officer offered, going down a road they'd both walked more than once before. Time to secure more intel, time to work out who on the Palestinian side was actually funding this. Perhaps most importantly—*time to find another way.*

"The administration is never going to let that happen," Lay countered, speaking a truth they both knew, the reality of their work. So much of it, coming down to *politics* in the end. "Taba represents their very last chance to achieve peace on their way out the door. This is about the President's legacy, and delaying the talks—even a week—sacrifices all of that. They won't do it."

Shoham just looked at him, a sad smile passing across the Israeli's features. "There's not going to be peace, David, not for my people. Not in the next two weeks, not in the next hundred years. It's a dream, that's all it is. Not reality. I know you see that, perhaps more clearly than most."

"I know," Lay said, nodding slowly. "But as long as the dreamers are the ones setting policy. . .men like you and I will be needed to try to keep the whole affair between the lines, whatever that takes."

And good men will have to keep going out into the night, he didn't add, his gaze drifting over the maps spread out on the table before them. Men like those whose lives they were prepared to sacrifice this night.

"*L'Chaim,*" he heard Shoham murmur, the traditional Hebrew toast sounding more like a prayer from his lips. Or. . .a eulogy.

To life.

7:34 P.M.

"All right, you all understand the role you're to play in this operation," Ariel began, glancing around at his assembled team as they began to go over the plan. *One final time.* They'd be loading up within the hour, awaiting the final "go" order. *Launch at 2200 hours.* "It's three kilometers from the drop zone to the target. We're going to need to regroup on the ground as rapidly as possible and start pushing in."

"Ze'ev, you and the rest of the team are with me. Colonel Silbermann," he continued, his eyes meeting those of his old comrade from the *Duvdevan* as he reiterated the orders he'd given earlier, "your team will take the lead on the ground, forming a skirmish line to cover our advance on the target. If you encounter resistance, take them out as quickly and quietly as possible. These aren't regular Army, these are Republican Guards—they're bound to have thrown out perimeter security."

Silbermann cleared his throat, taking a step forward. "Where are we at on updated strength assessments?"

It was a question that had come up before, and the answer hadn't changed. "We aren't. Based on what signals intelligence we've been able to garner, we believe Hadi's force to be relatively small—which would make sense if this transfer is, in fact, taking place without the official approval of President Hussein. But we haven't been able to verify that through other intelligence means. We have to be prepared for at least platoon strength."

Outnumbered three-to-one. It wasn't bad odds.

"The high ground is here," he said, indicating a spot on the map where the contour lines suddenly closed in on each other, "three hundred meters to the north of the target."

Take the high ground. A military mantra that went back centuries. Millennia, even. For as long as men had gone to war.

"We take that, we have command of the area for the range of our rifles and Sergeant. . .'Black,'" he said, hesitating as he indicated the American, "can work his magic. If things go well, we accomplish our mission without firing a shot."

If they don't. Well that was something they'd just have to deal with, if it came to that.

9:03 P.M. Arabia Time
Prince Sultan Air Base
Al Kharj, Saudi Arabia

The F-15E Strike Eagle was bathed under the harsh glare of the runway lights as Capano walked out on the tarmac, men in Air National Guard fatigues swarming over the plane.

Carolina boys, just like himself. Out here in the middle of a country most of them could never have dreamed of ever seeing.

Getting ready to bomb another one, he thought, catching sight of the pair of long objects slung beneath the plane—one under each of the F-15's wings, the familiar shape of the GBU-16 Paveway II. Over fourteen feet long, finned at both nose and tail. One *thousand* pounds of high explosive, combined with a targeting package that could guarantee its delivery to within four feet of the target.

Whatever that target might be.

He shook his head, still not completely capable of processing the reality of what was going on. Of what he was about to *do*.

The man had been CIA, of that he was sure—or at least as sure as he was of anything.

"Stop talking, Lieutenant. I don't want to hear another word." His CO's response when he'd attempted to take up the matter with him. *"You've been given a legitimate target. That's all I know. That's all you need to know."*

A legitimate target. *Reckon we're going to go bomb the crap out of it, then.*

All he really felt certain of, looking at the plane, was that whatever their target was. . .there wasn't going to be much left of it after those bombs hit.

Not much left at all.

8:34 P.M. Eastern European Time
Incirlik Airbase
Adana, Turkey

". . .and understand, under no circumstances are you or your team to approach the vehicles after they are destroyed," Shoham continued, his voice low as the two of them walked across the American military base, drawing up just short of the runway. "Understood?"

Ariel nodded, Shoham's anxiety only too revealed in the words. They'd been over all this, a dozen times before.

Having the team pack chemical warfare suits along for the jump had been ruled out as infeasible early in the planning stages, meaning that they couldn't risk even the slightest exposure to the nerve agent by getting close to the blast area.

Final confirmation of the weapons' presence was going to have to wait for later—days later, a team slipped across the border from Jordan. One, maybe two people. In and out.

Simple. Just like their mission tonight would be. . .with luck.

"Go with God," Shoham said heavily, putting a hand on his shoulder. The older man's face grim in the darkness of the night. "May He guide your footsteps toward peace."

An ironic smile touched Ariel's lips at the words, recognizing part of the *Tefilat HaDerech*—the prayer of the wayfarer.

He nearly replied, but let it pass—half-formed, unsaid. This night had nothing to do with peace, and they both knew it.

"I'll see you later on," he said finally, gripping Shoham's hand as he began to turn away, toward the aircraft. "After all this is done. After I bring my people back."

"*Shalom.*"

9:57 P.M.
The rendezvous point
Al-Anbar Governate, Iraq

"I understand," the Iraqi lieutenant colonel responded, holding the satellite phone against his ear as he listened, staring out into the desert night beyond their bivouac, the trucks masked with canvas to obscure them from overhead reconnaissance. It was a clear night, clear and nearly as cold as the noon day had been hot, a thousand stars twinkling down from the heavens above. The sliver of a crescent moon casting a faint, ghostly light over the forbidding landscape.

The symbol of his faith, ever since the days of the Ottomans. *His faith.* And what would Allah think, of any of this?

It was a question he had rarely asked of himself over the years, the concerns of the soldier being so far removed from those of religion. Yet he found it plaguing him now.

Just get through this night. There'd be time enough for qualms of conscience later, after the job was done.

"Then we look forward to your soon arrival," he said finally, signing off and replacing the satellite phone on the seat of the old Russian military truck.

"Our Palestinian friends are on their way," Hadi announced, walking out toward where Captain Thamir stood perhaps ten meters distant. "Order the men into position, and tell them to get those fires out."

"At once, sir," Thamir responded, acknowledging the instruction with a salute as he turned on heel, heading off toward the campfires around which their men were gathered. Every inch the soldier, as Raffi had always been. He'd made it ten paces before Hadi's voice reached out after him, arresting his steps.

"And captain," he began, his voice hard, professional. *Back to business—* all doubts banished once more to the dark corners of his mind. He gestured toward the north, the dark shadow of the rise clearly visible, even in the night. "Put some men up on that ridge. I want to see them coming long before they get here."

9:02 P.M.
Incirlik Air Base
Adana, Turkey

Ariel sank back against the red webbing lining the interior of the C-130's fuselage, feeling the vibration of the engines through his ruck as the big plane started to roll, the roar of four giant Allison turboprops drowning out all else.

They were doing this. They were really doing this. The familiar adrenaline rush he always knew just prior to a mission surging through his body—red equipment lights their only illumination in the cavernous hold of the plane, casting the camouflage-painted faces of his team members in a macabre hue.

He caught Tzipporah's eye and she flashed him a grim, tight-lipped smile. As professional, as unflappable as ever. The only woman on the team, he knew some team leaders in the *Kidon* who would have insisted on her staying behind on an operation like this, not taking part in what was, essentially, a combat jump.

But he had too much faith in her to have done so—and they might well need her on the long gun before this night was over.

And then they were airborne, the C-130 pitching nose-up ever so slightly as it took off into the night sky, banking to the south over Turkish farm fields below.

Ariel glanced over to see Ze'ev sitting a few feet away on the nylon seats lining both sides of the plane, the older man's eyes closed, his lips moving in apparent silence.

Hear O Israel, he thought, knowing exactly what the man was saying, even if he couldn't hear the words over the noise of the engines. He'd heard him say them so many times before over the years. *The Lord is our God. The Lord is one.*

The opening of the *Shema,* supposed to be the final words an observant Jew said before death. A testament of faith.

A faith he hadn't known himself for. . .so very many years. Ariel's face darkened at the thought, his fingers balling into a fist. But no Jews were going to be dying tonight.

Not if he had anything to say about it.

9:27 P.M.

It wasn't the first time he had sent men off into the night, Shoham thought, standing on the deserted tarmac of Incirlik long after the transports had departed. Hands shoved into the pockets of his dress pants, his face turned toward the darkness of the sky.

Wouldn't be the last.

Once, it had even been him—out there so far beyond the front lines that there weren't even any lines any more at all. *In defense of Zion.*

And he would far rather have gone himself once more than have sent others to do what he no longer could. Blood on his hands.

The price of getting old. Of survival.

He let out a heavy sigh, turning to head back toward Hodja Village even as the cellphone in his shirt pocket began to pulsate with an incoming call.

There were few people who had his number. Fewer still who would be calling. . .

"Speak," he ordered peremptorily, flipping the phone open, the first words from the other end of the line chilling him to the very bone.

He shook his head, his face twisting into a bitter grimace. "Are you sure? Are you absolutely *sure?*"

". . .they're passing sixty kilometers to the east of Homs now," the USAF radar operator intoned, a pair of brightly-colored dots on the radar screens in front of them indicating the current positioning of Baton Flight, the pair of C-130 transports. *Syrian airspace.*

And no problems, as of yet. Lay ran a weary hand over his face, taking a step back from the screens and picking up his cup of coffee from off the table.

There shouldn't have been—they'd been flying KC-135 Stratotankers into Syrian airspace to refuel their Northern Watch assets for years, and it would take a sharp Syrian radar operator to sort out that these planes weren't on a similar mission.

Still, penetrating the airspace of multiple countries in a single night was a dicey affair—which is why running the whole operation out of Saudi Arabia would have been so much *simpler.*

He snorted, raising the cup of steaming liquid to his lips. Like that was even within the realm of possibility. Some geopolitical realities were. . .insurmountable.

"David," he heard Shoham announce from the door of the tent, a sharp note of urgency in the Israeli's voice—jarring Lay to the point of nearly spilling his coffee as he turned to face him. *Something was wrong. Very wrong.*

"We have a problem," Shoham began, his voice low as he pulled Lay to one side, away from the Air Force personnel tracking the planes on radar. "I just received a phone call from Tel Aviv. One of our assets in Jordan has made contact."

"And?"

"And the Palestinians' trucks are already at the border crossing."

He just looked at Lay, the implication all too clear. *They had pulled out early.* Once they were through the Jordanian checkpoints, it was the shortest of drives to the rendezvous. Twenty minutes at most, and that was being generous—even on bad roads. Their window to interdict the transfer had just slammed shut.

"How long before they're on the ground?" the Israeli asked, the wheels almost visibly turning in his head as he evaluated one possibility after another, rejecting each in turn.

"Thirty, thirty-five minutes, minimum." And that was *"on the ground"*, not at the target, as they both knew.

"What about your strike aircraft?"

"Still on the tarmac at Al Kharj," Lay responded, shaking his head. "And without someone on the ground to visually identify and designate the target— the release of the aircraft for the mission was conditional on our being able to do precisely that. We go bombing Iraq blind and we're in completely uncharted territory, Avi. Presidential disavowal of the mission, Congressional inquiries. . .the Agency itself might not survive something like that."

"We are talking about the survival of my *country!*" Shoham exploded, his dark eyes flashing with anger. His outburst attracting the attention of the airmen on the other side of the tent, all eyes on the two of them in that moment.

"And that is why I am trying to *help* you," Lay responded, keeping his voice low. Every word measured. "Despite everything has gone before, on both our sides. But there are lines even I cannot and *will* not cross, and this is one of them. Without a means of positive target identification on the ground, we can't proceed. That's non-negotiable."

The Israeli glared at him for a long moment before seeming to subside, his shoulders sagging as he turned back toward the map table.

"You are right, of course, David. We both have our respective loyalties, ultimately, and it is unfair of me to ask of you what I myself would not do were our situations reversed." He paused, and Lay could hear him curse bitterly, shaking his head as he stood over the table. "But there *has* to be a way!"

"Your man in Jordan—is he in a position to perhaps. . .delay them at the border crossing?"

"He has already been given such orders," Shoham replied, seeming unconvinced of their efficacy, "but there's only so much time he can buy us."

Not enough.

10:36 P.M. Arabia Time
Al-Karameh Border Crossing
Jordan

"Delay them as long as possible. Whatever it takes." Lieutenant Salim Farajat rubbed sweaty palms against the sleeves of his uniform fatigues as he opened the door of the guardhouse, the words of his Israeli case officer still ringing in his ears. *Whatever it takes.*

It had all seemed so straightforward back when he'd first been approached by the man who now acted as his controller.

The money was good, enough to enable him to get married—making up the difference where a junior officer's salary had always fallen short. And all he had to do was keep track of vehicles passing through Al-Karameh—like he was doing already. So *simple.*

In the beginning.

And now he no longer had any choice, in any of this. Gravel crunched beneath his boots as he walked out into the glare of the headlights filling the night, circling around the front of the trucks to the driver's side of the lead vehicle.

"Is everything in order?" the driver, a heavyset Arab in Western clothes, demanded loudly as he leaned from the window of the heavy military truck—impatience written across the man's face. "I was told that there would be no problem, and there—"

"Your papers appear to be legitimate," Farajat replied, handing them back to the man. Summoning up every reserve of courage for what he was about to say. What he *had* to say. "But I am afraid it makes no difference. There have been many smugglers caught here on the border in recent months and we must search your trucks. Step out of the vehicle."

"This is absurd," the man exploded in protest, his face twisting with rage. "I was assured—"

"Out of the vehicle," the lieutenant cut him off, placing a hand on his holstered pistol for emphasis as he repeated the order. "Now. *Yalla, yalla!*"

10:43 P.M.
"Baton-One-Zero", the lead C-130
Syrian airspace

"We just received a transmission from Incirlik," Ariel announced, raising his voice so as to be heard by his team as he returned to his seat alongside the cargo hold of the C-130. "Our timeline has been moved up—the Palestinians are already at the border crossing."

He saw Ze'ev shake his head, a curse escaping the older man's lips.

"Is there any way we can get on the ground more quickly?" he heard Nadir ask, turning to see the dark face of the youngest member of the *Kidon* team.

The one question that was truly out of all their hands.

"Not much of one," he conceded, catching the eye of the American, "but our friends up front are going to see just how much more they can get out of these engines. We cross into Iraqi airspace in twelve minutes."

10:47 P.M.
Al-Karameh Border Crossing
Jordan

"If you do not let us proceed at once, there will be trouble," the man protested, his hands spread across the hood of the military truck, his eyes flickering back to where Jordanian soldiers were still going through the back. "You are going to be finished. *Finished!* Do you hear me, you son of a—"

"Quiet," Lieutenant Farajat responded, the collar of the man's shirt twisting around his hand as he shoved his face into the hood, the man's curses mingled with a cry of pain. "I've heard enough from you."

This had been easier than he had feared, any misgivings he might have felt over the dangers he ran stopping the trucks melting away with the discovery of five Type 56 assault rifles—Chinese copies of the more easily recognizable AK-47—badly hidden in the back of the second truck. More than enough to justify the stop before his superiors, if it came to that. He—

The sound of another vehicle approaching the border crossing interrupted his thoughts as he looked up to see a white BMW pull to a stop not ten meters away. A man in the uniform of a Royal Jordanian Army colonel emerging from the driver's seat into the checkpoint lights.

"What is going on here, lieutenant?" he demanded, striding up to Farajat even as the young officer brought his hand up in an instinctive, nervous salute. "What's the meaning of this?"

"Weapons, sir," Farajat responded, feeling a sweat break out on his forehead as the colonel's eyes bored into his own. An unrelenting gaze. "We caught these men trying to cross the border with arms, and they have no explanation for their possession of them. They—"

"You will let them go, lieutenant," the colonel replied, the tone of his voice brooking no opposition, "without further delay. Do it *now.*"

10:54 P.M.
Prince Sultan Air Base
Al Kharj, Saudi Arabia

"Palmetto One-One, this is Tower," Capano heard the flight controller intone, the woman's voice coming clearly through his headset as he adjusted the throttle, steering the F-15 toward the center of the runway. "Winds 260 at five knots, runway 35 left, heading 355. You are cleared for take-off."

Heading 355, aye, he thought, watching the indicator align as the aircraft turned toward the north, the horizon shrouded in darkness out there beyond the runway lights. "Winds 260 at five knots, runway 35 left. Cleared for take-off. Palmetto One-One."

"Good hunting."

Good hunting. Whatever that meant on this night.

He shook his head, his eyes focused on the heads-up display as his gloved left hand closed around the throttle, pushing it steadily forward as the F-15 accelerated into a rolling take-off—light flaring suddenly behind him as the afterburners fired, their thunderous roar penetrating his helmet, enveloping him in sound.

And then the ground seemed to drop away from beneath him, Garrison's voice in his ear as the Strike Eagle rose into the night sky over Al Kharj, climbing rapidly to thirty thousand feet before turning to the northwest.

Aimed toward the Iraq border, seven hundred miles away.

Half an hour, give or take.

9:56 P.M. Eastern European Time
Incirlik Air Base
Adana, Turkey

"They've crossed the border," Avi ben Shoham announced heavily as he replaced the phone in his shirt pocket, glancing at his wristwatch. "Our man couldn't hold them back any longer."

The Israeli ploy had bought them time, Lay thought, staring at the radar screens. But was it *enough*?

Only time would tell, and time still wasn't something they had much of. Cutting it so very close.

"Where are the planes?" Shoham asked, coming up behind him.

"Just crossed over into Iraqi airspace a couple minutes ago," the CIA officer responded, turning away from the screens. "Nine minutes from drop."

Nine minutes in which literally anything could go wrong. And if anything did. . .

Lay swore softly, turning back to the map table and picking up his coffee. It would be an international incident like nothing in living memory.

It wasn't the first time he'd found himself wondering if his career was destined for a swift and ignominious end—there'd been many of those times in Berlin.

But somehow, even in those darkest moments of the Cold War, the stakes had never seemed quite this high. The costs of potential failure so. . .*total*, not only to himself and his agents, but to the Agency as a whole.

And the men he'd sent out there, into the darkness. Perhaps that was the problem, at the heart of it. To be the sender, no longer the sent.

"It's hard, isn't it, David?" He heard Shoham ask, looking up to see the Israeli standing there a few feet away. A grim smile on his face.

"What is?"

"Letting go. Recognizing that at some point in your life, you have to step back and let others do what you once did so very well." The Israeli leaned back against the table, every movement displaying the tension pervading his body. As though he was finding his own advice impossible to take. "We are no longer young men, you and I—the front lines of this. . .shadow war are no longer where we belong, no matter how much we might wish it otherwise. And we must trust that those who have come after us are every bit as good as we once were."

His dark eyes twinkled with the first flash of humor Lay had seen from him since his arrival. "Maybe even better."

True enough. If no easier to accept, for all that.

He started to form a reply, but it died on his lips as an Air Force sergeant at the other end of the room suddenly ripped off his headphones, shock clearly written in the man's eyes as he half-turned to face the intelligence officers."

"Sir, it—it's the planes, they've broken radio silence. They're getting lit up by fire-control radars."

11:01 P.M. Arabia Time
"Baton-Two-Zero", the second C-130
Iraqi airspace

"They're tracking us," Colonel Silbermann heard the American announce, his arm resting on the back of the co-pilot's seat as he stared over the man's shoulder at the screens. "Seconds away from lock."

The final step before missile launch, the *Duvdevan* commander thought, cursing silently. Infuriated by his own impotence. There weren't *supposed* to be Iraqi surface-to-air units anywhere near their flight path. The gap between intelligence and reality never more apparent. Or more painful. "Is there anything you can do?"

"We've got some chaff," the co-pilot responded tersely, his eyes never leaving the screen. "A few flares, for all the good they'll do. We—"

His voice broke off suddenly, faltering ever so slightly as he announced, "They have lock-on."

"Baton-One-Zero"

Four minutes to drop. If he closed his eyes, Ariel could almost hear the Iraqi radar in his imagination pinging off the hull of the Hercules transport, bouncing back to the mobile launchers far below.

Signing their death warrants.

There was no time to think about how their intelligence could have been so terribly wrong. No time for regret, for recrimination.

There was only the mission, or what remained of it—as they flew into the very maw of the lion.

"The moment—the very *moment*—we're over the drop zone," he said, raising his voice over the throbbing engines of the transport as he looked around at his team members, "we go out. Until then, find something to hang onto. It's about to get rocky."

10:03 P.M. Eastern European Time
Incirlik Airbase
Adana, Turkey

Tense silence reigned in the operations tent, all eyes focused on the radar screens, the pair of small, moving dots representing the transports. The dark, oppressive silence of a tomb.

"Is there any way to take them out before they can launch?" Shoham asked finally, clearing his throat. "Your Southern Watch assets, perhaps?"

If only. "They were sent a flash as soon as the launchers were first detected," Lay responded, "but we're not patched directly into their comms network. It's going to take time to work its way through the chain of command."

Time, and far too much of it.

"What about the F-15 from Prince Sultan?"

"Still twenty minutes out." *Minutes, when seconds were what counted.* *All* that counted.

Shoham lapsed into silence once more, only for it to be broken moments later by an airman's loud curse.

The man's eyes opening wide as he stared at the screen, two more tiny blips emerging on-screen near the transports.

"We have missiles in the air."

11:04 P.M.
"Baton-One-Zero"

Ariel felt the plane lurch drunkenly as it banked suddenly hard right, wallowing like a large boat caught in a trough of the ocean—the fingers of his right hand entwined in the webbing as the maneuver threatened to pitch him across the aircraft.

He heard the transport's countermeasures fire, clouds of foil chaff from the dispensers filling the night sky around them. Enough to distract the missiles.

If they were lucky.

"A minute to drop," the co-pilot's strained voice in his earpiece informed him, even as the aircraft seemed to level out once more, the ramp slowly opening to reveal the cavernous abyss of the night beyond, the slipstream curling around their bodies. "SAMs eleven kilometers out and closing, heading one-five-five."

His eyes fixed on the red light over the ramp. *Fifty-three seconds. . .*

Just hold on. He caught sight of Ze'ev standing on the other side of the hold, just inside the now-open ramp—and the older man nodded tightly.

He'd lead the stick off the ramp, just as planned. Ariel remaining just behind to boot out anyone who hesitated.

None of his people ever had. *Thirteen seconds.*

"SAMs two kilometers out, heading one-two-nine." He heard the copilot's breath catch, immediately followed by a cry of exultation. "*Trashed* one!"

One missile down. *Three. . .two. . .*

The light went green in that moment, his voice yelling hoarsely, "Go! Go! Go!" as Ze'ev threw himself from the ramp and into the night. *Twenty thousand feet down.*

The American sergeant following immediately after—and then Tzipporah.

"The SAM's turning away," Ariel heard in his ear, a sense of relief washing over him as he saw Nadir drop, pushing himself away from the webbing. "No longer tracking."

And then, even as he took his own final steps to the brink, hurling himself forward into the night—he heard and saw the explosion.

11:05 P.M.
The rendezvous point
Al-Anbar Governate, Iraq

"What was *that*?!?" Umar Hadi demanded, a distant *crump* assaulting his ears as he glanced up and toward the northern sky—way, way up—a brief flash of fire blossoming across his vision before disappearing entirely.

Thamir shook his head, the look on the captain's face clearly revealing concern. "I don't know, sir."

Hadi swore loudly, glancing at his wristwatch. *No sign of the Palestinians yet.* And something was going wrong.

"Get on the radio to that Iraqi Army unit north of us," he ordered, "they have radar on those launchers. They should be able to tell us what's going on, if anyone can."

"But, sir," Thamir protested, "you have been very clear that we should not compromise our mission by any contact with—"

"Just do it, Raffi," he responded, turning to transfix his subordinate with a hard stare. "*Do it now.*"

10:07 P.M. Eastern European Time
Incirlik Air Base
Adana, Turkey

". . .Baton-One-Zero, I say again, what is your status?" David Lay heard the Air Force sergeant demand, keying the microphone of his radio once more as he leaned forward, his body rigid. *Filled with tension.* "Baton-Two-Zero, how copy?"

No answer. Nothing but static since the sound of the explosion. Lay swore quietly, his heart in his throat as he stared at the radar screens, both of the Baton Flight aircraft and the missiles themselves now obscured in the cloud of "noise" produced by the dispensed chaff.

"I say again, Baton-Two-Zero, do you copy?"

No. He glanced over to see Shoham standing there, the stricken look on the Israeli's face mirroring his own. You always knew there was a risk, sending men out into the night. A risk they might not come back. The implicit bargain, ever-present in their work.

Didn't mean you ever expected it to happen. . .like *this.* So many good men.

He nearly came out of his skin when the radio crackled once more with static, the shaken voice of one of the pilots announcing, "Control, this is

Baton-One-Zero, we've made the drop. I say again, the drop has been made. We're coming about for our return to base. How copy?"

"Reading you loud and clear," the Air Force sergeant responded. "Do you have contact with Baton-Two-Zero?"

"They—"

Another burst of static interrupted the transmission, another voice coming through. ". . .this is Baton-Two-Zero, we are aborting the mission. I say again, mission abort. Missile exploded a few hundred meters off our wing— we've lost power to No. 4 engine and No. 3 is on fire. We have to RTB, *now*."

Return to base. Lay traded a look with Shoham, reaching forward to pick up the microphone himself. "Baton-Two-Zero, this is Control. What is the status of the mission? Have you been able to complete the drop?"

Priorities. They were cold and brutal things, but no less necessary. If only one of the teams had made it to the ground. . .

"That's a negative, Control," the pilot's voice responded after a long, agonizing moment. "They're still with us."

"Can you make another pass over the DZ?" The CIA officer asked, wincing even as he did so. But it was a question he had to know the answer to.

"Not possible, Control, we're bleeding fuel from the right cell and struggling to keep this thing in the air on just two engines. We're going to be lucky to make it back to Incirlik."

And if they didn't. . .

Lay shook his head. *Syria, Lebanon, Saudi Arabia*—there was no good place for them to set down. No place they could ditch the plane without completely compromising a mission already gone so far sideways as to be well-nigh irrecoverable.

"Godspeed, captain," he said finally, handing the microphone back to the Air Force sergeant. Shaking his head as he turned back toward Shoham.

"We'll get Southern Watch assets in there to neutralize the SAMs and clear the way for the helicopters, but your people. . .they're on their own now."

It was going to have to be enough.

Al-Anbar Governate, Iraq

With a muffled sound, Ariel's parachute billowed open above him, jerking him out of freefall.

Five hundred feet from the ground.

Glancing down and to his right, he could make out another pair of chutes drifting in the darkness a hundred feet or so below him. Tzipporah and Nadir, most likely. Ze'ev and Sergeant Black would be below them—or on the ground already, if they were lucky.

His dark, painted face twisted into a grimace.

Luck seemed to be something they were running short of this night, their plan—*all of it*—going out the window with the loss of Silbermann's team.

Now, he thought, looking up into the vastness of the desert night—they were going to have to make it up on the fly. Adapt. *Improvise.* And hit an enemy which might already suspect they were coming.

11:13 P.M. Arabia Time
The rendezvous point

". . .no, Major, you may not," Umar Hadi responded brusquely, holding the field radio up against his ear as he listened to the regular Army officer. "You already know everything that you *need* to know. Hold your positions and remain vigilant—be sure to inform me of any developments as they arise. You've done good work tonight, I shall be sure to mention your name to the President."

Which he would most certainly not *be doing*, Hadi thought, letting out a heavy sigh as he signed off, replacing the radio inside the truck. But it had ensured that he got the man's attention and that sufficed for his purposes.

If Saddam ever learned of what they had done out here this night. . .

He shuddered involuntarily, turning to face Thamir and finding the question clearly written in the captain's eyes. "What is it, sir?"

"Major Kazim's unit," Hadi responded, gesturing toward the radio, "picked up a pair of planes crossing into Iraqi airspace from Syria. Once they had entered the engagement range of his missiles, the major opened fire and, he believes, succeeded in striking one of the planes."

Captain Thamir shook his head, seeming nonplussed. "What does any of this have to do with us? We are in the no-fly zone, American warplanes fly over us every day and every night."

"But these, Raffi," he began heavily, "were apparently *not* ordinary planes. I have never used radar equipment, but from what I understand—their radar cross-section was different than that of the fighter planes the Americans usually send. Major Kazim believes they may have been transports."

"Then. . ." Shock spread across Thamir's face, his eyes opening wide. "*Ya Allah*. You mean—"

He nodded. "I do. Put your men on alert, we are going to have to—"

The lieutenant colonel broke off as the radio crackled once more from inside the truck and he reached in through the open window to retrieve it, hearing the voice of one of his soldiers through the static.

"Sir, we have trucks inbound from the west along the border road."

And none too soon. Hadi shook his head, acknowledging the transmission with a curt reply as he retrieved his maroon beret from the seat of the truck. Adjusting it to his head as he nodded at Thamir. "Let's go welcome our guests."

11:14 P.M.
The drop zone

"Did you see any sign of him, Tzipi?" Ariel asked, glancing back over his shoulder at Tzipporah and Nadir as he knelt down by Ze'ev's side, a frown passing across his face as he tied the makeshift bandage tight around the older man's upper arm.

The former *Shayetet-13* operator had jumped into the middle of a firestorm, flaming debris raining down around him as he descended. A red-hot piece of metal—from the plane, from the missile, only God knew which—embedding itself in the flesh of his upper tricep, the heat nearly cauterizing the wound.

She shook her head, on one knee in the desert sand as she scanned the southern horizon through the night-vision scope of her SV-98. The sniper rifle was of Russian manufacture, deniable like the rest of their personal weapons.

And a bolt-action, Tzipporah's usual preference—trading speed in follow-up shots for unmatched precision.

He grimaced, glancing up at the sliver of crescent moon as he straightened, getting to his feet. None of them had hit the drop zone precisely, the chaos surrounding the jump—debris from the explosion falling all around them—throwing them all off course.

But he'd linked up with Tzipporah and Nadir quickly before coming across a wounded Ze'ev as they made their way south. The American remaining the only one unaccounted for.

The American.

Arguably the member of the team he most *couldn't* do without as much as he would have preferred otherwise, the AN/PEQ-1 SOFLAM laser designator he carried vital to the success of their mission.

"We drifted apart in freefall," Ze'ev offered, gritting his teeth against the pain as he pushed himself up, leaning back on his good arm. "I had everything I could do just to focus on getting the ripcord pulled in time."

If he hadn't... well, he'd rather have lost his own right hand than Ze'ev. It wasn't something he cared to dwell on, not with so much yet hanging in the balance this night. He retrieved the night-vision goggles from his ruck, weighing once more the advisability of breaking radio silence in an attempt to contact Black.

Their radios were encrypted and supposed to be secure. *Supposed* being the operative word in any such sentence, as you learned so quickly out in the field. The Iraqi SAMs weren't *supposed* to have been there either.

"Then we'll have to push on without him, trust that he knows enough to catch up." *Move toward the sound of the guns.* That was, after all, what Americans did. Wasn't it? He shook his head, assessing his options. Without Silbermann's team to screen their advance, they were going to have to do it themselves—just another piece of a night gone sideways. "Nadir, you take point. Tzipi, you'll pull rear security and I—"

Noise from behind him arrested his attention, and he turned on heel—his rifle coming up to confront the threat.

"*Shalom*," a distinctly non-Hebrew voice said from the darkness, the American's empty right hand raised in greeting as Black advanced, his paint-darkened face just recognizable in the faint moonlight. "I got here as quickly as I could."

"Your gear survived the drop?" Ariel asked, his eyes searching the American's face.

"Everything's still in one piece," came the reply. Black winced. "Can't say the same for the second transport, looked like they took a pretty close one."

Too close. He could only hope they could manage to limp back to Incirlik. But they had to.

Just like they had to accomplish their mission. Time to move out.

"All right then, let's get going," Ariel said, looking around at his team. *What remained of them.* "Sergeant Black, you're on me."

He glanced toward where Ze'ev sat, seeing a grimace of pain cross the former *Shayetet-13* operator's face as he started to rise.

"You good?" he asked, shifting the Kalashnikov to his left hand as he extended his right.

The older man nodded, ignoring the proffered hand as he pushed himself painfully to his feet—straightening to look Ariel in the eye. A look of determination. *Defiance.*

"I'm good."

11:19 P.M.
The rendezvous point

"We will tread them down until the strong are humbled."

"Until the spoils are divided," Lieutenant Colonel Hadi replied, watching the smile broaden across the Palestinian's wide face as he finished the code response.

He was a big man, and heavy—the loose civilian shirt he wore doing nothing to disguise his fleshy bulk.

"Major Walid Halawa," the man said, extending a hand. "Of the Force 17 commando."

If the man before them had ever been a "commando", it had been many years and a very many meals prior, Hadi thought, trading a glance of thinly-veiled contempt with his subordinate.

The Palestinian security forces were rabble, nothing more. Corrupt, undisciplined, fanatical. Not to be relied upon under any circumstance.

Which caused him to question once more what Siddiqi was thinking in allying himself—and *them*—with such degenerates. But the general had a plan, of that he had no doubt. *Whatever it was.*

He pointedly didn't respond to the introduction, instead sweeping his hand back toward the trucks. "We have the shells that you asked of us. And you, you have our money?"

"We do," the Palestinian major responded, waving forward one of the men who stood behind him, gesturing toward the briefcase in the man's hand. "All of it."

"Relief money," he said, laughing as if he had made some huge joke. "From the United States."

There was an irony there, that much was impossible to deny. Perhaps most of all that money intended to *help* the Palestinian people was instead being used to ensure their destruction. For there could be no other outcome to this.

Hadi shook his head, gesturing for Captain Thamir to take the briefcase as he turned to lead the way back to the trucks.

Casting a wary glance toward the dark shadows of the northern ridge even as he did so. As if he expected any moment to hear the crackle of small arms fire break out from the soldiers he had dispatched to take up positions on its height.

They couldn't wrap up this business any too soon. And if they could do so without the Palestinians realizing anything was wrong, so much the better.

10:21 P.M.
Incirlik Airbase
Adana, Turkey

The night without was cool, the winds of early winter swirling down out of the Taurus Mountains to the north—but Lay's shirt was damp with sweat in the operations tent, a thin sheen of perspiration forming on his brow as he adjusted the radio headset, staring at the radar screens.

"Baton, this is Control," he began, catching the eye of the Air Force sergeant whose seat he had taken, "give me your sitrep. What's going on?"

"Control, this is Baton-One-Zero," the voice of the pilot of the lead, undamaged C-130 responded—considerably calmer now, the immediate danger passed. *Now that missiles were no longer filling the air.* "We're in Syrian airspace now, heading three-one-five—maintaining our position off Baton-Two-Zero's wing."

Close enough to mark their position if they ditch, was Lay's morose, unvoiced observation. Wasn't much else they could do.

"Baton-Two-Zero reports that the fire in No. 3 engine has been extinguished, with power levels back to forty-five percent. No. 4 engine is still dead, and the wing surfaces appear to have taken major damage, really chewed up. They're going to be cutting it close on fuel. Requesting authorization to divert to Ramat David."

An Israeli Air Force air base located in northern Israel, southeast of Haifa, Lay thought, wincing at the realization. Only a couple hundred miles to the southwest of the planes' current position—far, far closer than Incirlik.

Far easier to make on the damaged aircraft's remaining fuel. *Minimize the risk of losing both plane and crew.*

He glanced over at Avi ben Shoham, the unspoken question clearly visible in his eyes.

The Israeli shook his head, his face grim with the knowledge of what the decision could mean. But they'd been over all this, a dozen times before.

If Syrian radars picked up the planes entering Israeli airspace, it would be only a matter of time before that intelligence reached Baghdad. And when it did. . .

Their cover would be blown, all their efforts in vain.

"That's a negative, Baton Flight," Lay said finally, toggling the mike. "Request denied."

To hold life and death in your hand, weighed in the balances. *And found wanting.*

"Control, that is going to be—"

"Absolutely necessary," the CIA officer responded, a cold edge entering his voice with the words. "You must make it back to Incirlik. Control out."

He sat there in silence for a long moment as the transmission ended, staring straight ahead. The weight of what he had done, bearing down upon him.

"Sir," he heard a woman's voice begin, glancing up to see an airman first class standing there behind his chair, "we've just heard from the Navy. A pair of EA-6B Prowlers from the *Abraham Lincoln* have responded to our warning about the Iraqi SAMs and are inbound on the target, ETA six minutes. They'll be taking the launchers off-line then."

Taken off-line. Such a tidy, *sterile* way to refer to it. The death and destruction those Navy pilots would be bringing with them. But there was no help for it.

You pays your money, and you takes your choice. And the Iraqis manning those launchers had made theirs.

"Good," Lay said, shoving back his chair and removing his headphones as he stood. "Make sure the helicopters get the all-clear—we need them ready to go in as soon as the SAM threat has been neutralized."

As soon as we've heard from the field team, he thought, mentally acknowledging the elephant filling up the room.

With the Mossad team under strict orders to maintain radio silence until they called in the plane, they were flying blind here. No way to determine how things were actually progressing on the ground.

Or *if* they were.

"I am sorry, David," Shoham said quietly as he approached, pushing past him to the map table—Lay's knuckles resting against the hard metal as he leaned forward, surveying once more the terrain their men were going to have to traverse. "Your men, they have risked so much for my country. . .it seems ungrateful. I wish there was another way."

But there wasn't and they both knew that.

"Save it, Avi," Lay responded, shaking his head. "No one's dead—yet. And if we're lucky, we can keep it that—"

"Sir," the airman first class broke in, an urgency in her voice, "You need to hear this. We're receiving a transmission from Palmetto Flight."

"And?" Lay demanded, hustling across the tent and taking the headphones from her outstretched hand.

"He's over the target."

11:25 P.M. Arabia Time
"Palmetto One One"

Nothing but darkness met Capano's eyes as the young lieutenant put the F-15 over into a steep bank, gazing out through the bubble canopy.

Darkness stretching down through the faint moonlight to the ground, twenty-eight thousand feet below the strike fighter's wings.

"Copy that, Control," he responded, checking his heads-up display once more as he toggled his headset mike. "We have no targets. I say again, no targets."

"Just sit tight, Palmetto," came the terse response from the man on the other end of the line. "It'll be there, give it time."

Time. The Air National Guard lieutenant took a deep breath, clearing his throat. "That's not something we have a lot of, Control. Used up quite a bit of fuel just getting here, what's left is only going to let me remain on-station so long."

There was a long pause, only static filling the silence. And when the man spoke again, his voice had changed. Become guarded, wary. "How long are we talking about, Palmetto?"

Capano shook his head, glancing down at his gauges. "Fifteen, twenty minutes at the outside. Then we're bingo-fuel."

11:26 P.M.
Al-Anbar Governate

The night-vision goggles revealed the rugged terrain of Anbar in stark relief as Ariel moved forward, his Kalashnikov held at low ready. Every detail picked out in ghostly shades of green, dark and granular.

His team spread out on either side of him in the darkness, forming a skirmish line as they pressed on toward the ridgeline, now less than a third of a kilometer away. A dark shadow, looming before them in the ambient moonlight.

And then he saw it, a line of soldiers moving up the western slope of the ridge, their shapes just visible as a light green against the darker landscape. At least eleven men, maybe more.

A low hiss escaping his lips as he dropped to one knee, glancing left and right—gesturing for his team to take cover.

Had the Iraqis seen the explosion? Been alerted by the mobile SAM unit? He swore beneath his breath, only too aware of the reality. *Why* didn't matter, what mattered was that they were reinforcing the ridgeline in strength.

And they were going to have to root them out before they could accomplish their mission.

"Move in and pass the word along," he whispered, finding Ze'ev on his left and the American on his right. "Pick your targets and take them out on my mark. Do it quietly."

11:29 P.M.

"Nine 130mm artillery shells," Umar Hadi announced, throwing back the canvas to allow one of the junior Palestinian "officers" to climb into the back of the truck and inspect the two massive footlockers resting on the bed. This was eating up precious time, but he couldn't very well refuse. "Designed to be fired from the Russian-built M-46 field gun. And filled with sarin gas by Iraqi scientists during our war against the *safawi*."

Iran. It seemed so long ago now. And yet all that they had done then remained with them to this day. Embodied in nothing, perhaps, so much as these shells.

"Good, good," Major Halawa grinned, clapping Hadi on the shoulder in an unwelcome gesture of familiarity. "May God be praised. This will give us the ability to strike back against our oppressors at last."

And be crushed for your pains, the Republican Guard officer thought, adding his own perfunctory *"Insh'allah."*

As anyone could reasonably expect following the deployment of such weapons. Madness, all of this.

"If you would take my advice, you—" Hadi began, cut off suddenly by Captain Thamir's voice, his subordinate emerging from the darkness near the front of the trucks.

"Sir, you're wanted on the radio," came the urgent warning, a chill sense of foreboding darting down the lieutenant colonel's spine with the words.

He excused himself briefly from the Palestinians, leaving his soldiers to stand guard as he hurried after Thamir. "What is it?"

"It's the army missile commander. He says we have a plane in the air above us. An American fighter."

11:30 P.M.
The ridge

Sergeant Saleem Jabouri paused on the crest of the ridgeline, only the silence of the night surrounding him as the Republican Guard NCO took his left hand off the foregrip of his AK-47, glancing back over his shoulder as he signaled for his men to spread out further across the ridge.

Paratroopers? It seemed hard to imagine—unfathomable, almost—but there had been no mistaking the tension in the captain's voice when he'd given the order. He'd served with Thamir too long not to recognize that tone when he heard it.

His hand slid along the Kalashnikov's receiver, his finger resting against the safety as he dropped to one knee, peering out into the darkness as he searched for targets—for any sign of *life*—and finding nothing. His men passing behind him as they moved to take up positions.

It was then that he heard it, a muffled sound like hands clapping together—something warm and wet spraying across the back of his neck.

He rose half out of his crouch, catching the sight of one of his men toppling backward, his rifle clattering to the rocks—half his head blown away.

Jabouri's mouth opened in a cry of warning, his own rifle coming up, but the sergeant never made it—a 9mm slug slamming into his temple, smashing through the dense bone of his skull as it mushroomed into his brain.

He was dead before his body hit the ground.

The rendezvous

"You wished to speak with me, Major Kazim?" Umar Hadi demanded, glancing back at Thamir as he picked up the radio. His own concern mirrored in the captain's eyes.

It only made sense for an American fighter to be dispatched to the area following the targeting of coalition aircraft, and if the planes Kazim's unit had fired upon earlier *hadn't* been aimed at interdicting the weapons shipment—if he had brought American attention down upon the area this night due to his rash action—Hadi swore softly. He would *find* a way to put the man on report, no matter the consequences.

It was a few seconds before the Army officer's voice came through the static, and when it did, it sounded breathless—as though he had just been running. And from the first words out of his lips, it was clear that a solitary American fighter was no longer chief among his concerns.

"Sir, we have multiple contacts inbound on our location—still a hundred kilometers out, but they're closing fast. Heading straight for us."

Hadi was caught speechless for a moment, overwhelmed by the sheer stupidity of it all—and then the words came pouring out, like waters through a broken dam. "Get your radars powered down. Do it *now!*"

11:31 P.M.
Fifty miles to the southeast

"Magnum away."

An AGM-88 HARM missile dropped from beneath the Prowler's wing, disappearing in a blinding flash of fire across the night sky as its rocket motor ignited, boosting the missile to speeds close to Mach 2.

Homing in on the electronic transmissions emitted from the Iraqi radar systems even as the Navy plane pulled up, the distinctive cougar insignia of VAQ-139 visible on the Prowler's tail as his wingman moved into position, the second pilot's voice coming clear through the radio.

"Magnum away. . ."

The rendezvous

Hadi could hear the Army officer barking orders in rough, panicked Arabic over the open radio, his own breath caught in his throat as he listened. Paralyzed—helpless to intervene, to *alter* what had been set in motion.

And then he heard it, the force of a massive explosion buffeting his ear for the space of a half-second before the transmission dissolved into white noise, only static filling the line.

The lieutenant colonel swore loudly, throwing the radio onto the seat of the truck as he pushed past Thamir, hurrying back toward the trucks—anger distorting his features.

Kazim's men may have died due to their commander's stupidity, but he had no intention of joining them.

"Get the lockers loaded onto the trucks," he bellowed, shoving the Palestinian major to one side as he addressed his own startled soldiers. "*Now. Yalla, yalla!*"

The words had barely left Hadi's lips before he felt the Palestinian flinch at his side, the crackle of small-arms fire breaking out through the night. His head snapping up and to the left, just in time to catch sight of muzzle flashes flickering along the ridge to the north.

His every fear confirmed in that moment. *They were here.*

11:32 P.M.
The ridge

Ariel pressed his back against the rock shelf, his rifle in his hands, taking cover as bullets whined in overhead—smashing into surrounding rocks, pieces of rock spraying around him.

The Iraqis had been clustered too closely together on the ridgeline to have allowed for them to all be taken quietly. They'd halved their number, at the very least, in the opening fire—but those who remained were fighting back with more tenacity than he might have expected.

And if they could pin them down *here*—on the northern slope of the ridge—long enough for reinforcements to move into position, then their mission was going to be in major trouble.

Like it wasn't already.

He raised himself up over the rock, muzzle flashes seeming to blossom in slow-motion before his eyes through the night-vision goggles as he brought the Kalashnikov to bear, getting off a controlled burst at a cluster of shadows moving perhaps forty meters away. Seeing the dark form of a Guardsman pitch forward, a body sprawling in the dirt. Catching sight of Nadir, perhaps ten meters to his right, engaging the enemy.

He ducked down and to the side as return fire came his way, bullets hammering into the rocks. His breath coming quick as he clutched the rifle, glancing over to see Sergeant Black crouched behind another rock perhaps five meters away. *Across open ground.*

Bent over his radio as Tzipporah stood over him, her SV-98 still slung over her back—the American's Kalashnikov in her hands as she fired.

Another building crescendo of fire struck Ariel's ears even as he felt someone slide into position behind him, scrabbling across the rocks.

"These fools—they can't shoot to save their lives," Ze'ev laughed grimly, raising his voice to be heard over the sound of gunfire as he ejected a mag from his rifle, replacing it with another from a pouch on his belt.

The older man was bleeding, a deep scar across his right cheek as if hit by a flying shard of rock, the blood mixing with the stubble of his beard.

Something in his voice belying the forced levity. They needed to break the deadlock. *And do it soon.*

Ariel pushed himself up on one knee, placing a hand on the older man's shoulder. "Going to make a run for it—need you to give me covering fire."

A nod and then he was off, crouched low—the death rattle of Ze'ev's rifle sounding behind him as he ran—the whine of bullets in the air over his head. *Move. . .*

10:34 P.M. Eastern European Time
Incirlik Airbase
Adana, Turkey

"Anything?" Lay asked for what had to be the third time in the last five minutes, running a hand across his chin as he turned, beginning to pace back across the tent toward the radar screens.

The Air Force sergeant shook his head mutely, his face mirroring the anxiety written on Lay's own. *No word from the fighter or the field team.*

No confirmation that the mission was even still on-track, let alone close to being accomplished.

He swore in helpless frustration, glancing once more at his watch.

Ten minutes. That was how long they had until the F-15 ran low enough on fuel to be forced to turn back to Prince Sultan.

After that. . .they'd have to cut their losses and abort the mission. Pull their people out.

As best they could.

11:35 P.M. Arabian Time
The ridge
Al-Anbar Governate

Ariel threw himself into cover as he reached the rocks, landing beside the American, his knees scraping against the hard ground.

"Where are we at with the radio?" he demanded, heedless of the pain as he pushed himself up, staying crouched in the shadow of the rock.

Black shook his head, a curse escaping his lips as hot brass from Tzipporah's rifle showered over both men—his face lit briefly in the muzzle flash.

"Nothing yet—haven't been able to raise the fighter. And," he began, glancing over his shoulder to the south—toward the rendezvous point, "I don't even have line of sight on the target."

Thirty meters. That was probably all it was, he thought, the topographic map of the ridgeline displayed in his mind's eye as he followed the sergeant's glance.

Thirty meters and they'd reach the southern face of the ridge—the sheer drop-off eighty feet to the desert below. A direct vantage point on the rendezvous point less than half a kilometer away.

If they could make it.

"All right," he said, ejecting the half-empty magazine from his rifle and tucking it into a pouch on his vest as Tzipporah dropped down on one knee beside him, "both of you on me. We move out together, cover to cover—lay down fire as we go."

Ze'ev and Nadir would have to bring up the rear, as best they could.

Tzipporah nodded wordlessly, leaning back against the rock as she braced herself for the charge. Determination in the set of her jaw, her face flushed with the heat of battle.

He caught a nearly imperceptible nod of assent from Black as the American drew his sidearm, briefly press-checking the weapon to confirm a round in the chamber. *Ready.*

He retrieved a magazine from his own belt, taking a deep breath as he rocked it into the mag well. Time to do this.

And then he was up and on his feet, the Kalashnikov already raised to his shoulder as he came out into the open, a bellow escaping his lips as he fired again and again.

Move.

11:36 P.M.
The rendezvous point

"We need to be leaving, Colonel Hadi—we need to be leaving at once."

There. The lieutenant colonel heard the tailgate of the old Soviet military truck slam shut behind him, his eyes still fixed on the northern ridge—the gunfire seeming to swell in intensity even as he watched, ignoring the entreaties of the Palestinian officer at his side. The rest of his men spread out in a skirmish line twenty meters in front of him, weapons trained to the north, protecting the trucks.

"Sir," a Guardsman announced, coming up behind him—the man still breathing heavily from his exertion with the footlockers, "the shells—the shells are loaded as you ordered, sir."

Good. And not a moment too soon.

"We have to get out of here," Major Halawa repeated, his voice rising higher as panic seemed to overwhelm him—the jowls of his face quivering as he stared at Hadi, his eyes wide with fear. "*Now.*"

"Yes, you do," Umar Hadi replied contemptuously as one of his soldiers handed him a rifle, unable to conceal his disgust for the Palestinian. "*Go.* My men and I will provide security to the border—do not fear, we will protect you."

Because the consequences of your worthless carcass being found here on Iraqi soil are too great for us all, he thought but didn't add. He would have shot the coward himself if he could have gotten away with it.

Halawa nodded quickly, his Adam's apple bobbing like a ball on a string as he swallowed, seeming too preoccupied with the prospect of his own safety to notice the insult.

Another moment and he was gone, disappearing on the far side of the trucks—followed by the sound of engines roaring to life a few moments later, the first of the trucks beginning to roll out across the desert sand back toward the border road.

Hadi turned to his old friend, shouldering his weapon. A grim smile passing across his face in the darkness. "Let's go finish this. We'll be back in Baghdad by sunrise."

11:38 PM
The ridge

Target. Target. Ariel squeezed the Kalashnikov's trigger once more, a three-round burst ripping from the barrel as the rifle recoiled into his shoulder, firing as he moved. A dark shape sprawling across the ground like a broken doll. *Target down.*

Another burst, and the rifle's bolt locked back on an empty magazine, his weapon useless for the moment as he ejected the mag, his support hand flying toward his belt to retrieve another. The night-vision goggles restricting his peripheral vision.

"Get down!" he heard the American bellow, briefly glimpsing a figure emerging from the rocks in his blind spot not even ten meters distant—near the cliff itself—before Black shoved him roughly down and to the side, his pistol coming up in his hands.

A pair of shots resounded as one, the figure staggering backward from the impact of the double-tap before Black put another shot into him and he toppled from the cliff, an anguished scream filling the night as he fell. The Iraqi line on the ridge faltering, on the verge of crumbling under the weight of their losses—the ferocity of the Israeli assault.

Almost there. Ariel slammed another mag into his rifle, bringing it up to engage another threat as he saw Ze'ev move in from the side, firing as he came. As dependable as the morning sun.

Another five meters, and they'd be above the southern face of the ridge. The Guardsmen's attempt to cut them off thwarted.

He glimpsed a line of men in the darkness below, advancing on the ridge—falling to one knee as he fired several short suppressive bursts, not even taking the time to aim carefully. Just enough to keep their heads down.

And then he saw it. *The trucks.* Moving out onto the road, easily four hundred meters away already and farther with every passing moment. Picking up speed. Rolling westward, back toward the Jordanian border.

The last few grains of desert sand trickling through their hourglass.

He looked back, finding Black still engaging the enemy on the ridge with his pistol—the laser range-finder secured to his pack. No way he could get it deployed in time, even assuming they were able to make contact with the plane. They had to. . .

Flame blossomed from the muzzle of his Kalashnikov as he triggered another burst, falling back until he found himself beside Tzipporah, placing his hand on her shoulder as he gestured out through the darkness toward the receding taillights of the trucks. "Can you take them?"

A nod was her only response, bullets cracking around them as she coolly unslung the SV-98—going prone on the hard rock. Her gloved hand reaching forward to deploy the rifle's bipod, steadying the buttstock against her shoulder.

Cover her, Ariel thought, raising himself up from behind the boulder—heedless of his own danger as he emptied the rifle down-range, seeing muzzle flashes flicker in the night below him.

If she failed to make the shot—if those trucks made it back across the border into Jordan—none of this was going to matter.

All the bloodshed, the risks they had run this night. None of it *mattered.* Only this shot.

The empty magazine clattered against the rocks as he ejected it, his hand moving to his belt to retrieve another—realizing only as he brought the fresh magazine up in his hand that it was his last. *Almost out.*

He hesitated only a moment before rocking it into the mag well, his gloved hand finding the Kalashnikov's charging handle and pulling it back. *There. Now to—*

The single powerful *crack* of a rifle bullet splitting the night shattered his train of thought, his head coming up just in time to see the Russian-made sniper rifle recoil into Tzipporah's shoulder as she fired, her hand already up and moving to work the bolt, chambering another round.

His gaze shifted out over the desert, just as the first of the Palestinian trucks lurched drunkenly before swerving sideways out into the middle of the road—the truck behind it trying and failing to stop fast enough, the metal shriek of grinding brakes audible even over the distance as it slammed into the side of the lead vehicle.

11:40 P.M.
The rendezvous point

A sniper. That was Hadi's first thought, the solitary sharp *crack* so distinctive—so familiar—rising above the chaos of the battle. The sound of death.

And then he heard the crash, swearing loudly as he turned to watch the military trucks collide—the lead vehicle spilling over on its side, the third truck managing to avoid the collision by a hair's-breadth, grinding to a halt behind its fellows.

Leave it to the Palestinians, he thought bitterly, rising from his crouch and moving to Thamir's side—heedless of the incoming fire from the ridgeline as he placed a hand on his subordinate's shoulder.

"Captain," he began, almost shouting in the man's ears to be heard over the small arms fire, "take a dozen men and go help right those trucks. *Move!*"

Somehow, perhaps, they could yet salvage something out of this situation.

11:41 P.M.
The ridge

Yes, Ariel thought, suppressing a cheer at the sight. Victory—or something close enough to it, their fortunes reversed in the space of a moment even if their danger was far from past.

He rose from his crouch even as Tzipporah fired again, taking on the rear vehicle as he sprinted across the ridge, bent over at the waist.

"Sergeant Black!" he bellowed, sliding into position beside the American, his hand on the man's shoulder. "The convoy has been stopped—get on the horn to your planes. Do it *now!*"

Black nodded his understanding, turning back toward the cliff—toward Tzipporah and their targets beyond.

Call the plane, Ariel thought, breathing heavily as he rose up to follow him. That was all they needed now.

Call the plane, light up the target—then begin extricating themselves from this mess. *Simple enough*. Nothing they hadn't done a score of times before.

Ze'ev materialized at his side in that moment, the older man's face drawn and grim in the darkness. "He's down."

"What are you talking about?" Ariel demanded, a cold chill seeming to trickle like ice water down his spine—scarce able to process the words, raising his voice to be heard over the staccato *crack* of the rifles—the whine of incoming rounds.

"Nadir's down," Ze'ev repeated flatly. "I saw him fall, couldn't get to him. He's—"

Another burst of fire from somewhere close by—*very* close by—assaulted Ariel's ears, followed almost immediately by the sickeningly wet sound of a bullet striking flesh.

Time itself seeming to slow down as Ze'ev's knees buckled, the former *Shayetet-13* operator staggering into him, dropping his weapon. *No.*

It wasn't possible.

His own rifle clattering to the rock as he wrapped his right arm around his friend's back, struggling to keep him from falling. An Iraqi soldier coming into view over Ze'ev's shoulder—no more than seven meters away.

Only seconds before he opened fire once again, fire blossoming from the muzzle of his weapon. Blood spraying over the fingers of Ariel's right hand as more bullets tore into Ze'ev's back—hammer blows seeming to strike his own Kevlar plate—and then they were both falling, the air driven from his lungs as he went down hard on his back, Ze'ev landing on top of him.

A dead weight. The two of them locked in a macabre embrace, Ze'ev's mouth open, his face blurred in the haze of the night-vision goggles. His breathing heavy and labored, his blood still staining Ariel's hands.

Half of his team taken out of the fight, just like that. And when they had been so *close*. . .

It wasn't going to end like this—not like *this*. Ariel could hear footsteps drawing nearer, struggling to get his breath as the Iraqi guardsman closed in, his own weapon hopelessly out of reach.

His left hand closed around the holstered Beretta on Ze'ev's hip, jerking it free as he rolled his friend's body off him—revealing not one but two Iraqi soldiers approaching, only a few feet away.

Close enough to make out the looks of surprise on their faces as he brought the pistol up, the weapon describing a painfully slow arc as it came to bear. His vision narrowing to a tunnel focus on the men. *Targets.*

One, two shots. Echoing out through the night. Striking his target squarely in the chest. *Center mass.*

The man's legs went out from under him and he went down—his partner managing to get his own rifle up before Ariel fired again, the bullet ripping through his throat and out the back of his neck.

Target down. Ariel watched as the second Iraqi collapsed in a heap on the rocky ground, his breath coming fast and shallow as the adrenaline slowly faded from his body, his vision clearing as he searched the night around him for further threats. *Nothing.*

Nothing except the continuing chatter of fire from the cliff, reminding him of their danger. *Ze'ev.*

He dropped the pistol, pushing himself painfully to his knees as he bent over his friend's body—the older man's face deathly pale in the night.

"Stay with us," he whispered fiercely, clasping Ze'ev's bloodstained hand in his own as he began to perform a blood sweep, checking his body for wounds. The multiple ragged holes in the *front* of the man's Kevlar already telling him everything he needed to know. The bullets had struck his friend in the back, traveling through his body and exiting *through* the front plate—the hammer-like blows he had felt against his own vest. "Hang on, just stay with me. We're going to get you out of here, we're going to get you home."

Dear God, *we're going to get you home*, Ariel thought, scarcely conscious of the prayer. He saw Ze'ev smile, seeming to grip his hand with renewed strength, his lips moving as if he was trying to speak.

"Save it," he ordered brusquely, beginning to unstrap the damaged vest from Ze'ev's shoulders, "you're going to need your strength."

His old friend shook his head, gripping Ariel's bloodstained hand tightly in his own.

"*Hear,*" he whispered, his voice desperately weak, but seeming to grow in power with each passing moment, every word striking Ariel's ears like a death knell. "Hear, O Israel, the Lord is our God."

The Lord, He is one. . .

11:43 P.M.
Palmetto Flight

". . .that's a negative, Control," Capano responded, glancing once more at his gauges as he brought the big strike fighter around to the south for a final pass over the target area. "I've hung around here as long as I dare—already pushing the envelope on fuel. We have to RTB at once."

"Just give it a bit more time, Palmetto," the voice insisted, for the second time in as many minutes. "Our men are on the ground."

"And that's where we're going to be if we stick around, sir," the lieutenant responded sharply. Wishing for the thousandth time that he knew where this man fit into the command structure. *How far he could go.* "On the ground, out of gas. I—"

His voice broke off suddenly as a third, unfamiliar voice came on the radio net, breaking up for a moment in a haze of static before coming through loud and clear. "Palmetto, this is Dogpatch. Do you copy?"

10:43 P.M. Eastern European Time
Incirlik Airbase
Adana, Turkey

Thank God, David Lay breathed, grabbing up the microphone. "Palmetto, this is Control. You are cleared hot. I say again, you are cleared hot."

He took off the headset, pacing back across the tent toward the map table where Shoham stood.

"We're still in the game, Avi. Still in the game."

11:44 P.M. Arabian Time
The ridgeline
Al-Anbar Governate, Iraq

"Reading you loud and clear, Dogpatch," came the pilot's reply through Black's headset as he set up the AN/PEQ-1 SOFLAM laser designator, spreading out the legs of the tripod on the hard rock of the clifftop before mounting the designator itself atop it. "What's your status?"

It was a moment before he replied, rifle bullets caroming off the rocks around him as he switched the unit on, aiming it through a narrow gap in the rocks. The Israeli woman was up and moving, trying to draw fire away from him—the rest of her compatriots nowhere to be seen, not since Ariel had sent him back to the cliff face.

A bullet spattered off the stone nearby, sending chips of rock flying into his face, cutting into his cheek. He winced at the sudden flash of pain, shaking his head as if shooing away a fly.

He hadn't been under fire this intense since Somalia, seven years before, skinnies hunting him and his fellow Rangers through the streets of Mogadishu.

Twenty-four hours the like of which he'd never forget. *No matter how hard he might try.*

"We are in position, Palmetto," he responded finally, keeping his voice steady with an effort as he took aim through the side-mounted night-vision sight, the soldiers clustered around the trucks clearly visible in the sight's magnification. "I have eyes on the target."

"Copy that, Dogpatch," came the pilot's voice after another moment, "we are cleared hot. Stand-by ten seconds."

Hurry up, he thought, watching his targets through the sight. The SOFLAM was vastly superior to the units he'd used just a few short years before in Kosovo and yet—

"Laser on," the pilot announced, the soft drawl of the Carolinas tinging every syllable.

There. *The order he'd been waiting for.*

Let's do this. Black heard movement across the rocks behind him in that moment, jerking the Beretta on his hip from its holster as he turned to confront the threat. *Ariel.*

He lowered his weapon, cursing beneath his breath at the close call as the Israeli team lead emerged from the darkness, crossing the open space bent low at the waist before throwing himself into cover.

Alone, he thought, glancing into the darkness from whence the Israeli had come as if expecting to see the other members of the *Kidon* team following close behind.

Nothing.

"Do you have the plane?" Ariel demanded, a raw edge to the words, his face obscured by the night-vision goggles as he glanced over.

Black nodded wordlessly, a round impacting less than six inches from his hand as he reached forward, flicking the switch on—taking a deep breath to calm his nerves as he adjusted his eye once more to the sight.

Seeing the trucks painted in a beam of infrared light, the laser "firing" a rapid stream of pulses toward the target to be reflected back up into the night sky. "Palmetto, Dogpatch, lasing the target. How copy?"

Another agonizingly long moment passed, the Beretta clutched tightly in Black's left hand as he held his position, forcing himself to ignore the fire, the staccato chatter of Ariel's Kalashnikov as the Israeli opened up. *Come on, baby. Make it rain.*

Then his radio crackled with static once more. "Dogpatch, Palmetto, we have the spot. Target locked."

He took his eyes off the scope for only the space of a second, glancing over at Ariel to mouth a silent warning.

Get down.

11:45 P.M.
Palmetto Flight

Here we go. The F-15 Strike Eagle came around once more from the north as Lieutenant Capano brought the fighter down to ten thousand feet, throttling back as they approached the target zone.

"I have the spot," he heard Garrison announce once more from the backseat, re-affirming that they were locked on to the designator's beam. "Ten seconds. . .five. . .three. . ."

He felt the stick vibrate into his hand, the entire airframe shuddering as a thousand pounds of ordnance dropped off the F-15's left wing.

"Stores away, stores away."

The trucks

Chaos. Captain Thamir flinched involuntarily as another bullet came in over his head, the sniper who had already killed two of his men keeping them all under fire as they tried to extricate the wrecked trucks from each other, the men straining to roll the second truck back onto the road, its tire shredded by a bullet—Major Halawa cursing them as they worked, the Palestinian's broad face purplish in the pale moonlight.

"Push, you fools!" he screamed, his voice sounding as though it was on the brink of cracking. "What are you—women? *Push*. We have to get out of here. We have to—"

"Get ahold of yourself," Thamir warned, cutting him off as he stepped in close to the Palestinian, seizing hold of his arm. Smelling the stench of fear off the man, wide-eyed panic written across his face. "We're going to get you out here, we—"

He never got to finish the sentence, a peculiar whistling sound from somewhere in the night above interrupting his words. He started to look up. . .and that was the last thing Captain Raffi Thamir ever saw in this world, stars shining down from above.

Exploding in fire.

11:46 P.M.

Umar Hadi felt the earth rumble and shake beneath his feet, nearly throwing him off his feet as he threw out a hand to catch himself. The shockwave rippling over him, tearing his maroon beret from his head.

He looked back, his ears still ringing from the force of the explosion, seeing a pillar of fire, smoke, and dust ascending into the night. The broken rear half of one of the Soviet military trucks falling from the sky to crash into the desert barely eighty meters distant, nearly two hundred meters from the epicenter of the blast.

My God, the Republican Guard officer thought, feeling a tide of panic break over him as he watched in horrified awe, seemingly rooted in place. *Unable to move.*

The other two and a half trucks, the Palestinians, all gone—vanished in a fiery cloud of smoke and ash. Along with his men. *Raffi.*

Echoes of American airpower in Kuwait, years before. Memories of stragglers from once-proud Army divisions, fleeing back across the border in abject terror.

Fleeing the carnage of what the Western media would come to call the "Highway of Death", but there had been no escape. The sheer *power* of it all. . .

Now come for them this night.

Another large piece of flaming debris from the wreckage crashed down into the desert sand not twenty feet away from where he stood, seeming to jar Hadi from the stupor which had fallen over him.

He felt a soldier run past him, nearly bowling him over in his panic and he reached out, grabbing the man by the arm and pulling him roughly back toward him, cursing violently as he did so.

"You run, you die," he hissed, his face only inches from the soldier's. He took the man by the collar, gesturing back toward the ridge, where the man who had called in that airstrike had to be sheltering. "The only way you live— the only way *any* of us live—is to take that ridge."

11:47 P.M.
The ridgeline

"Palmetto, Dogpatch, confirm target destroyed. I say again, the target has been destroyed," Black repeated, keeping the elation out of his voice with an effort. They weren't home just yet.

218

Long way yet to go.

"Shift south," he continued, taking advantage of the momentary cessation in fire to reposition the SOFLAM, this time aiming the laser directly at the Iraqi base camp. "Lasing secondary target."

Destroy their vehicles. *Cut off their means of giving pursuit.*

"Stand by, stand by," came the response, the strike fighter describing a turn in his mind's eye as it came back for another attack run. "We have the spot. Target locked. Ten seconds. . .five. . ."

The American sergeant took his eyes off the scoped night-vision sight at the last possible moment, throwing himself into cover behind the rocks just as the night erupted once more into fire—the ground trembling and shaking beneath his feet.

11:48 P.M.

Umar Hadi had barely made it into the cover of the shallow wadi which ran along the foot of the ridge perhaps fifty meters from its base—extending a hand back to help one of his men down—when the second bomb struck.

The night behind them lit up by a flash as powerful as a bolt of lightning, the shock wave throwing both men into a heap at the bottom of the wadi.

Screams of pain and fear ringing hollowly against his battered eardrums, sounding distant, far-off as he extricated himself from beneath the other man, seeing only then the jagged piece of metal—as big as a man's hand—buried in the soldier's back with the precision of a throwing dagger, inches from the spine.

Devastation. That was all that greeted the Republican Guard officer's eyes as he pushed himself to his feet, absently wiping away blood from a long cut across his cheek.

The trucks which had transported him and his men out into the middle of this desert, now reduced to flaming, unrecognizable wreckage on the brink of a yawning crater. Their communications, their supplies. *All gone.*

Soldiers who had been caught closer to the blast staggering away from its epicenter, dazed—clothes nearly torn from their bodies. One of the survivors struck down by an unseen sniper even as he watched, brains exploding from the back of the man's head—the shot barely even audible, only the explosion ringing again and again and again in his ears.

The man seeming to collapse in slow-motion, falling to his knees on the hard earth before pitching forward. Dead before he hit the ground.

And he knew in that moment, a premonition as certain as the coming of the dawn. *This is where he would die.*

Here in the desert, like so many soldiers before him.

But that was *how* he was going to die—on his feet, like the soldier he had been all his life.

The lieutenant colonel stooped down painfully, picking up his rifle—his own voice echoing faintly in the dark corners of his mind as he rallied his remaining men around him.

Another sixty meters down the wadi and they'd be able to ascend the ridge out of the view of the cliff—mount an attack from the flank, take their enemies off-guard.

If they were going to die. . .they wouldn't be alone.

11:50 P.M.
Palmetto Flight

"Confirm target destroyed, Palmetto," Capano heard the ground controller announce, the relief clearly audible in the man's voice. "I say again, secondary target is destroyed."

Yes, the National Guard lieutenant thought, pumping his clenched fist exuberantly into the air as the F-15 banked over the desert—the oily pillar of smoke and fire visible even from ten thousand feet in the air.

It wasn't his first strike, but there was something about blowing things up that never really got old. Reminded him of why he'd become a fighter pilot in the first place.

"Anytime, Dogpatch," he replied, his smile fading as he looked once more at his fuel gauges. "Anytime."

10:51 P.M. Eastern European Time
Incirlik Airbase
Adana, Turkey

"Good work, Palmetto Flight," Lay announced, keying his mike as he exchanged a tense smile with Shoham. The mission was far from over, but their objectives. . .those were achieved. "Come on home."

Their men, achieving the impossible. *Once again.*

"Sir," he heard the Air Force sergeant begin, "we just received an updated status report from Baton Flight. They're approaching the Turkish border, and—"

He started to turn toward him, only then hearing Black's voice once more over the Air Force comms network. The transmission breaking up into static but the tension in the Delta Force sergeant's voice coming through crystal clear.

"Palmetto, Dogpatch. . .request—requesting a gun run against OPFOR ground targets."

Opposing force. He was asking for a strafing pass, down low and fast— apparently the Iraqis were still present in strength.

All their plans for extraction threatened, if that were the case.

There was only silence on the radio net for a long moment, until Lay interjected, "Palmetto, this is Control—can you do it?"

"That's a negative, Control," the young National Guard officer responded, the exasperation clearly audible in his tones. "I've overstayed my welcome—gonna be lucky just to make it back to Prince Sultan with the fuel I've got left. If I go down on the deck for a gun pass. . ."

His voice trailed off, the implication only too clear. *No way.* Lay closed his eyes, steeling himself against the realization of the truth.

There was nothing they could do. Not a thing, and that was the hardest burden of command you could ever bear. To become the man on the *other* end of that phone.

"Dogpatch, this is Control," he began, pain in every word, "I'm afraid that's not going to be possible. Our air assets have used up their time on-station. Extraction is less than thirty minutes out, you're going to have to hold on your own until then."

There was another long pause of silence, only static crackling across the radio. Then he heard a curse and another voice came on the 'net, as if he had taken the radio away from Black.

Ariel.

"In another thirty minutes," the Israeli team lead responded, his voice clear and even. *Lifeless.* "The only thing those helicopters are going to need to bring are body bags. I've already lost good men on this ridge tonight—not going to lose the rest of them if I can help it."

". . .*lost good men.* . ."

A cold chill seemed to grip Lay's heart at the words, a look at his counterpart's stricken face revealing that the Mossad officer had heard the radio transmission as well. "Dogpatch, this is Control, I need your sitrep."

Nothing. Only silence meeting his request, the faint crackle of static over the net

"Dogpatch, this is Control—requesting a sitrep. . .Dogpatch?"

11:53 P.M.
The ridge
Al Anbar Governate, Iraq

Cursing bitterly, Ariel ripped the headset off his head—shoving it into the American's hands as he shouldered his rifle, ejecting the magazine and hefting it briefly in his hand before shoving it into the pouch on his vest and replacing it with one of the full mags he had taken from Ze'ev's body.

"Kit up, they'll be here before we know it," he said brusquely, hearing barked orders in Arabic drifting up from the desert below, along with the tormented screams of the dying. *The crackle of flames.* "We're not going to have much time."

He glanced back up the ridge toward the west, feeling Tzipporah's eyes on him as he did so, knowing the question which lay unasked and unanswered in their depths. Doing his best to ignore it, focus on what little he could yet change.

"We fall back on that rise," he said, indicating the slightly higher ground to the west, near where the ridge began to narrow—reducing their front. "Make our stand there."

"Ze'ev, Nadir," he heard Tzipporah begin, a slight tremor in the words, unable to refrain from asking any longer, "are they. . .?"

"They're both dead," he replied, his voice flat, emotionless. Unable to get the image of Nadir out of his head—the youngest member of his team, an American kid from Brooklyn who'd made his *aliyah* to the Jewish homeland along with his parents at the age of eleven. Laying there dead in the rocks, a single hole in the middle of his forehead—he'd been dead before he hit the ground.

"Let's move," he said finally, finding no words to further express the emotions roiling within him. "On me."

Palmetto Flight

". . .you're not listening to me, Control," Capano retorted, frustration building within him as he listened to the man's voice. He didn't know what was going on down there in the desert below him, suspected he didn't *want* to know. He did know the consequences for losing a plane, particularly on a mission that was never officially supposed to have happened. "If I *could* provide close support, I would—but if I take this plane down low for a pass, I'm not going to make it back to base. I—"

"Make the run, Palmetto," came the reply, firm and unequivocal. "Then return to base, here to Incirlik. On my authority."

It could just work, the pilot thought, glancing at his gauges once again— the change of base cutting several hundred miles out of the return flight. And perhaps the logistics didn't matter, in the end.

He knew an order when he heard one.

"Solid copy, Control," he replied finally, pulling the strike fighter into a hard bank as he came back around toward the target area—pitching the nose down as he began to descend toward the desert, twelve thousand feet below. "Dogpatch, Palmetto, come in. Dogpatch, how copy. . ."

11:57 P.M.
The ridge

Fire. Ariel felt the Kalashnikov recoil into his shoulder as he squeezed the trigger, getting off single, aimed shots, out into the darkness in which Ze'ev and Nadir had both given their lives—seeing a dark shadow fall in the night even as a burst of fire tore through the air past his ear. The Iraqis closing in on them, faster than even he had expected.

Move. And then he was up and running, his boots pounding against the hard earth as he ran back, further west along the ridge, glimpsing the muzzle flash of the American's weapon ahead of him—blossoming across his night-vision.

Providing covering fire.

He slid in beside Black, sheltering behind a boulder as he reloaded the rifle—glancing around him in an effort to get his bearings. Catching sight of Tzipporah, just off to his left—her face like stone as she raised herself up, Ze'ev's rifle in her hands as she returned fire down-range.

The ridge narrowed at this point to scarce more than fifteen meters across, defensible, even with just the three of them—*if* they could drive their attackers to ground, force them to take cover.

Keep them at a distance.

For as long as ammunition held out, Ariel thought morosely, only too aware that wasn't going to be long enough, even with the magazines they'd managed to scavenge from the dead.

He pushed himself to one knee, leaning out from cover just long enough to get a sight picture, the rifle's staccato chatter filling the night. *Target. Target.*

There—he felt something tug at his arm, a blinding flash of pain exploding across his mind as he fell back into cover, nearly dropping the rifle. Looking down to see the sleeve of his shirt stained with blood, his left arm hanging nearly useless at his side. Had to have hit the bone, or something close to it.

Out of the fight. He swore viciously at the folly of it all, another round splattering into the rocks just overhead, blood trickling out between his fingers as he clamped his hand tight over the wound, fighting against the pain.

Reaching down to undo his belt for use as a tourniquet, knowing he only had so long before he went into shock.

He heard Black call out, his voice faint and indistinct—the words lost in the cacophony of small-arms fire surrounding them.

"I have the plane!" the American sergeant repeated, closer this time, reaching over to place a hand on his shoulder. "It's coming in for the run. I'm going to need covering fire so I can set up the designator, I—"

His voice broke off in that moment as he saw the look on Ariel's face, saw the wound. "Do you—"

No. Ariel shook his head angrily, bracing the folding stock of the AK-47 tight against his right shoulder as he struggled to push himself up, his knuckles whitening around the pistol grip as he raised the rifle in one hand, trying to get a sight picture.

"Just call the plane. Do it *now.*"

11:59 P.M.
Palmetto Flight

". . .lasing the target. How copy?"

"Copy that, Dogpatch," Capano responded, the SOFLAM's beam clearly visible on his HUD as the F-15 Eagle swept down over the desert in a steep dive. "We have the spot."

His fingers slick with sweat as he clutched the stick, every fiber of his body at full alert, the desolate landscape of the desert looming large in the night. Everything looked different down here. *At night.* A mission he had never trained for, never expected he would be asked to perform. So much that could go wrong, so quickly, at this altitude. If he failed to pull out in time. . .

A single movement wrong, a single *twitch* and they'd be into the ground before he could react—a thirty-one-million-dollar airframe turned into the desert version of a lawn dart.

Both of them dead.

Forty-five hundred feet. . .three thousand. . .twenty-one hundred. . .

His finger wrapping around the trigger as he saw the firing reticle center in the target area, men suddenly visible on the ground beneath him—scattering like ants as the fighter roared in, the aircraft shuddering as the 20mm Gatling beneath the Eagle's fuselage spat fire into the desert night.

"Guns, guns, *guns!*"

12:00 A.M.
The ridge

Pain. Surging through his veins like liquid fire.

Chaos. Filling the night around him as Ariel lifted the rifle once more in one hand—fighting against the nausea, the weakness that threatened to overwhelm him as he fired, again and again into the darkness. Struggling to stay on his feet, to stay in the *fight*.

For as long as he could.

And then he heard it, a distant sound at first, barely perceptible over the gunfire—building to a throbbing roar, penetrating the darkest recesses of his mind, overpowering all else.

The American jet sweeping in out of the night, the unearthly sound of the Gatling heralding its arrival, the ridgeline thirty meters in front of their position suddenly churned into a maelstrom of swirling dust, flesh, and earth by the impact of dozens of 20mm shells.

Men torn apart, dying in agony. Staggering out of the cloud of dust in a frenzied panic. *Trying to get away.*

Target. Target.

Palmetto Flight

Yeah! Capano struggled to suppress a cheer of exultation as the F-15 pulled out, climbing nearly straight up into the sky—his heart pounding wildly against his chest—the g-force pushing his shoulders hard back into his seat.

"Dogpatch, Palmetto," he began, his voice still trembling with adrenaline and excitement as he toggled the mike, "how copy?"

It was a long moment before the forward controller came on the net, and when he did, Capano could hear the sound of gunfire—close, *very* close—as if the man had just fired his own weapon.

"Good work, Palmetto," he said then, pausing as if to fire again, the reverberations of a gunshot nearly drowning out his next words. "One more run ought to do it, if you can give us one."

One more run. One more breathtakingly low, high-speed pass across the desert.

The National Guard lieutenant swallowed hard, guiding the big strike fighter into a hard turn back toward the south—willing his heart rate to calm down. "Copy that, Dogpatch. On our way."

12:05 A.M., January 9th
The ridge

They just kept coming. Inexorable as the tide, broken, ragged—but seemingly unstoppable, driven on by desperation. Another Guardsman falling in the night, crumpling to the dirt even as Ariel fired.

The AK's bolt locked back on an empty chamber and he threw it aside— falling to one knee as he struggled to draw his sidearm.

His fingers moving slowly, as if lost in a dream—feeling like wooden stubs as they closed around the pistol butt. *No.*

Pain flooding over him, clouding his brain as everything around him seemed to fade away, sounding so very distant. Far away. He had to keep going—had to stay in the fight as long he could—had to. . .

The Beretta came out in his hand, but he lacked the strength to raise and aim it—the pistol falling from nerveless fingers as he pitched forward, catching himself on his good hand for a moment before slumping to the earth.

He felt hands on his shoulders, heard a voice calling his name but he found himself incapable of responding—darkness closing in all around. . .

And then everything went black.

12:06 A.M.

So this is how it ends, Umar Hadi thought, lying there on his back on the hard earth, looking up at the stars in the night sky above him, fading in and out of his vision as he struggled to retain consciousness.

A military career which had begun so long before in a little village on the banks of the Tigris, come to. . .*this*, bleeding out here in the desert—his right leg hopelessly mangled below the knee, torn apart by the impact of a shell from the American jet.

So many wars, so much fighting—all across the years, from Iran to Kuwait to Basra, crushing the revolt of the deserters—all of it ended here. In this moment.

He heard the steadily growing sound of jet engines in the distance—even over the desultory fire from what remained of his men. Knew what it meant.

It was coming back.

Death, coming to claim him. Not to be denied. He gritted his teeth against the pain, his mind wandering—brief snatches of the Qur'an coming to his lips and passing, unspoken as he moaned in agony, fighting to remain silent.

He had never been a religious man and yet. . .perhaps when the deeds of his life were weighed, it would be enough to face the Questioners. *Who is your Lord? What is your religion? Who is your Prophet?*

The roar building louder and louder in his ears as he tried to roll over onto his stomach, the primal desire for survival taking over in the last moments of his life, his lips silently forming the words of his creed as he began to drag himself across the broken ground. *There is no God but God. . .and Muhammad is His Prophet. God is—*

And the plane swept in.

11:14 P.M. Eastern European Time
Incirlik Airbase
Adana, Turkey

"I understand, sergeant," David Lay said heavily, staring ahead into the blank side of the tent as he listened to Black's voice on the other end of the comms network.

He felt no surprise at the soldier's words, just sadness—the kind of sadness which comes from having every worst fear confirmed. He had known from the moment that the second transport was forced to abort that they wouldn't be getting everyone back alive. Five men—no, four men and a woman—sent to do the job of ten, when even ten might have proved insufficient.

"Hold where you are, sergeant," he said finally, signing off, "and radio in if you encounter further opposition. The helicopters will be with you soon."

"Well?" he heard Shoham ask as soon as he removed the headset, a great weight seeming to settle over Lay's shoulders at the sound of the question.

"The mission was a success," he began, choosing his words with painstaking care. "The shipment of weapons was successfully interdicted, with both the primary and secondary targets completely destroyed. The threat to the peace summit has been neutralized."

"And?" He looked up, meeting his counterpart's eyes—seeing in their dark depths recognition of the truth. *He already knew.*

That premonition of evil which comes only from having had blood on one's hands, so very many times before.

"And two of your men are dead," Lay announced flatly. *No way else but to say it.* "Your team lead took a pair of rounds to the left arm in the final skirmish with the Iraqis—lost a lot of blood. My man is working to try to stabilize him as they await extraction."

He took a deep breath, watching Shoham stiffen at the first impact of the words—resignation slowly spreading across his face as he came to terms with their reality.

"I'm sorry, Avi," he began. "There are no words that can adequately express my—"

"It's not necessary, David," the Israeli replied, cutting him off with a brusque shake of the head. "This is the price my people have always had to pay for a place in this world—a price paid, as ever, in our blood. We—"

"Sir," one of the Air Force officers interrupted, gesturing to catch Lay's eye. "We have Baton-Two-Zero on final approach."

The former station chief exchanged a glance with Shoham, swearing underneath his breath as he pushed his way past a female sergeant, emerging into the chill night in his shirtsleeves—not taking time to stop for his jacket as he hurried toward the runway, the Israeli not far behind.

May we lose no more men this night. . .

The flashing lights of emergency vehicles lend a macabre cast to the scene as Lay reached the runway, Air Force personnel clad in firefighting gear barking orders—hoses snaking out across the ground toward the tarmac as men prepared for the landing of the crippled transport.

And then he saw it, the landing lights of the C-130 clearly visible off to the east as it approached, barely a shadow against the darkness of the night.

So very many things that could yet go wrong, the CIA officer thought, a chill seeming to wash over him as he watched, reduced to a helpless observer in these moments. Glancing over to see Shoham standing beside him, the Israeli's lips moving as if in silent prayer.

Perhaps that was all any of them could do now.

The C-130 came in nose-high, its damaged wing and smoldering, fire-blackened engine readily apparent in the runway lights as it descended, the prop blast from the remaining engines swirling around them as the aircraft passed just overhead.

The sound of rubber squealing against asphalt filling the night as the battered transport touched down farther down the runway, men all around them tensed—ready to run forward should it burst once more into flame.

It rolled forward another thirty meters before coming to a stop—and then it was down. *Safe.*

Lay let out a breath he didn't even realize he'd been holding, running a hand over his forehead as he turned away. So much remaining to be done this night.

But they were safe.

12:27 A.M. Arabian Time
Al-Anbar Governate, Iraq

"*. . .need to get an IV in, or we're gonna lose him. He's still bleeding. . .*"

Lights, flashing in the darkness. Voices, distant and far away—fading in and out. A dull, throbbing roar—filling every recess of his mind, seeming to drown out all else.

He could feel hands under his shoulders, his body seeming to lurch to the side as they lifted him roughly—a curious feeling of suspension seeming to overcome him as he was carried. Pain, washing over his body with every halting step.

"Hear, O Israel. . ."

Ze'ev. He could still see the shock, the surprise frozen across the older man's features as the bullets struck home. And then they were falling. Falling, falling, falling down. Into the abyss.

"The Lord is our God, the Lord. . ."

And he seemed in that moment to be transported back across time and space, seeing a young man in the fatigues of a soldier, his hair freshly cropped, standing by an old car outside a modest home in West Jerusalem. His hand on the open door of the car, his voice raised in anger.

Anger directed at the man standing only a few feet away in the doorway of the house—an older man, his hair not yet grey, his clothing marking him as one of the ultra-Orthodox. ". . .how could you? How could you do this to me? To your mother?"

A bitter curse exploding from the young soldier's lips as he shook his head, spitting upon the ground. ". . .I want nothing, of any of this. . . .you can have your God. . ."

Seeing the older man recoil as if he'd been struck at the words, sadness in his own eyes. Sadness mixed with his own anger, now boiling to the surface. ". . .if you do this, David, know that you are no longer my son. You are no longer welcome here. . ."

And the soldier's face turned toward him, revealed only then to be. . .his own.

"The Lord, He is One. . ."

So much death. So much destruction, Black thought, kneeling beside the corpse of the older Israeli as he worked the body bag up over the man's shoulders, the rotor wash of the helicopter hovering just up the ridge from where he knelt whipping at his clothes.

Two men dead, a third clinging to life—the Israeli team lead already loaded onto the Blackhawk, Air Force pararescue jumpers working to save him as he slipped in and out of a fevered delirium—the wound sending him into shock.

The Israeli team effectively wiped out, in the space of a half hour. *Less.*

You always knew it could happen, just always hoped it wouldn't happen on your watch. And perhaps it was inevitable that it would, given enough time—the odds growing against you with every successive mission back out into the field.

That one of these days it was going to be one of your people. That one of these days it was going to be. . .*you.*

The pitcher that goes to the well. . .

"Ready?" he asked, looking up into the eyes of the Israeli woman, his words nearly carried away by the sound of the rotors.

She nodded wordlessly, moving to take her position at her fallen teammate's feet as he zipped up the bag over the man's face, pausing to grip his shoulder in one final gesture of comradeship. *Brotherhood.*

Her face an impassive mask as they lifted the body together, staggering back over broken ground toward the waiting helo.

Still in the fight. He had to hand it to her—she'd seen most of her fellow team members die in front of her and kept fighting, at his side until the guns at last fell silent, the F-15's second attack run breaking the last vestiges of Iraqi resistance.

Whatever she felt, it was locked away. Saved for later. *After* the mission. Like the professional she was.

He lifted the man's shoulders up onto the floor of the hovering helicopter as they reached the door, sliding him in alongside the body bag containing his fallen comrade.

Taking a final look around him, his eyes scanning the barren wastes of the desert as the Israeli woman pulled herself up into the helicopter behind him— seeing the wrecks of the military trucks off in the distance, still smoldering in the night.

Success? It seemed wrong, somehow. . .and yet they had done what they'd come here to do. *No matter the cost.*

He shook his head, heaving himself up onto the floor of the helicopter, his AK-47 gripped in one hand—his legs still dangling from the door as he glanced back, signaling the pilot with his free hand. *Take off.*

Time to go home.

3:47 P.M. Israel Standard Time, January 22nd
Mossad Headquarters
Tel Aviv, Israel

". . .with the Israeli elections just two weeks away, the Israelis and Palestinians are debating a new peace accord which could weigh heavily on those elections. CNN's Jerrold Kessel has this report."

Avi ben Shoham glanced up from his desk as the image on the screen of his television changed to show footage of a white-bearded Israeli journalist standing outside of Ehud Barak's home, protesters visible in the background behind him.

"That's right, Andria," Kessel said, leaning into his microphone as the shouting behind him grew louder, "We're here outside the Israeli prime minister's home, where Mr. Ehud Barak is convening his senior ministers as supporters and opponents demonstrate without. In just over two weeks, Mr. Barak faces the Israeli people at the polls. But the embattled Israeli leader is first engaging the Palestinians again, responding to Yasser Arafat's proposal for a last ditch peace talks effort. . ."

Doomed to failure like all the rest, the Mossad officer thought, muting the television with a click of his remote as he returned to his paperwork, shaking his head. There would be no peace, not this time—just like all the times before.

An Israeli high school student had been murdered only five days before, lured into the Palestinian Authority by a young Arab woman he had met on the Internet, posing as an American tourist.

He'd been found a day later, his bullet-riddled body stuffed in the trunk of an abandoned car on the outskirts of Ramallah.

Ramallah. Where this had all begun, so many months before.

This chain of events that had led his men from the streets of France to the islands of the Mediterranean to the deserts of Iraq. . .to their *death*, in the case of Ze'ev and Nadir.

Two of their best. Sacrificed for peace, or at least averting a greater tragedy.

As of last he had heard, Ariel was still in the hospital, recovering from his wounds. But he *was* recovering, and that was what mattered.

The road back, however, would be a long one for the *Kidon* team lead—the second of the two rounds which had smashed into his arm penetrating further and breaking his shoulderblade.

Putting him out of commission for the time being. Maybe longer.

A knock on the open office door, and Shoham looked up to see Eli Gerstman enter, glancing briefly at the television as he closed the door behind him. "Taba?"

Shoham grunted a "yes" by way of reply, scribbling his signature at the bottom of the cover sheet before opening the folder. "Is there something I can do for you, Eli?"

"There is," the senior officer responded, remaining on his feet even as Shoham gestured toward an available chair. "The presence of chemical weapons at the site of the operation—where are we at with obtaining confirmation?"

Ah, yes. They needed proof, beyond the American communications intercepts—physical proof that the weapons had ever been there to begin with. The kind of proof the field team could never have obtained in the heat of the firefight.

He rose from his chair, handing Gerstman the folder and indicating that he should open it. "Our people will cross the border tomorrow. An hour, two—should give them all the time they need to collect soil samples from the bomb craters and make it back into Jordan. Our asset there at Al-Karameh will ensure that they pass unchallenged."

At least that was the plan. No one knew better than they just how many things could go wrong, but he'd done his best to prepare for every eventuality. To the extent that you ever could.

"Good," Gerstman said finally, returning the folder with a nod as he turned to leave. "Let me know as soon as you have answers. And, Avi?"

"Yes?" Shoham asked, looking up to see Gerstman standing there with his hand on the door.

"What about General Siddiqi?"

Siddiqi. The man who had set all of this in motion, from the very beginning. Been responsible for so many deaths, attempted to cause so many more. Shoham pursed his lips, his eyes betraying nothing as he met Gerstman's gaze.

"It's being handled."

5:03 P.M. Eastern Standard Time, January 26th
Fort Bragg, North Carolina

Coming home. There was always something strange about it, as if something of himself had been left behind. Back there, in the desert sand. *In the war,* if that's what you chose to call it.

Black glanced out the open window of his rental car as it idled not twenty feet back from the gate of the military base, the chill air biting at his bearded face.

It felt like snow, though he doubted they'd see any here at Bragg—cold air blowing down from the mountains to the west. Such a contrast with the desert. The world he'd left behind him. *For the moment.*

The car in front of him pulled forward, driving on into the base and he looked up to see the uniformed MP waving him forward.

"Your identification?" the soldier asked, a scowl passing across his face at the sight of Black's civilian clothes—his long, non-regulation haircut and beard.

So typical.

He grinned, handing his military ID through the window to the MP, watching as the man scanned it, his expression changing as he did so.

"All right," he said, nodding as he gave the ID back, taking a step away from the vehicle, "you're free to proceed, Sergeant Kranemeyer."

1:57 P.M., January 27ᵗʰ
CIA Headquarters
Langley, Virginia

". . . and has brought us to a stage where we can definitely say that we, Israelis and Palestinians, have never been closer to an agreement between ourselves than at this point. We have embarked on a technical and also principle-based discussion. And certainly we can say that we have a basis for an agreement, which will be able to be implemented and achieved after the elections in Israel."

Now there's the voice of optimism. David Lay shook his head, packing his personal effects once more into a cardboard box as he prepared to vacate the temporary office he had occupied since returning to Langley—the image of Shlomo Ben-Ami, the Israeli foreign minister, on-screen as he continued to speak.

Announcing the conclusion of the Taba Summit, brought to an end without reaching an agreement. Just as Shoham had predicted.

Just as he had known would be the case.

Cynicism, never more useful than when speculating on outcomes in the Middle East. And he was going to have plenty of use for it over the next few years, Lay thought, a wry smile crossing his face as he picked up the picture of his ex-wife and daughter, gazing at it for a long moment before placing it in the box, on top of his papers. Time for another move—another one of so many they hadn't known with him. *Out of his life.*

And perhaps it was all for the best.

Coming back from his three-year tour as Chief of Station in Tel Aviv, he had expected he would be receiving a promotion, most likely to SIS—the Senior Intelligence Service—making him roughly the equivalent of a flag officer in the military. The logical next step up the ladder of Agency bureaucracy, given his experience and the postings he'd known over the previous decade and a half.

But there had been no victory lap to take upon his return stateside—the threat might have been defused in the end, but that didn't make the seventh floor any happier about the way the decision to run Mustafa al-Shukeiri as an asset had blown up in their collective faces.

A decision which hadn't been *his* to make, but a chief of station made a convenient scapegoat in times like this, as the Agency scrambled to make the transition to a new administration. To smooth over mistakes, leave embarrassments in the past.

So it was back to the Middle East for him—or more precisely, in charge of the DO's activities in that region from here at Langley. "Chief of the Near East Division, Directorate of Operations", as the nameplate on the door of his new office read.

Not a promotion, more of a lateral move—back to something he'd done once before, before the Tel Aviv posting came his way. Shunted off to the side, out of the way.

Out of trouble.

He placed the lid on the box, covering his wife's face as he prepared to leave. Leave all of this behind him

Reaching over to grab the remote and turn off the television—the CNN anchor's words arresting him in that moment.

". . .in other news from the Middle East, we have a report just today from Baghdad, where General Tahir Kamal Siddiqi has been announced executed for treason this morning. A member of President Hussein's inner circle, Siddiqi had long been viewed as a rising. . ."

Siddiqi. Lay stopped, staring open-mouthed at the television as the woman continued to speak, providing voice-over for video showing a man being led to the scaffold—a noose being placed around his neck.

He shook his head in disbelief, knowing all too well what he was witnessing, whose hand was behind all of this. "Avi, you clever devil. . ."

11:31 A.M. Israel Standard Time, January 29ᵗʰ
Har HaMenuchot Cemetery
Jerusalem, Israel

A Star of David was freshly chiseled into the granite at the top of the new headstone, just above the name written there. *Major Natan Tsukerman, Israeli Defense Force. March 29ᵗʰ, 1963—January 8ᵗʰ, 2001.*

Ze'ev, Ariel breathed, stooping down awkwardly—his left arm supported by a sling, his balance unsteady as he dropped to one knee in the soft earth, running his fingers over the letters.

All the years they'd worked together, and he'd never known the man's actual name. *Until now.*

Now as he lay here, dead, on this hillside overlooking the city of Jerusalem. *Of peace.*

Not so very far from his own grave, Ariel thought—the headstone his father had erected after disowning him for joining the military. The stone beneath which David Shafron was buried forever, the date of his enlistment listed as the date of his death.

And perhaps it had been. The death of an old life, the birth of a new.

But for Ze'ev, laying here now. . .there was no birth, only death. *Hear, O Israel. . .*

Ariel shook his head, bitter remorse washing over him once more—pain shooting once more through his body as he jostled the arm, rising to his feet.

He could still remember his old friend standing there in the safehouse in the Golan, planning the operation against Mustafa al-Shukeiri. Advocating for bringing the weapons in through the marina, like the Navy man he had always been.

It seemed wrong, somehow, to think he had met his end in the desert—so far from his beloved sea.

"Ariel," he heard a familiar voice announce from behind him, turning to find Avi ben Shoham standing there just up the hill from the grave—the senior Mossad officer's SUV visible on one of the access roads above them. "They told me I could find you here."

That was about right. He hadn't been getting out much, still far too early in the recovery process for him to know much mobility. But he had asked to be brought here. To pay his respects.

"He was a brave man," Shoham said, joining him at the grave, his head bowed for a moment in silence. "And a good father."

Oh, yes. He remembered now, seeing the pictures.

The one part of Ze'ev's life he had opened up about, his twin stepdaughters. Couldn't have been more than ten, and now without their father. *Again.*

"A true loss. He and Nadir both." The older man shook his head, straightening as he took a step back from the grave. "How's the arm?"

"Improving, day by day," Ariel replied, gesturing with his good hand. "It'll be a while before I can get back out in the field, but I'll be there, with time. I—"

He stopped short, seeing the look in the senior Mossad officer's eyes. Sensing danger.

"I had intended to wait for another time," Shoham began, choosing his words slowly. "But perhaps it is all for the best. I'm pulling you out of the field, Ariel—for good."

No. It was everything he had done. . .for *years.* Ever since leaving *Sayeret Duvdevan.*

"Why?" he asked, controlling his voice with an effort.

"It'll be a year before you're combat-effective again," the older man replied, his tone brooking no argument. Signalling that the decision had already been made, by others—somewhere else. That telling him in person was a courtesy. Nothing more.

"Maybe longer, depending on just how well the arm mends," Shoham went on, his voice softening as he continued, "And you lost over half your command out there, it would be unwise to underestimate the impact that will have upon you, upon your judgment in future such situations. Losing people. . .it changes a man."

The voice of experience. The Mossad officer had seen two full-scale wars, known decades in the defense of the Jewish state. "I understand you've refused to see the staff psychologist."

Ariel nodded, not even looking in Shoham's direction—his face set in a bitter mask as he stared out over Jerusalem. Toward Mount Zion in the distance. He had.

It was the last thing he needed, someone poking and prodding their way through his psyche—analyzing the grief, the loss. Placing it under a microscope.

"I want to bring you back in, once you've recovered—put you in charge of training new operatives," Shoham continued without waiting for a response. "Men and women like yourself, doing the job you've done these past few years. The knowledge you can impart to them on the basis of the operations you've run. . .it will be invaluable. Will you do it?"

He turned then, looking the older man in the eye. "I don't have a choice, do I?"

A shake of the head, confirming what he already knew. *Take it or leave.* For good.

"The chemical weapons," Ariel began, changing the subject. *Moving on.* "Have we been able to confirm that they were in the trucks we destroyed?"

"They were in the trucks," was the simple response—alarm bells going off in his brain, something in Shoham's voice warning him there was something he *wasn't* saying.

"And?" he demanded, a fierce intensity creeping into his voice as he turned on Shoham.

He saw the older man take a deep breath, still not looking at him. "And, based on heavy sarin residue collected in soil samples from the area surrounding the site. . .we believe the nerve agent had been rendered inert by age. Fifteen, twenty years since its original manufacture—that's a very long time for sarin to retain its viability as a weapon. Siddiqi was selling the Palestinians a defective product. Worthless."

Then. . .that would mean—*no.* It wasn't possible, it wasn't real. That it had all been. . .

"You knew, didn't you?" He spat, suddenly identifying what was wrong. His dark eyes flashing fire. "You *knew!*"

"We knew," Shoham assented, sadness written across his face. "We knew, and couldn't take the chance of being wrong. The stakes were simply far too high."

"The stakes?" Ariel shook his head, his voice carrying across the desolate Judean hillside—the repressed anger finally spilling over. *Finding a target.*

"I can tell you about the *stakes.* I lost men out there in the desert that night—I lost a *friend,*" he said, his voice trembling with raw emotion as he gestured back toward Ze'ev's grave. "And now you're going to stand there and tell me that it was all for nothing. That he *died* for *nothing.*"

It seemed an eternity before Shoham replied, his eyes never leaving Ariel's face. "No, not for nothing."

"Then for *what?*"

"Ze'ev, Nadir. . .they died as they had lived, in the service of their country. For *Zion.*"

Zion. He turned away from Shoham wordlessly, standing there looking out over the hillside as the older man walked away, his footsteps against the grass fading into the distance, the sound of a vehicle starting up heralding his departure—the city of Jerusalem spread out below him. The city of peace, riven by violence for so many centuries. The city of. . .*Zion.*

Hear, O Israel. . .

The End

An author lives by word-of-mouth recommendations. If you enjoyed this story, please consider leaving a customer review(even if only a few lines) on Amazon. It would be greatly helpful and much appreciated.

And if you would like to contact me personally, drop me a line at Stephen@stephenwrites.com.

For news and release information, visit www.stephenwrites.com
and sign up for the mailing list.
Stay in touch and up-to-the-minute with book news through social media.

On Facebook: https://www.facebook.com/stephenenglandauthor

And join the Facebook group to discuss the books with other fans:
Stephen England's Shadow Warriors

On Twitter: https://twitter.com/stephenmengland

Read more from author Stephen England!

The *Shadow Warriors* Series

NIGHTSHADE
Pandora's Grave
Day of Reckoning
TALISMAN
LODESTONE
Embrace the Fire
QUICKSAND

Also by Stephen England

Sword of Neamha

Acknowledgements

Eventually, all things—even good things—must come to an end. And so it is as I come to the close of this trilogy.

When I first began to delve into this world in the summer of 2015, I couldn't have accurately predicted just how much fun I would have telling Ariel's story, or the places it would lead.

My thanks to all those who have come on this journey with me, and all those who have helped along the way.

Special thanks to both Russell Blake, providing the initial impetus to tell this story, and his artist, Ares Jun, for his fantastic artistry for the trilogy.

To friends in Israel for, as ever, providing a sounding board for research and ideas—and to a handful of retired US fighter pilots who provided technical input. Any remaining errors or moments of "artistic license" are mine and mine alone.

To the members of the advance team for the volumes of the trilogy, for their diligence in working through the manuscript to supply invaluable feedback: Tyler Donoghue, Joe Walsh, T.J. Lowther, Brock Wilson, Paula Tyler, and Bodo Pfündl.

And to my readers, without whom all this would be nothing more than a personal hobby. Your enjoyment of these stories has meant the world to me, and though this trilogy may be over—I look forward to many more years of exploring the *Shadow Warriors* universe together. There are so many stories to tell.

May God bless you all, and may God continue to bless the United States of America.

Made in the USA
Columbia, SC
20 May 2019